HOME
IS THE
SAILOR

LILLIAN MAREK

**CAVEL
PRESS**

Kenmore, WA

A Camel Press book published by Epicenter Press

Epicenter Press
6524 NE 181st St.
Suite 2
Kenmore, WA 98028

For more information go to:
www.Camelpress.com
www.Coffeetownpress.com
www.Epicenterpress.com
www.lillianmarek.com

Cover design by Scott Book
Design by Melissa Vail Coffman

Home Is the Sailor
Copyright © 2024 by Lillian Marek

Library of Congress Control Number: 2023950855

ISBN: 978-1-68492-173-7 (Trade Paper)
ISBN: 978-1-68492-174-4 (eBook)

*To my grandchildren
Arthur, Ellie, Emilie, and Owen*

PROLOGUE

May 5, 1801

IT WAS A LATE BREAKFAST AND A QUIET ONE, as was inevitable after a night that had seen the consumption of more bottles of port and brandy than courtesy would note. The two footmen in attendance moved with silent caution, taking care to pour the coffee without a glug and to set down the cups without a clink.

Viscount Claremont, the tenth to bear that title, was a gentleman whose sixty-eight years had settled comfortably around his middle. He peered nearsightedly at the missive that had been laid beside his place. "Here. Read this," he said, tossing it to his oldest son, the Honorable George Dormer.

George, who had been trying to decide whether it was safer to lift his cup to his mouth or lower his head to the cup, gave up the conundrum and picked up the letter. He broke the seal and, with some effort, brought the contents into focus.

"Condolences? Why is . . ." He turned to the signature. "Why is Harry Sunderland sending you condolences?"

George's cousin Frederick, wearing his usual slight sneer, said, "Perhaps if you actually read the letter?"

"Oh, right." George frowned with the effort. *"Offer my condolences on the death of your son . . ."* His head snapped up. "What's he talking about? I'm not dead and neither is Augustus."

Augustus began to nod in agreement but winced and decided not to move his head unnecessarily. "Right. Not dead," he said.

Frederick sighed, plucked the letter from his cousin's hands, and scanned it quickly. "It's Will who's dead."

The others looked confused for a moment before remembering the youngest brother.

"Ah yes," said the viscount. "Will."

"Sunderland saw his name in the casualty lists in the Gazette. It was after that naval engagement up by Denmark," Frederick said, summarizing the letter. "Captain William Dormer. Will a captain? That can't be right."

After a moment's thought, Augustus said, "I think that's right. He was made up to captain after some other battle. Mentioned in dispatches and all. Somebody told me that."

George was frowning again. "Does that mean we're expected to go into mourning?"

His father shrugged. "I'll tell the vicar to say something in the sermon on Sunday and we can wear black gloves. That should be enough. Not as if we have to actually bury him if he died at sea."

"Yes, but Isabella will probably want to order new mourning gowns," said George. "Her mother too."

"Your wife always wants to order new gowns. She's never been anything but an expense. Useless creature." The viscount's complaints dwindled to a mutter.

Augustus had been thinking, and the process brought a pained expression to his face. "Do you suppose there is anything for us to inherit? He must have had prize money."

Frederick gave a short laugh. "If he did, he won't have left it to any of us."

That was so obvious to the others as to need no comment. Instead, the viscount said, "At least he's no longer a problem."

CHAPTER 1

September 8, 1802

CAPTAIN WILLIAM DORMER, LATE OF His Majesty's Royal Navy and now the eleventh Viscount Claremont of Belford Park, was in a foul temper. This was not unusual. He had been in a foul temper for almost a year and a half now and felt entirely justified.

From behind the library desk, he glared at the steward with his good eye. The other one, the one covered by the patch, was part of the reason for his mood. Another part was the fact that the steward was talking to him at all. His father should have been handling this, and failing his father, his brother George, and failing George, his brother Augustus. Fools they may have been, but they still should not have been idiotic enough to get themselves all killed at once in a drunken midnight carriage race that ended at the bottom of a cliff. Not when that left him saddled with the running of an estate about which he knew nothing.

Will heaved himself up from behind the desk with the help of his cane and made his way over to the window, keeping clear of any furniture that could impede the arc of his wooden leg. That was his other souvenir from the battle at Copenhagen, and the fundamental reason for his foul temper. Nor had his temper been improved by all those well-meaning spreaders of good cheer who kept telling him how lucky he was to be alive.

Luck had never been on his side—not good luck, at any rate.

He glared out the window. Off to the side was the orchard the steward was bleating on about. The apples, which were apparently good for cider and nothing else, had the unlikely name of Foxwhelp.

Dammit, what did he care about apples? He knew about ships. He could command a ship, steer it through storms, lead it through battles. The sea had been his home for twenty years. He knew her in all her moods. Hell, he could smell a coming change in her even before the wind shifted, and his crew knew that he could. They depended on him. He belonged on a ship, with the open sea stretching off beyond the horizon.

Now that horizon was bounded by an apple orchard. *Apples!* He snorted in disgust.

The steward, who answered to the ridiculous name of Hopworth, kept bleating away.

Leaning on his cane, Will managed to turn around not too awkwardly. "If it's time to pick the apples, why not pick them? Do we need to hire people for the job?"

"No, no, we have plenty of workers, and they are all familiar with the task." Hopworth was now smiling and bobbing.

"Then why are you coming to me?" It was difficult not to sound exasperated, and Will doubted that he was successful. After all, he hadn't tried very hard.

The ingratiating smile was still on the steward's face. "I apologize. I hadn't meant to bother you, just thought to let you know in case you saw the men in the orchard and wondered. No, the reason I came to see you was about Harry Parsons. He's not going to be able to pay his rent come Michaelmas, but I've another man willing to take over the Parsons farm at the same rent, so there won't be any loss of income."

Will looked at the steward more closely now. Hopworth was a scrawny fellow who stood a bit hunched over. He hadn't the look of a farmer—too pale, for one thing, and too weak to do a decent day's work. He looked more like a bookkeeper, and that was probably all he really was. But he looked entirely too pleased at the prospect of evicting this Harry Parsons. Was Parsons some kind of troublemaker? A ne'er-do-well? Will felt a certain curiosity.

"How do you know Parsons won't be able to pay the rent?"

"Oh, it's certain enough," Hopworth said cheerfully. "He's been laid up ever since he fell off the cider mill roof and broke his leg. His boys are too young to be of any use, and his wife tried, but she couldn't bring in the crops. And his own apples won't ripen until November, so he can't sell them in time."

A broken leg. That was certainly something that Will could sympathize with, something he could envy, in truth—a leg that was merely broken. Though why this should make the steward *cheerful* he did not know. Then there was the location of the accident. That gave him pause.

"The cider mill roof. The *estate* cider mill?" Will wanted to be sure.

"Your cider mill, yes." Hopworth nodded, still smiling.

Will smiled back carefully. "Just as a matter of curiosity, what was Parsons doing on the roof?"

"Repairing it. Some of the slates had been blown off in a storm."

Will kept his voice soft. "So Parsons was injured repairing my mill, leaving him unable to manage his farm, and he is now going to be evicted? Do I understand that correctly?"

Hopworth looked confused. "There was nothing unusual in his working on the roof. All the tenants who use the mill are obliged to help keep it in repair."

Will stared at the steward for a minute and watched as he began to twitch nervously. Then he swung over to the door, flung it open and bellowed, "Gibbs!"

A footman who had been waiting in the hall jumped to attention. Will turned to him—he thought the fellow's name was John—and snapped, "Find Gibbs and send him to me right away."

John scurried off, leaving Will free to turn back to the study. He made his way slowly to the desk, not looking directly at the steward but watching him from the corner of his eye. The man was too uneasy for this to be a case of nothing more than callousness. Will seated himself carefully, adjusting his wooden leg under the desk so it could not be seen by anyone coming into the room, and laid his cane across his lap so it was invisible as well.

Only then did he look directly at Hopworth. "Any other evictions planned for the end of the quarter?"

Hopworth licked his lips. "Two others."

"And you have people ready to take over their farms too?"

The steward's eyes widened. "But that was settled before you arrived. Mr. Frederick Dormer approved them. Your cousin," he added helpfully.

"I know who Frederick Dormer is," Will snapped. He needed to calm down. He lost his temper too easily these days. "That approval is herewith rescinded. There will be no evictions until I know more about the situation. Leave." *There. That sounded calm enough.*

Hopworth looked as if he wanted to protest, but he scurried out, sidling through the door around Gibbs, who had just arrived and filled most of the doorway with his bulk.

Like Will, Gibbs still wore his hair tied back in a queue, navy fashion. Once the bo'sun serving under Captain Dormer, he was now ostensibly Viscount Claremont's valet. More accurately, he was the one man at Belford Park that Will trusted. Together they were trying to make sense of the estate.

In one way it wasn't all that different from a ship of the line. There was a chain of command—or rather, there were several chains of command, and none of them were supposed to overlap. At the top was the viscount, the captain of the ship. And like the captain, the viscount needed regular and accurate reports from his officers.

Reports that he obviously wasn't getting. Not if one of his men had been injured in the line of duty—and repairing the roof was apparently one of the man's duties—and was being punished for it rather than assisted.

Gibbs understood Will's outline of the situation quickly enough. His massive bulk and placid air masked a quick mind, and he knew the importance of protecting his crew from abuse. He also knew the importance of discipline. He could be trusted to determine whether or not the evictions were justified.

Gibbs nodded, then hesitated before he turned to leave. "I'll be taking the gig. You could come along. Pleasant day today."

Will stiffened, then answered calmly enough, "No. People will talk to you more freely if I'm not there." It was a sensible enough reason, hard to deny.

He didn't relax until the door closed behind Gibbs. Damn the man. He couldn't stop fussing. Gibbs may have fished Will out of the sea when the ship went down at Copenhagen—and Will wasn't sure the bo'sun had done him a favor there—but that didn't give him the right to keep pushing.

Will knew the way people reacted to the sight of his mutilated face. It hadn't been so bad in the hospital, where they were all damaged one way or the other. Outside was a different story. A woman had screamed and half fainted when she met him in the doorway of an inn on the journey here. The servants in the house were still barely able to look him in the face, and that was after two months.

Better to be a hermit than a monster to frighten children with.

His glace fell on the letter sitting on the desk in front of him. The letter he had been trying to ignore. It had been forwarded from the Admiralty and arrived that morning. Addressed to Captain William Dormer, it had to be from someone who didn't know that a cannonball had knocked him out of the navy and that three deaths had then transformed him into a viscount.

It might be from someone seeking a favor. That could be easy enough. At least he could still write a letter of recommendation or send some money if that was all that was needed.

But it might be from a friend. There had been some good friends in the navy. Unfortunately, they would want to know what had happened. They would ask how he was. They would seek explanations—and he wasn't ready to give them—not when he would get pity in return. He could drown in the amount of pity that flowed over a one-legged, one-eyed, scarred ex-sailor.

He continued to stare at the letter, trying to work up the courage to read it. Finally, he finally cursed himself for a coward, snatched up the paper knife, and broke the seal.

He looked at the signature first. Robert Garland. Captain Garland. His first captain in the Navy, the man who had taken a frightened ten-year-old boy under his wing and taught him to be a sailor. To be a man. Garland had never mollycoddled him, but he had always been there to encourage him, teach him, and eventually praise him. More of a father than his own had ever been. This would not be a letter he could ignore.

Garland had been badly wounded when they were at the Battle of the Nile. Letters had been few and sporadic, but he knew that Garland had been invalided out—like himself. No, not quite like himself. Garland probably had not inherited a title and an estate. Did he have prize money? Probably. But if he did not, he would be existing on half pay at best, and he had a wife and daughter.

Perhaps Will had been fortunate after all, at least in financial terms. The possibility made him uneasy. Had he been indulging in self-pity? That was an uncomfortable thought.

He shook it off and picked up the letter. As he suspected, Garland knew nothing of what had happened. It was an invitation to visit if Will was ever in England now that there was peace—however temporary—with France. No. It was more than an invitation. As he read between the lines, he saw that it was almost a plea. There was something Garland wanted to ask, but needed to ask in person. As if there were a favor Will could deny him!

But to travel? Will checked the address. Widham? That was

near Portsmouth. Travel to a village near Portsmouth? Such a trip would take at least three days; probably four. There was no longer any need for him to travel on a public stage—as Viscount Claremont, he was possessed of a comfortable traveling coach—but he would have to stay overnight at an inn at least two times.

He put the letter aside, pushed his chair back, and pulled himself up once more. Gripping the cane firmly, he pounded his way over to the window. There was no longer much pain, but a battered ship limping into port moved with more grace. Could he inflict the sight of his grotesque self on innocent travelers?

The window was open to let in a breeze. Gibbs was right. It was, in truth, a pleasant day—the sun still warm, only a few leaves beginning to turn. Perhaps he should go out and take a turn on the terrace.

FREDERICK DORMER STROLLED ALONG THE TERRACE, George's widow on one arm and her mother on the other. Mercifully, the women would soon be out of mourning. Isabella, of course, looked beautifully tragic in black with her dark hair and creamy skin. Her mother, Lady Blackwell, on the other hand, looked like a crow, all points and angles.

He considered taking them along one of the garden paths but saw that the gravel had not been raked recently, and he did not wish to risk scratching his boots—one of Will's decision's, no doubt. The gardeners were probably off picking fruit when they could have been keeping the pleasure grounds in trim. As usual, the thought of his cousin, the new viscount, sent a spasm of pain across his face.

"Is something wrong?" Lady Blackwell pounced on his expression. "I do hope I am not hanging too heavily on your arm. It is so good of you to allow me to walk with you."

"Not at all. I was merely pained by the state of the paths. The viscount does not appear to consider the upkeep of the gardens important. I suppose the maintenance of a nobleman's estate is not something a sailor would understand."

"Ah, Mr. Dormer, it is too, too dreadful. A grotesque figure like that as Viscount Claremont! How much better it would have been had you come into the title." Lady Blackwell smiled ingratiatingly. "You are so much the elegant gentleman and would have been an adornment to the peerage."

"I could hardly wish for my cousin to have died, though it is what everyone thought had happened." Frederick trusted that he kept any trace of bitterness from his voice.

"It was a surprise, wasn't it," said Isabella in her placid way. "Quite like something in a novel. The missing heir is discovered. What a pity he is so hideously disfigured. And the ridiculous way he dresses, in those ill-fitting coats, to say nothing of his hair. No gentleman of fashion wears his hair in a queue these days."

"At least you are the heir presumptive," said Lady Blackwell, patting Frederick's arm consolingly. "And Captain Dormer—I mean Lord Claremont—does not look well. I doubt he will make old bones, as they say."

As if Frederick had not noticed that, as if he did not study Will's complexion each morning to make sure the pallor continued. But he managed not to snap at the stupid woman and lifted a shoulder dismissively. "He is still young. He might marry and have children."

"Do you think so?" Isabella turned her lovely face to him with a look of puzzlement. "I would not have thought so. After all, his appearance is so very hideous, I cannot imagine that any lady of sensibility could bear to marry him."

WILL CLUTCHED THE WINDOW FRAME and watched them stroll around the corner, out of sight and out of hearing. Bile rose in his throat. It was bad enough he had the responsibility of the estate. Did he have to be saddled with those three vultures as well?

The presence of Isabella and her mother he could understand. Both were widowed and had little by way of a jointure. Their other relatives did not seem eager to offer them a home, so here they were. Well, he could put up with that. The house was big enough to ensure that they rarely met. Lady Blackwell even justified her existence by running the household, or so he was told.

Frederick, though—why was he here? He had grown up here and had been Will's tormenter throughout childhood. The one good thing about being sent to the Navy was that it had meant an escape from his cousin. But here Frederick still was, no longer a child but a man in his thirties. Had he no career, no life of his own? Had he always been nothing but a dependent here?

Will decided he would have to check his father's will, ask the lawyers, and find out if he was actually obliged to house his cousin.

Right now, he needed to remove himself from Belford Park before he choked on his anger. Captain Garland wanted to see him? Very well. He would take Gibbs and travel to Widham to see his old friend . . . and if those he encountered on the trip were horrified by the sight of him, be damned to them!

CHAPTER 2

Widham, September 12

MARIA GARLAND FROWNED OVER THE ACCOUNTS. There was almost thirty pounds left from Papa's pay for the year, but the quarter's rent was due this month at Michaelmas, and that was ten pounds. She would have to pay the accounts at the shops, Maddy's wages were overdue, and they owed the doctor and the apothecary as well. That added up to just over six pounds.

There was enough coal to keep Papa's room warm, and the weather had not turned cold yet . . . at least, not very cold. They could do without fires in the parlor or bedrooms. When they weren't with Papa, she and Aunt Sophia could sit in the kitchen, and come December, the next payment of Aunt Sophia's jointure should arrive. If they needed more coal then, they would be able to afford it. Probably.

She sat back, gnawing on her lower lip. Yes, she was fairly certain that they would be able to manage through the end of the year, at least. Perhaps it was foolish to think even that far ahead. Dr. Petersham looked more and more gloomy each time he stopped by.

And afterwards . . .

She would not think about afterwards. Whatever came, she and Aunt Sophia would manage. After all, Aunt Sophia had an income of two hundred pounds a year. Surely they could live quite nicely on that, but not in this house, of course.

She looked around and shook her head at the elegant parlor with the finely-carved woodwork over the doors and fireplace, the intricate plasterwork on the ceiling, and the brocade drapery at the windows. Papa had taken this house five years ago—back when Mama was still alive, before his prize money had been lost.

They had not been good years. They had been filled with illness and death. When the time came, she would not be sorry to leave this house.

She gave herself a shake. There was work to be done—dinner to prepare, mending to do. There was no time for a practical, sensible woman to sit around thinking gloomy thoughts. She laid aside her pen, closed the bottle of ink, and began to straighten the pile of bills.

A knock at the door, a loud, heavy knock, demanded attention. She hurried into the hall, worried that the noise would disturb her father. Hastily swinging the door open, she prepared to scold but stopped in surprise when the visitor was not a village lad come on an errand.

On the doorstep stood a tall, gaunt man scowling down at her. He was obviously a naval officer, with his hair in a queue and his bicorn hat folded under his arm, but one who had been badly injured. His blue coat hung loose on him, he had lost his left eye, and that side of his face was badly scarred. Had he come here looking for assistance from her father? He was doomed to disappointment in that case.

He was a stranger, but something about him looked familiar. She could swear she had seen him before; she knew that face from somewhere . . .

Suddenly it came to her, a memory from years ago, from the happy years, and she smiled in delight. "Lieutenant Dormer! Is it really you? No, not Lieutenant. It's *Captain* Dormer now, is it not? You have come to see Papa! How very good of you. He will be so pleased. Do come in."

She stepped back to let him inside. As he swung along, his stiff left leg moving in an arc, she recognized the gait. He had lost a leg as well as an eye. Still, he managed his wooden leg quite well with the help of a cane. The injury cannot have been too recent. The North Sea encounters, perhaps. But that was unimportant. What mattered was that he was here. She was grateful for anything that might cheer up her father. He had few visitors these days, even though they were so close to Portsmouth. It was as if everyone had forgotten him; this was Captain Dormer, of all people. She could hardly believe it. Papa had always had a special fondness for him and was so proud of his success.

Once in the hall, he stopped to look at her in some confusion. "Miss Garland? Maria?"

She laughed, the first time she had laughed in a long time. "Of course you don't recognize me. It must be ten years since you saw me last, and I was still a schoolgirl then."

He smiled awkwardly as if he did not do so very often. "Still in pinafores, as I recall. And a mud-stained pinafore to boot. I am surprised that you remember me. You only saw me on that one visit."

She laughed again. It felt good to laugh. "Papa mentioned you so often in his letters that Mama and I thought of you as almost a member of the family."

How she remembered that visit. Fortunately, he could have no idea how vividly he had figured in her girlish dreams so long ago. He had been tall and handsome, with his dark hair and eyes—well, not perfectly handsome, perhaps. His face was too long and narrow for that, and his expression was almost always stern, surprisingly so for a lad of twenty. But even as a young lieutenant there had been something about him, something striking that drew the eye. And then every now and then there had been a smile, a shy, uncertain smile, that lightened his face.

He was attractive still, despite his injuries. No longer a youth, and despite the gauntness, he was now a powerful man, someone to be reckoned with. Those scars, slashing down from his eye and twisting the corner of his mouth, would fade a bit with time, and the patch over his eye gave him the air of a rakish pirate. Oh yes, he was still a man to give a girl dangerous dreams—even a girl like herself who knew better than to dream.

Then she bethought herself. "But where are my manners? Let me offer you something to eat and drink. Have you come far?" She ushered him into the parlor. "Please be seated while I see what we have."

"No, no. I need nothing," he said. "I was hoping to see your father. Is he at home?"

Her face fell. "At home? I had not realized . . . You did not know that he is ill?"

He looked surprised. "I knew that he had been wounded at Aboukir Bay, but I did not know he was still unwell. He did not mention that in his letter."

"It was the fever. He brought back some sort of fever, and it keeps recurring, leaving him a little weaker each time."

"That sounds . . . serious."

All desire to laugh had left her, and she felt the weight of their situation settle on her again. She did not even try to smile. "So the doctor tells us. My Aunt Sophia is sitting with him just now. I will see if he is awake."

HE WATCHED HER WALK OUT OF THE ROOM, not quite certain what had happened. She kept changing, right before his eyes.

When she opened the door, he had assumed she was a servant girl, and not a very well-treated servant girl at that. She looked overworked and underfed, wearing a shabby dress that seemed too big for her and an old-fashioned mob-cap that hid her hair completely.

Of course, the first thing he had noticed was not her appearance, but the fact that she had not flinched at his. She had looked up at him as if surprised to see a stranger, but nothing more. Those calm gray eyes showed no disgust, no horror, no fear.

And then she had smiled. A glorious smile that lit up her face and made her beautiful. A smile that wrapped a blanket of warmth around him, because the smile had been for him. It wasn't just that she had not looked horrified by the sight of him. She had looked pleased—not just pleased, but positively joyful to see him.

The smile hadn't really been for him, he reminded himself. It had been for Captain Garland's visitor. The joy had been on behalf of her father. She could not have been expecting him, had not even thought he was here to see her. Still, he could not remember if anyone had ever smiled at him that way. He shook his head in bemusement. A man would slay dragons to be rewarded with a smile like that.

She must be younger than he first thought. It was less than ten years since he had seen her, and she could not have been more than fourteen then, all legs and eyes, and full of questions.

Her letters had been like that too, at least the parts Garland read aloud. She'd wanted to know everything about the places they sailed and even the battles they fought, questioning the accuracy of the reports in the news sheets. A healthy skepticism, that. She had shown no illusions about the glory of battle, and had often included in her letters articles about new treatments for wounds.

Perhaps that was why she had been able to look at him without horror. She had grown up among seamen and must have seen the cripples coming out of the hospital in Portsmouth, the survivors coming off the ships.

She knew all that, had seen all that, and still could smile that glorious smile.

He looked around the room, noting that the elegance of the house seemed at odds with her apparel. It was a large room, at least in comparison with the ship's cabins he was used to, though not as cavernous as the rooms at Belford. One would think it the home of a wealthy, or at least well-to-do, gentleman. But despite the brocade at the windows, there was no sign of a recent fire on the hearth, and no coals were laid, though the room was certainly chilly enough.

Something was wrong here.

His eye was caught by the papers scattered on the desk, and he walked over to take a look. Someone had been doing the accounts. He knew he had no business prying into what was obviously private, but he looked anyway. It took no more than a quick glance to reveal that the family was in straitened circumstances.

He frowned at that. Garland might be on half pay now, but he must have won his share of prize money over the years. His family should be in more comfortable circumstances, not worrying about the butcher's bill.

The chill was beginning to feel oppressive. Leaving the desk, he moved to lean against the windowsill. That took the weight off his leg, which was beginning to pain him, and standing again would not be as ungainly as it was when he needed to rise from a chair. While he waited, he thought about a girl—a woman—who looked too old, too tired, too worn down for her years, but who warmed his soul with her smile.

The time passed slowly in the quiet house. He could hear the occasional murmur from what he assumed was Garland's room on the other side of the house, and footsteps hurrying along the hall several times. There was little noise from outside. Although the house was in a village, it was on a quiet lane that seemed to see little traffic.

He had told Gibbs to wait with the carriage, since the day was warm and dry enough to cause the horses no discomfort. When he looked out, he saw that the coach was causing no problem even though it took up most of the width of the road. Gibbs, however, seemed to have grown tired of waiting in the road and was walking around to the rear of the house.

Will smiled to himself. Gibbs would soon discover if anything was wrong here.

It was close to half an hour before Miss Garland returned, minus her smile this time. In fact, she looked uncertain. He pushed himself erect and tried to smile reassuringly. Her worry seemed to ease, at least fractionally, though it did not disappear.

"He wants very much to speak with you," she said, "but please, do not let him overtire himself. I fear you will find him much changed."

"I have some experience with the ill and wounded, as you might guess," he said dryly.

She seemed about to say something but changed her mind and turned to lead him into the hall. Stopping before a door toward the back of the house, she spoke again. "We made a room for him down here. It made it easier when he wanted to sit outside in the fine weather."

Opening the door, she stepped in and said cheerfully, "Here is Captain Dormer, come to visit, Papa." She turned back to Will and indicated an older woman, standing by the bed. "And this is Papa's sister, Lady Pellew."

The first thing that struck him when he stepped into the room was the smell. He knew it at once. It was familiar enough after all the time he had spent in hospitals. No amount of cleaning, no changing of linens, no bottles of vinegar or bunches of herbs could banish it.

It was the smell of death.

That gave him warning so he could school his features as he neared the bed. Even expecting the worst, he found the sight of Garland a shock. The strong, imperturbable captain who had led his men on the most daring of exploits without turning a hair had dwindled into a fragile old man.

Maria and her aunt had done their best for him. Garland was propped up to a sitting position on the pillows. His hair—what there was of it—was neatly combed, his face was freshly shaven, and he wore a clean nightshirt. But the hand that lay on the bed sheet seemed to be nothing but bones, and Garland's once piercing blue eyes were faded and dim.

The smile, though, that was still there—a bit faded, but still entirely honest, declaring unfeigned pleasure. This was where Maria's glorious smile had come from.

"Will. You came."

God, the voice was so weak. It tore at Will's heart.

Maria, standing at her father's side, caressed his cheek gently. "I'll leave so you two can have your visit." But as she passed Will on her way out, she whispered, "Not too long, please."

Will came to the bedside, trying to pretend his cane was naught but a fashionable flourish, but Garland's eyesight had not grown that dim. His smile faltered as he took in the limp and the patch. "Ah, Will lad, you too?" His mouth twitched. "Just another half-pay officer?"

"Not at all, Captain Garland," said Will, doing his best to sound hearty. "I've landed in a fine berth, softer than anything the navy has to offer. I'm a viscount now, with a fine estate and servants tripping over themselves to serve me. You must come for a long visit so you can be suitably impressed by my consequence."

"A viscount?"

"Aye. Lord Claremont at your service." Will managed a brief mock bow.

Garland simply looked confused. "Like Nelson? They gave the same honor to a captain?"

"No, no." Will kept his smile on, though it twisted a bit. "The title is no reward, just a matter of chance. Ill chance for some. My father and brothers managed to send themselves over a cliff in a midnight race, leaving no one to inherit the title but your humble servant." Will shrugged. "It doesn't seem to matter that I've no idea what I'm doing."

"That's all right, then." Garland leaned back and gave a sigh of relief. "Will . . ." He had to pause to take a few breaths and licked his lips before speaking again. "I'm dying, lad." When Will started to protest, he lifted a hand weakly. "No, there's no time for pretense. I'll not die this moment, but it won't be long. I've no right, I know, but I don't know where to turn. You must refuse if it is too much, but I have to ask . . ."

"Anything, Captain. You know that."

"It's Maria." He stopped and looked away for a moment before turning back to face Will. "I lost all the prize money, you see. Invested in a pair of ships that never made it home." He grimaced. "You'd think a sailor would have more sense, would know the risk. But now there's nothing for her. And there's my sister as well. Two women alone . . ."

It was not difficult to understand the fear that weighed down on the captain, but it was easy enough for Will to remove it. "No. They will not be alone," he promised, and took Garland's hand. "Rest easy, captain. I can take care of them. You were a father to me when I needed one. I will be a brother to them."

Will had to stop. Too much emotion was choking him. He swallowed, and managed a jocular tone. "Besides, there has to be something this fool title of mine is good for, never mind that great barracks of a house. It can be put to good use to protect them and keep them safe and secure."

Garland fell back against the pillows, breathing roughly until he could speak again. "Thank you. You were a good lad, Will, and now you're a good man. One of the best."

Will sat on the edge of the bed, still holding Garland's hand, until the older man fell asleep.

CHAPTER 3

MARIA WAS NOT QUITE SURE HOW it had come about, but apparently either Papa or Aunt Sophia had invited Captain Dormer—*Lord Claremont*—to stay at the house, along with his valet, though Gibbs seemed to be more a second in command than a servant.

At first, she had been appalled. How could they provide for a visitor? There were spare bedrooms, but they had not been used or even aired in ages. Lord Claremont would undoubtably want a fire in the bedroom—he was a *viscount* for goodness sake—and the chimney had not been cleaned since . . . well, she had no idea since when.

And what on earth were they going to feed him? How could she be expected to entertain him when she and Aunt Sophia spent all their time taking care of Papa? How could she possibly cope?

While Aunt Sophia sat with Papa, and Gibbs and Viscount Claremont returned to the inn to collect their things, Maria and Maddy, the Garlands' one remaining servant, set to work.

They scrambled madly to get a spare bedroom, with the adjoining dressing room for Gibbs, into something resembling decent shape. There were extra bedclothes laid away in the linen press, but the woolen mattress and bed hangings were a problem. The ones in the spare room looked decent enough, but they smelled musty and needed a thorough shaking to get the dust out. Maria was not going to allow them to be used by guests. She and Maddy replaced them with the mattress and the embroidered hangings from Maria's own room and dragged the others down the back stairs to the garden.

"We can take them up to my room this evening," said Maria. "They'll serve well enough once they've been aired."

Maddy looked dubious.

But when they reached the garden, they found it was starting to darken already. Clouds were gathering, and there was a damp chill in the air. Nothing could be left outside. It would end up soggy, not fresh.

When Maddy looked at her for a decision, Maria said, "We'll just leave everything here near the door. I don't need bed hangings tonight, and I can fold up enough blankets for a mattress."

The maid snorted derisively. Maddy may have been young, but she had very definite ideas about what was appropriate for a lady. "I'll go see what can be done," she said, heading back up the stairs.

Maria couldn't worry about the maid's approval or disapproval. What mattered now was dinner. She had left a kettle of soup simmering on the fire, but it was only enough for the three of them. If she added enough water to stretch it for five, it would have no flavor at all. Perhaps if she put the stale bread in the bowls and poured the soup over that . . .

But when she burst into the kitchen, she found that the table was covered with a white cloth, one of the ones they used to use in the dining room, and places had been set with their silver and china. On the cupboard sat a roast leg of mutton, emitting an incredibly savory smell, and four covered dishes beside it promised further delights. Aunt Sophia was fitting a final candle into a large candelabra in the center of the table.

Maria skidded to a stop. "What . . .?" She couldn't be more specific because she didn't know where to begin.

Aunt Sophia hummed softly as she lit the candles . . . beeswax. Where on earth had Aunt Sophia unearthed beeswax candles? They hadn't used anything but tallow for months.

"Isn't this nice, dear?" Aunt Sophia looked up, smiling happily. She had fixed her hair and put on a fresh dress and the lacy cap that she kept for Sundays. "Lord Claremont insisted on having dinner brought from the inn since we had not been expecting guests. Such a considerate gentleman."

Maria opened her mouth to protest. They were not a charity case, after all. But then she closed her mouth. Accepting this bounty would be less humiliating than serving a viscount hot water over stale bread. Then she felt a moment of panic.

"Who's with Papa?"

"The viscount is sitting with him. So kind. And I think it gives your father comfort to have a friend with him. He seemed easier in his mind when I left him."

"But Lord Claremont won't know what to do."

"He said he has had a great deal of experience with illness, and if he has any questions, he will call for us." A slight frown crossed Aunt Sophia's face. "Don't you think you should clean up a bit before dinner? Mr. Gibbs heated some water, and there is plenty left."

Undoubtedly it was so. If the rest of her was as grimy as her apron after the frantic cleaning, she must look like a chimney sweep. It was bad enough having to accept charity. To look as though she needed it would be intolerable. She filled a pitcher with some of the water—it was indeed good and hot—and hurried upstairs.

Following her aunt's example, Maria put on a fresh, lacy cap. It covered her hair effectively, and that was the best that could be expected. She had no time to brush out the dust and dirt, and she could pin it up only in a simple coil. Her dress, though clean and neat, was a sturdy and serviceable garment of practical brown linen. She annoyed her sensible self by regretting that it was not more fashionable and becoming.

As she descended the stairs, the regret was overtaken by gluttony. She paused momentarily to savor the scent of the roasted mutton. How long had it been since she tasted roasted mutton? Her mouth watered as she pictured it on the plate, a thin—no, a thick—slice lying in its juices, the fat crisp around the edge. She breathed in the pleasure of it before she hurried on down.

It was a strange meal, yet no one but Maria seemed to notice the oddity of it. Lord Claremont carved while Gibbs carried the plates around and Maddy set out the dishes of creamed turnips, roasted potatoes, carrots, and a loaf of fresh bread. Aunt Sophia sat at the head of the table, with Lord Claremont on one side of her and Maria on the other, while Gibbs and Maddy sat at the foot.

Maria had a panicked moment when she thought that Papa was alone, but Gibbs assured her that her father was asleep. "The lad from the inn's sitting with him and will let us know when he wakes."

The lad from the inn? But how were they going to pay him? She wanted to protest, but how could she?

Everyone else seemed to think that this dinner was the most natural thing in the world. Even if they did not really believe it, they at least behaved as if it were true.

"Are you settled in this part of the world now that you are no longer in the navy, Lord Claremont?" Aunt Sophia was being the aristocratic Lady Pellew, the gracious hostess of a dinner party, tilting her head inquiringly as she sought to draw out her guest.

Their guest seemed inclined to go along with the pretense and smiled courteously. "No, my lady. My estate is in Somerset. The sea is nowhere in sight, and the view is all of apple trees."

"We must have Maddy make one of her apple tarts for you then, to make you feel at home."

The courteous smile slipped a bit. "No need for that. I have not been there long enough—or rather, I have been away too long—for apples to loom large in my notions of home." He picked up a bottle of wine and turned to Maria. "Please allow me to fill your glass, Miss Garland."

Maria did not ordinarily drink wine, but she was beginning to think that a glass might make this meal seem less bizarre, so perhaps two glasses. She smiled at the viscount. "Please."

He hesitated as if startled, but then filled her glass. She sipped and examined him over the rim.

He had a good face, she decided. Strong. Even without the scars, he would not look at all like a pretty boy. His was a man's face, resolute. His eyes—his eye—was dark, and his hair was too, so dark as to look black in the candlelight. She had always liked dark hair. His movements were economical—a sailor was accustomed to tight quarters—but did not lack grace. Perhaps that was one reason he resented his wooden leg. It made it impossible to walk gracefully. But his hands were graceful. She watched him gesture as he described something to her aunt—graceful but also strong.

She looked down at her plate and realized that it was empty. She had even wiped up the juices from the mutton with her bread . . . and though the viscount had refilled her glass, it was now as empty as her plate. That was wrong of her. A lady should always leave something on her plate and in her glass, lest people think her greedy. She shook her head to scold herself.

"Perhaps you ladies would like to make an early night of it. Gibbs and I will take care of Captain Garland tonight, and you can both get some rest."

The viscount's voice was a deep, reassuring rumble. It seemed to wrap around Maria like a shawl, a lovely, soft shawl. She felt herself swaying as she turned to him and thought that she really shouldn't have had that second glass of wine. She opened her mouth to say something, though she wasn't sure what, when she heard Aunt Sophia speaking instead.

"Thank you, my lord. That is very kind of you. Come along, Maria. You can share my bed tonight. Say goodnight to everyone."

Maria said goodnight. At least, she thought she said goodnight. She didn't really remember much more until she awoke the next day, feeling fully rested for the first time in ages.

By the third day, Lord Claremont's presence had begun to seem perfectly natural. Despite her best efforts to feel guilty for imposing on him, his presence made such a difference in the household that Maria simply felt grateful. At the very least, there were two more people to sit with Papa, but it was more than that.

Lord Claremont was a surprisingly easeful presence. He not only made no demands on the household, but accommodated himself to their situation.

No, that was not true, she realized after a moment's thought. He had not accommodated himself at all. What he had done was take charge of the household, but so skillfully that she had not at first seen what was happening. She ought to protest. This household was her responsibility, after all. She would protest, but not just yet. Not while Papa was so much easier in his mind.

At first glance, Lord Claremont appeared stern and forbidding, but she soon realized that the lines on his face had been etched there by pain, not ill temper. He was a proud man and seemed resentful of the limits imposed on him by his injuries. Thank goodness she had said nothing when she saw him descending the stairs yesterday morning. His progress had been slow, one step at a time, and almost certainly painful. Her first thought had been to offer him a room on the ground floor so he could avoid the stairs completely. It was just as well that her second thought had been the realization that he would consider her offer a humiliating display of pity. He had stiffened defensively when he saw her and eased only after she had smiled and said nothing more than, "Good morning."

Once he realized that no one was going to make a fuss over his injuries, he relaxed.

She was grateful for the food, of course, and the coal, but most of all she was grateful for the change he had wrought in her father. It was not that Papa's health had improved. She was not so foolish as to hope for a miracle, and her father was still fading away a bit more every day. But Lord Claremont's presence seemed to have brought him peace. Papa no longer fretted constantly. His worries seemed to have eased. He even seemed to breathe more easily.

Nonetheless, gratitude could not make the guilt disappear entirely. There was food on the table—roasted meats, fowl, ragouts, fresh white bread, wine, tea, and sugar to sweeten it—and there was plenty of coal for fires, even in the bedrooms. These were luxuries they could not possibly afford—had not been able to afford for quite a while.

She had tried to speak of this to Aunt Sophia yesterday, but the older woman was standing by the fireplace with her eyes closed and a faint smile trembling on her lips, looking unworried for the first time in many months. She even looked younger, more like the pretty, petted woman she had once been, before her husband died and the extent of his debts was disclosed.

That simply added to Maria's sense of guilt. Aunt Sophia may have come to live with them because she had nowhere else to go, but what had they offered her beyond a roof over her head, and a chilly roof at that? Papa had already been ill when Aunt Sophia arrived, and she had immediately been put to work helping to care for him. Not once had she complained, though it was obvious that she was lending a hand at unfamiliar tasks. If Lord Claremont's charity meant ease for Papa and comfort for Aunt Sophia, how could Maria refuse it?

Truth be told, she could not be certain she would refuse it even if she did not have the others to worry about. She was warm, well fed, and with two more people to sit with her father, she even had enough time to sleep. To refuse to accept these gifts, she would have to be a fool. Besides, on a purely practical level, it was far easier to accomplish her tasks when she was not hungry and tired all the time. At least that was the sop she threw to her conscience.

She only hoped that Lord Claremont could afford all this bounty. He had arrived in an impressive carriage, true enough, but he did not have the look of wealth about him. His unfashionable clothes fit badly, as if they dated to a time before his injuries. His linen was of good quality but worn almost threadbare. He may have inherited a title, but a title did not necessarily mean wealth. Aunt Sophia's situation was proof enough of that.

She hoped that he was not giving more than he could afford, because there was no way she would be able to repay him. The only thing she could think of was to suggest to Gibbs a pad of lamb's wool to cushion his stump where it rested on the wooden leg. It might lessen his pain.

CAPTAIN GARLAND CHUCKLED APPRECIATIVELY at Will's tale of the horror felt by one of his fellow patients at Yarmouth's naval hospital. The young midshipman had survived storms and battles, mayhem and maelstroms, but had come close to passing out from sheer embarrassment when a visiting vicar's wife lifted the sheet on his cot to examine his wounded leg. Will smiled at the memory himself, but now that Garland looked cheerful and even easy in his mind, he had some questions.

"By the by," he said casually, "you mentioned that your daughter had lost her fiancé. That must have been terrible for her. How long ago did he die?" What he really wanted to know was if Maria was still mourning him, if her heart was still broken, if that was the reason for the sadness in her eyes. But he had no right to ask such things. He would have to be indirect, and this was not easy for him.

Garland lost his cheerful look. "He didn't die. As soon as he heard I had lost the prize money, he broke off the engagement."

Will snapped to attention. "He did *what*? What kind of scoundrel would do such a thing?" It was inconceivable. How could any man bear to give up a woman like Maria?

"A practical fellow." Garland's mouth twisted in a sneer. "He has since married a woman whose father made a fortune in naval stores and bids fair to make another when the war resumes."

"If that's the sort of fellow he is, his loss was no loss at all." Will remained tense, his hands clenched on his cane. "Who was the bastard?"

"Son of a local merchant. Now what was his name? Cuttlebush. That was it. Jeremy Cuttlebush." Garland sneered slightly. "A pretty boy, but no more to him than that."

Will longed to thrash the fellow, to pound him into a pulp. Never had the loss of his leg brought greater frustration. The fellow had dared to insult Maria? To cause her pain? "But your daughter. How did she deal with such a betrayal?"

Garland leaned back and appeared to give the question some thought before he answered. "Do you know," he said slowly, "I believe the greatest injury was to her pride. I remember her seeming surprised, affronted, but not, I think, heartbroken. I do not think she could have carried it off so well if her affections had been deeply engaged."

Will frowned. "If it was not a love match, why did she agree to it?"

That drew a slight smile from Garland. "My fault, I fear. I believe the great attraction was that he was a landsman, or at least not a seaman. I was away throughout most of Maria's childhood— most of her life, for that matter. I was not even here when her mother died, and it fell to Maria to nurse her through the months of her illness. Then when I finally did return, it was as a dying man. A husband who would be there when she needed him must have seemed desirable." There was pleading in his eyes when he looked at Will. "Find her a good husband, one who will take care of her and protect her. She has had to spend too many years taking care of others."

Will nodded. He could do that.

Over the next week, there was a steady stream of visitors from Portsmouth. Men who had served under Garland, fellow captains, veterans of campaigns in the Caribbean and in the Mediterranean—they all came to visit Garland, sharing memories and bringing news and gossip. When the captain began to look tired, Will saw to it that they retreated to the drawing room to share their reminiscences with Maria and Lady Pellew.

At least now they could offer the visitors tea and cakes, even brandy.

On the evening of the second day, once the last visitor had left, Maria cornered Will. "Lord Claremont, I must thank you," she said.

He looked at her as if surprised. "Whatever for?"

"For all these visitors."

"Nonsense," he said, not meeting her eye. "They are nothing to do with me. If visitors are coming, it is because of the affection and admiration they feel for your father."

"Now it is my turn to say nonsense. His old friends came at the beginning, but eventually drifted away. Now they are back, and you are the one who made it happen."

She stood there in silence until he felt obliged to speak again. "Well, Gibbs may have mentioned something to a few friends when he went into Portsmouth the other day."

"So, it was all Mr. Gibbs' doing, then? At a word from him, captains and commodores leave their ships to visit my father's sickbed?" She laughed softly. "If you prefer. I am still exceedingly grateful. Papa was feeling useless and forgotten, and you have given him back some measure of dignity. To say nothing of everything else you have done for us. We are all of us in your debt." She looked embarrassed, as if she had said too much, and hurried off.

Will watched her walk away. He felt able to do so only when she was not aware of his scrutiny. She was far prettier than he had realized at first. No, not pretty like those dainty little dolls, but beautiful, like a queen, with those eyes that looked directly at him as if they could see everything about him, and that wide, generous mouth with its glorious smile. How had he not seen it immediately? Perhaps it was simply that she was no longer so tense. There were no longer lines of strain around her mouth. It would be pleasant to think that he was responsible for lifting some of her burdens.

At least she had discarded that dreadful mobcap in favor of a smaller lacy cap and he could now see some of her hair. It was pinned up, and mostly under the cap, but it was no longer completely hidden. What he could see of it was a sort of light brown. Was he supposed to know a word to describe that shade? He didn't, any more than he knew a word for the color of her eyes. He didn't dare try to peer at them too closely, but he had been able to descry flecks of blue mixed in with the gray, like the winter sky. Did such a mixture even have a name?

Ah, what was he doing, thinking about such things? He should just be grateful that she didn't shudder at the sight of him.

She was grateful to him? These past days had been the first comfortable days he had spent since he received word of his inheritance. At least he had something to do, something he could do. He knew enough officers in Portsmouth to spread the word about Captain Garland. And those men knew enough not to bring sad faces with them. They wouldn't pretend that Garland wasn't dying, but they wouldn't make it worse for him by maudlin psalm-singing.

No, he was the one who should be grateful. The meals he ate at the kitchen table here were the first enjoyable meals he had eaten in ages. It wasn't simply that the food was better—plain, decent English food, not hidden under the odd-tasting sauces that seemed to cover every dish at Belford Park. It was the company. Far better to share a meal with the servants than with people who resented his existence.

THE END, IT TURNED OUT, HAD NOT BEEN FAR OFF. Within the fortnight, Captain Garland died, with both his daughter and Claremont at his side. Maria kissed her father's cheek one last time. Will closed the dead man's eyes and then held Maria as she trembled until the tears finally came. Then he took her to sit with her aunt while he and Gibbs dealt with the details of death.

The funeral took place with all the proper pomp and solemnity. Many of the neighbors were surprised to see the number of high-ranking naval officers who came to the church and followed the coffin to the cemetery. Afterwards, they returned to the house and trooped into the parlor. Miss Garland and Lady Pellew offered sherry and biscuits and accepted the expressions of sympathy with quiet courtesy. That their mourning garb was a few years out of fashion only underlined their grief and lent them dignity.

Lord Claremont had removed himself to the inn after Captain Garland's death for reasons of propriety, though he left Gibbs behind to protect the household. After the visitors had departed, he remained behind to confer with Gibbs. Maria had managed admirably over the past few days, but the strain was beginning to show. She was pale, and once again there were lines of tension about her mouth. Lady Pellew looked no better. Perhaps Gibbs could slip something in their wine to help them sleep. Then tomorrow he could talk to them about the future and assure them that they would be taken care of.

Mr. Garrison, the elderly lawyer who handled the captain's affairs, also remained behind to approach the ladies. After appropriate expressions of sympathy, he took Maria's hand and patted it. "I know how much you will miss your father, Miss Garland. I just want to assure you that you need not worry about your future. Nor you either, Lady Pellew," he added, turning to the older woman.

"Not worry?" Lady Pellew asked hopefully. Maria looked at him as if he had lost his mind.

"I was not certain Captain Garland explained everything to you." The lawyer smiled gently and patted Maria's hand again. "He left everything in Lord Claremont's hands, so you need have no concerns."

Will's head snapped around when he heard that. He had intended to wait until morning to bring up the matter. Maria had been too distressed the last few days. Death, no matter how expected, is always a shock, and she had been in no state to have a calm discussion about her future. He knew all his tact would be needed to make certain she did not refuse assistance. It had been difficult enough, getting her to accept food and coal. She would not have done so had it not meant ease for her father's last days.

Expressions of confusion and irritation chased each other across Maria's face. She snatched her hand away from the lawyer and glared at Will before turning back to Garrison. "Thank you, sir, but neither I nor my aunt is in need of a guardian, and as my father had no wealth to bequeath, there is nothing to leave in Lord Claremont's hands."

"No, no, no, I think you will find that things are not nearly so bad as all that." Mr. Garrison continued to smile gently. "And his lordship is not your guardian, of course. Simply your trustee. As such, he will see to your welfare."

Maria turned her back on the lawyer and faced Will, hands fisted at her sides. "Papa cannot have asked you to assume responsibility for us. That is really too much. We are already too deeply in your debt."

"Nothing of the sort," said Will stiffly. He was seriously annoyed with Garrison for bringing this up now, and so bluntly, as if Maria were a child. Did he think her unable to take charge of her own life? Will knew better. He simply wanted to make it easier, safer for her. "If there is any debt, it is the one I owe to Captain Garland. Looking after his family is the least I can do for him. I assure you, Belford Park is more than large enough to accommodate you and your aunt."

Lady Pellew gave a small gasp and looked hopeful at that. Maria gave a gasp too, but it was an angry one. "Belford Park?" she said. "Your estate? That is absolutely impossible."

He could not help but feel slightly affronted. After all, his dislike of the place came from his memories. She had not even seen it. Did she dislike it simply because it was his? "You could, of course, remain here if you prefer," he said.

"No we could not." Maria was quite emphatic. "You do not seem to understand. We will not be your pensioners. Aunt Sophia and I will find a cottage somewhere, and we will manage quite nicely on her income."

Will did not fail to notice that Lady Pellew seemed far less certain of this than her niece did. Indeed, Lady Pellew looked rather horrified by Maria's assertion.

Ignoring both Will and her aunt, Maria turned to Mr. Garrison. "If you wish to be of assistance, you might see if anyone knows of a small cottage that we could rent, perhaps with room for some chickens and a vegetable plot."

With that she sailed out of the room, pennants flying, proudly defiant. Will could not suppress a small smile of admiration. She was a wonder.

Lady Pellew fluttered in distress, murmuring, "Oh dear oh dear." Finally, she gathered herself up to follow Maria, but just as she was at the door she looked back. "I do hope you aren't offended, Lord Claremont. My niece is upset, of course, and I fear she is not, at the moment, as sensible as she usually is."

Will smiled reassuringly at her. "Don't distress yourself. Things always look better in the morning." They didn't, of course. Sometimes they looked far worse. But that was an aspect of reality that Lady Pellew would not choose to face. It was something Maria knew, though.

His problem was going to be trying to convince her that things *could* be better.

CHAPTER 4

IT WAS SUCH AN OBVIOUS SOLUTION Will could not imagine why he had not thought of it immediately.

Sitting by the fireside in the inn's private parlor, he took a swallow of his brandy and considered. He could not see a flaw in the plan. It was perfect.

That Miss Garland could manage in a cottage, raising chickens and vegetables, he did not doubt. She had run the household for years, caring first for her dying mother and then for her father, doing the work of the servants when the money ran out. She had courage and determination enough to do whatever was necessary, and she would survive.

Her survival was not what her father had asked for. She deserved more.

Even if he found her a cottage near Belford Park, where he could watch out for her, she deserved more.

What she needed was a husband who could protect her, provide her with security, and guarantee her a respectable place in society. Seeing to it that she married a man who could offer her those things would be the best way—indeed, the only way—for him to fulfill his promise to Garland.

He, on the other hand, needed a wife and, it was to be hoped, children. He needed a wife to help him run the estate, and he needed heirs who would ensure that Frederick did not get his greedy hands on it.

It was an eminently practical solution for both of them.

If they married, he would be in a position to take care of her in ways that would in turn fulfill Garland's hopes for her. He could protect her. The damned title all by itself would protect her. As a viscountess, she would have a more than respectable place in society, and he could see to it that she had all the material security anyone could desire—her aunt as well.

He could not offer her love, of course, nor would he expect it from her. He knew what he looked like. But at least she did not recoil in horror at the sight of him. Perhaps she would not find the idea of marital relations too repugnant. In the dark, she would not even have to see him. And if she could not bear it, he would not insist. He would have to make that clear.

But how he hoped she would agree! Just the thought of having her in his bed had his blood racing.

And she did not shrink away at the sight of him.

His body was tight with longing at the mere thought of her. He tossed down the rest of the brandy and tried to bring his body under control.

Could he make her see the advantages to such a marriage? The disadvantages were obvious, not only insofar as she would have to accept him, a grotesque excuse for a man, as her husband.

She would also have to give up any hopes for the sort of romantic love match found in novels, and many women seemed to want that. But perhaps she was not a romantic. She was a sensible woman. According to her father, she had once before accepted a man for practical reasons. Perhaps she would be willing to do so again.

Then there was the problem of pride. This was a thorny issue. She hated being the recipient of favors—he had seen that from the outset. It had been difficult enough providing decent meals for the household. She would have refused if she could. It was only because she was presented with a *fait accompli* that she did not. The fact that the food was already on the table or in the kitchen, and that her aunt was so relieved, forced her to accept.

But in this case, the truth of the situation was that she would be the one conferring a favor. He was the one in need. Could he convince her of that? He could explain about the estate, tell her that he needed someone to help him run it, that he needed to keep it out of Frederick's hands.

Perhaps he shouldn't say too much about Frederick. After all, he didn't want to frighten her away, just show her that he needed her. He needed a wife and, it was to be hoped, children.

If he presented marriage as a practical, mutually beneficial arrangement, she might agree.

It was a pity he did not have a better-fitting suit of clothes. He had not bothered with a visit to a tailor since he left the hospital, not seeing any need to put fine feathers on his grotesque body. Fortunately, Gibbs had somehow unearthed new linen—shirts and cravats. Someone here at the inn could polish his boots and brush his coat.

A man should look his best when making a proposal, no matter how pragmatic.

MARIA SAT IN THE ROCKING CHAIR near the kitchen fire, her hands wrapped around the teacup, letting the scented steam caress her face. There was so much to do, but she was having difficulty rousing herself to begin. She had slept badly, when she had slept at all, tormented by her thoughts.

What on earth had Papa done? And why couldn't Aunt Sophia see how impossible it was? She could not possibly become Lord Claremont's pensioner, his dependent. It would be too unbearably humiliating. Not even for Aunt Sophia's sake could she do it.

She had had it all planned. They would find a cottage with room for a kitchen garden in the countryside. She had cared for chickens when she was a child and could do it again. She even had some seeds saved for the garden. Aunt Sophia had agreed to it all. But that was before, when there really was no other choice.

Now along came Lord Claremont, and all Aunt Sophia could see was how much easier their lives would be if they went with him. It was all the little luxuries he had provided, the soft bread, the tea she was holding right now. These were things they would no longer be able to afford, and she would miss them too. But she could not accept his charity. If only he had never come! But his presence had made Papa's last days so peaceful as if . . .

Good heavens.

She sat back with a start, sloshing the tea on her hands.

Suddenly it all made sense.

That was why Papa had been so peaceful at the end. He had stopped worrying because Lord Claremont had promised to take care of her and Aunt Sophia.

She wanted to weep. How could Papa have done such a thing. If it had been anyone else, it would not have been so bad. She might even have accepted, if only for Aunt Sophia's sake. But to be dependent on Lord Claremont, to live humbly on his charity? It would be more than she could bear.

"Beg pardon, miss, but that Mr. Cuttlebush is here." Maddy was twisting her hands in her apron uncertainly. "He said he wanted to see you, so I put him in the parlor."

"Jeremy?" Maria asked. "What can he possibly want?" All her worries were replaced by irritation. How dare he intrude at this time? He could not possibly think he was welcome.

"I dunno, miss. Should I tell him you're not here?"

Maria frowned. She would like to say yes, but she had no idea why he had come. It could not be for any good reason. What new disaster awaited? Best to face it now, she supposed, along with all the other problems.

"No," she said to Maddy. "I'd best see why he has come." She went to the sink to wipe the tea from her hands with a damp cloth, shook out her skirt, and patted her hair into place. Her old black dress was hardly becoming, a relic from her mother's death four years ago. Now the skirt was too short and the bodice too tight. She would have liked to be more becomingly dressed for an encounter with Jeremy—it would have soothed her pride—but this was really all he was worth. She held her head high and glided, like an elegant lady, down the hall.

The door to the parlor stood open, and she could see Jeremy standing by the fireplace, examining the cards on the mantle. He looked surprised to see so many. Did he assume that because he had deserted them, no one else cared about her father? Surprised or not, he looked very prosperous, his hair neatly trimmed, his gray tail coat with its high color fitting snugly across his shoulders, and his legs encased in a fashionable pair of trousers.

He turned as she entered and smiled broadly, walking toward her with his hands held out. "My dear Maria. How are you?"

She evaded his hands as she stepped into the room. "Well enough, at this sad time, Mr. Cuttlebush, thank you."

"Such formality? Between us?" Ignoring her reference to her father's death, he continued to smile and stepped toward her again.

She gave no answering smile, only a look cold enough to stop him in his tracks. She had once thought him handsome, but she could not now see why. His chin was weak, and his full mouth looked petulant when he was denied. "What brings you here, Mr. Cuttlebush?" She repeated the name deliberately.

He let his hands fall and offered her his rueful smile. "You have not forgiven me, have you? But you must know that I had no choice. No matter how much I loved you, I had to marry someone who could replenish the family coffers."

She kept her face impassive. "That is the past. What brings you here today?"

"How could I not come? I know how close you were to your father, and I know how badly off he must have left you."

And that knowledge brought him here with a smile on his face? What was he about? "How kind of you to come offer your condolences in person. However, the funeral was yesterday."

"Not my condolences." He was smiling again. "I have come to offer my assistance."

She raised her head a bit higher. "I am sure that is kindly meant, but I have no need . . ."

"Maria, Maria, there is no need for pretense between us." He was coming closer again and seemed to be trying to back her up against the wall. "I know what your financial situation is, and I have come to help you."

"My financial situation has not changed in some time. I do not recall any offers of assistance from you in the past." She sidestepped his advance again.

"Well, I could hardly expect you to come away with me while your father was still alive. But now that he is no longer with us, I have come to offer you my protection." He looked rather pleased with himself.

She froze in place, not entirely believing what she heard. "I beg your pardon?"

"I know your father was angry with me, but there is no longer any reason why we cannot be together."

"Surely I misunderstand you. You are now a married man, and it sounds as if you are proposing to set me up as your mistress."

"Be realistic, my dear. What other choices do you have? Your father has left you penniless. You need a man to protect you. You know I have always found you attractive, and you did not appear indifferent to me. It was only the lack of money that tore us apart. But now I can afford to keep you in the comfort you deserve." Taking her silence for interest, he continued, "I'll be spending most of my time in London now, so I'll take a house for you there."

She held up a hand for silence, but lowered it immediately as she noticed that it was trembling with fury, turning into a claw. "Using your wife's money, I presume."

Looking affronted at the remark, he sniffed dismissively. "The money is mine now that we're married."

"What a vile toad you are, and what a lucky escape I had." She spoke so softly that it took a moment for her words to register. Then he flushed angrily.

He reached out and grabbed her by the arm. "Now see here . . ."

"Let go of me, you, you rancid jellyfish, you bilge scum, you dunghill!" She pulled back a fist to swing at him and almost stumbled when she connected with empty space.

Lord Claremont was standing there, holding Cuttlebush by the neckcloth, twisting it so that his captive was turning a bright red. "Are you all right, Miss Garland?" he asked. The rumble of his deep voice seemed to calm the charged atmosphere.

She took a deep breath and managed to smile politely. "Yes, thank you, my lord."

Good heavens. Lord Claremont was holding Jeremy up in the air with one hand while he leaned on his cane with the other and he didn't even appear to be straining. She had no idea he was so strong. It was a delightful sight. Behind him, she could see Maddy, her hands twisted in her apron, listening wide-eyed, a smile beginning on her face too.

"What shall I do with this piece of offal?" Lord Claremont spoke as calmly as if he often came to a woman's rescue and lifted villains up in the air.

Feeling somewhat lightheaded, she swallowed a giggle. Jeremy looked so ridiculous twisting in Lord Claremont's grip, his face turning red as he struggled ineffectually. "I expect that if you put him down, he will scuttle away."

Cuttlebush hit the floor with a thud and scrambled to his feet, carefully staying out of Claremont's reach. "I see my offer came too late," he sneered. "A lord, eh? So that's the way of it. Well, some women can stomach even a cripple when there's a title attached." He leaped farther out of reach as Claremont turned to him again and scurried out of the room. A moment later they heard the front door slam.

Claremont looked at Maria with a slight smile. "Rancid jelly-fish? Bilge scum?"

She could feel a blush rising and lifted her shoulders in an apologetic shrug. "What would you? I grew up in naval ports and acquired an inappropriate vocabulary."

"It appeared to be appropriate today." He nodded approvingly. "Who was that particular barnacle?"

"Mr. Jeremy Cuttlebush."

"Damnation!" He started to spin around but his wooden leg caught, and he had to grab hold of a chair to keep from falling. The next few words were muttered in an unintelligible undertone as he steadied himself.

Firmly erect once more, he turned his frown on Maria. "What was that . . . fellow doing here?"

His reaction to the name startled her, until she bethought herself. "My father told you about him."

"Had I known his name before he left, I'd have given him the thrashing he deserves." Claremont frowned. "How did he have the effrontery to come here?"

She closed her eyes. Humiliation piled on humiliation. Not only did he know that Jeremy had jilted her, but he had come upon her just as she was receiving Jeremy's degrading proposition. He must think no one considered her entitled to respect. But she had no intention of hiding the truth. She tilted up her chin and looked straight at him. "Mr. Cuttlebush was under the impression that since I am now alone and penniless, I would be grateful for his attention. He came to offer his protection and was affronted when I took offense."

Fury and outrage flashed across Claremont's face. Truly, he appeared to feel the insult to her even more than she did herself. He stabbed his cane on the floor as he swung over to the window. Cuttlebush was long out of sight.

Turning back to her, he said, "I cannot adequately express my regret that you should have been subject to such insult."

She managed a small smile. "I confess that I feel somewhat ashamed."

"Ashamed? Nonsense." His voice was an angry growl. "No reproach could possibly fall on you for his dastardly proposition."

"Not for that. I am ashamed that I was once such a fool as to be willing to marry that creature."

His features eased into a slow smile. "Then I conclude that you do not pine for him?"

"Hardly. And I do thank you for your intervention. I could not have humiliated him so effectively by myself."

They shared a companionable smile before she let hers fade. She spoke again. "However, if you have come to renew your offer of assistance, I would ask you to refrain. I am no more willing to be your pensioner that I am to be Mr. Cuttlebush's mistress."

Claremont flushed angrily. "You cannot think I meant . . ."

"No, not at all. I am certain that your offer to care for me and Aunt Sophia was honorably meant. But you must see how humiliating it would be for me to be your pensioner. I could not do it."

He cursed softly—too softly for her to make out the precise words, but the tone was unmistakable—and swung back and forth across the room, finally coming to a stop by the window once more. It had begun to rain, and he stared out at the drops splattering against the panes.

The rain, thrown by gusts of wind against the house, was loud enough to drown any fidgeting sounds she might make as she waited. She was not quite certain what she was waiting for, but still she waited.

He finally turned back to face her. "This is obviously not the most opportune time for what I have to say. The past weeks have been difficult for you, and the events of this morning cannot have eased your spirits. Still, I ask that you hear me out before you answer."

She nodded agreement. "I certainly owe you that courtesy at the very least."

He shook his head impatiently. "You owe me nothing." Then he turned aside slightly and took a deep breath. "As you know, I am now a viscount. What you may not know is that I never expected to inherit the title. I had two older brothers, and I have spent the last twenty years at sea. I know nothing about running an estate."

He paused. The pause went on so long that she felt obliged to say something. "Can you not find a competent steward to run things?"

He nodded dismissively. "Yes, that needs to be done, but that is not enough." He grimaced. "There seem to be all sorts of social obligations. And there are the servants. Tenants. Neighbors. People who need to be dealt with." He took a deep breath and looked straight at her. "And I need an heir. I need a wife."

What was she supposed to say to that?

"Yes, I can see that," she said cautiously. "But I do not see how I could help you. I do not know the sort of woman you would need to marry. I have never even been to London, no less mingled with the aristocracy."

That brought a scowl to his face. "You misunderstand. I do not want you to *find* me a wife. I want you to *be* my wife."

Maria sat down abruptly. More precisely, her legs ceased to hold her up, and she was fortunate enough to land on a chair when she collapsed. Had she just received a proposal of marriage? She realized that her mouth was hanging open, so she closed it. Then she opened it again to say, "You must be mad."

He looked as if she had slapped him. Obviously, she needed to explain.

"I know my father asked you to look out for us, but you are carrying charity too far. There is no need for you to sacrifice yourself on the altar of matrimony."

"Sacrifice myself?" He snorted. "You obviously misunderstand." He turned away, stomped over to the fireplace, and stared into the empty grate. Taking a deep breath, he began again. "I am the one in need, not you. It is not only the servants and the neighbors. There are relatives, dependents . . . and at the moment my heir is a cousin who . . ." He broke off with a grimace. "Suffice it to say that I would prefer that he not inherit."

She must have looked uncertain, because a note of pleading entered his voice. "You are a sensible woman, Miss Garland. We seem to rub along well enough. You can see that this is a practical solution for both of us."

Sensible. Practical. This was something less than a romantic proposal. But then, he was correct. She was a practical woman. But even as a practical matter . . .

She gave her head a shake to clear it. "This is most kind of you, my lord, but marriage?"

He turned to look at her, his face stern and unsmiling. "Think of it as a bargain. I can offer you a secure social position, with no financial worries, and provide for your aunt as well. You will no longer have any worries of that sort. In return, you can help me, stand between me and other people, deal with my tenants and neighbors, with the social obligations. That sort of thing." He waved a hand somewhat helplessly to indicate those incomprehensible matters.

"But, my lord, you are talking about running an estate, occupying a social position far above anything I have ever known. I have not the training for that sort of life. My family has always lived simply."

He shook his head. "I have had no training either, and I do not see that it requires training, only sense. I know that you can do it. I saw you these past weeks with your father's visitors. You knew precisely how to talk to them, and there were lords enough among them. They in turn admired you and enjoyed your company. You will have no difficulty with the gentry of Somerset. You will put them at ease, and they may eventually forget that the sight of me terrifies them."

Now that was exasperating. Why did he talk of himself in such a way? "I can hardly believe that your neighbors fear you."

Turning aside, he gave a careless shrug. "Fear me or simply find the sight of me repulsive, it matters not." He continued, his face devoid of emotion. "I know I am more the stuff of nightmares than the answer to a maiden's prayers. I want you to know that if you find the thought of marital relations too distasteful, I will not force you. I promise you that."

"What utter nonsense!"

"I have it on good authority from my sister-in-law that no lady of sensibility could bear my touch."

"Do stop this idiocy." She was truly irate and stood up to do some pacing of her own. "If your sister-in-law said any such thing, I think she must be a great fool. You have a few scars that are already fading and an eye patch that actually looks rather dashing. That is all."

"And a missing leg. Do not forget that." When she opened her mouth to argue once more, he shook his head. "No, you are kind, but I know how I appear. You are able to look at me without disgust. That is what gave me the courage to put this proposal before you. If you think you would not be able to bear life with me, you must say so."

Shaking her head, she said, "It is not your appearance. I assure you of that. Indeed, I find your looks quite striking and attractive." She paused and sat down again, gnawing at her lower lip. "It is just marriage . . . It is such a great step, you see." She stared at her hands, clenched in her lap, then looked up. "I need time to think," she said. "Could I give you my answer tomorrow?"

"Of course." He managed a half smile as he bowed over her hand to take his leave. "At least you did not reject me out of hand. I feared you would think I was no different from Cuttlebush, taking advantage of your situation."

"I would never think that of you."

No, she thought as she watched him leave, the two propositions were worlds apart. The offer of protection grew out of contempt, the offer of marriage out of respect and kindness. They were as different as the two men who made them.

CHAPTER 5

"MARRIAGE? HE PROPOSED MARRIAGE? OH, MARIA, my dear girl!" Aunt Sophia clasped her hands to her breast in an ecstasy of delight.

Maria had been fretting all day, and now that evening was settling in, she decided to confer with her aunt. After all, whatever decision she reached was going to affect both of them. So she had come to her aunt's bedchamber and told her what had happened. She was beginning to think that had been a mistake. Aunt Sophia was not being her usual practical self. Maria needed her to calm down and think rationally. She said so.

Unfortunately, Maria's flat tone made no impression on Aunt Sophia. She continued to burble happily about new clothes, fashionable entertainments, and servants to do the work.

"A lady's maid," she said with a happy sigh. "You will have a proper lady's maid to do your hair."

"Aunt Sophia, it is not that simple." Maria wanted to shake the woman. What was she doing, burbling on about a fairy tale future? They both of them needed to consider this realistically.

Her aunt looked at her in amazement. "Not that simple?" But then she finally recognized the absence of delight in Maria's face, and her own smile faded. "Oh dear. Do you truly dislike him? Is it his injuries? I know he is badly scarred, and he does have that wooden leg. Does his appearance truly bother you? I thought you were getting along quite well with him. But of course you cannot marry a man if you cannot bear the thought of his touch."

"It is not that at all." Maria began to pace about the chamber, picking up odds and ends—one of Mrs. Radcliff's books, a china shepherd—and putting them down impatiently. "His scars are nothing—I barely notice them. He is far more bothered by them than I."

Lady Pellew's face crumpled, and she sat down abruptly, as if she had somehow deflated. "Then you dislike him. I misunderstood. You seemed to get on so well with him that I thought you quite liked him. And I confess, I found myself liking him more and more when he was here. Were you just tolerating him for your father's sake?"

"Of course not." Maria turned on her aunt angrily. "How can you say such a thing? He is a thoroughly admirable man, kind, generous . . ." She needed to explain what her difficulty was, but it began to seem impossible. "That is precisely the problem. He is too kind, too generous. What if he does not actually want to marry me? What if he is making the offer only out of some sense of obligation to Papa? I know life will be much easier for you if I accept. It will be easier for me as well. I know that too. Everything sensible tells me that I would be a fool to refuse him."

She began pacing again. Over to the window to look out at the rain, then back to the fireplace. There was no fire because now that Lord Claremont was no longer here, they had returned to being frugal with the coal. If she refused, her aunt would be cold come winter.

She made a sound that was half sigh, half moan. "But how can I possibly spend the rest of my life not as a wife but as an obligation?"

Aunt Sophia looked at her curiously. "I think I begin to understand. You admire Lord Claremont then?"

"Of course I do." Maria waved an impatient hand. "Who could not?"

Her aunt smiled slightly. "But you are afraid that he does not admire you."

"How could he?" Maria turned to face her aunt. "Look at me. I am a drudge, a practical, sensible drudge, not a fine lady. Certainly not someone who could be considered an appropriate bride for a viscount." She collapsed onto a chair. "How could he possibly admire me? I don't even know how to use a fan."

A fit of coughing overcame Aunt Sophia. When she had recovered, she said, "I think you may have misjudged Lord Claremont's reaction to you." When Maria started to argue, the older woman waved aside her protest. "No, I understand perfectly what is worrying you, and if Lord Claremont does view you with such indifference, you should not marry him. That would be a cold marriage indeed, and I would never wish that for you."

"You think I should refuse him then?" It had been her first thought, but she found that she did not feel gratified to have her aunt confirm it.

"I did not say that." Aunt Sophia smiled at her. "You need to kiss him."

"Aunt Sophia! I couldn't possibly do such a thing."

Kiss him? Kiss Lord Claremont? Maria felt suddenly warm. She could imagine kissing Lord Claremont. It required no effort at all. Touching her fingers to her lips, she imagined the sensation of his lips there. She could feel color rising in her face. It was just embarrassment causing this flush, was it not?

"Of course you can. Couples should always kiss before they marry. I kissed all my suitors. That was how I knew that Pellew was the man for me. It is the simplest way to discover how things will go after the wedding. And if it is an unpleasant experience, it is best to discover that while you can still call it off."

"He will think I am dreadfully forward and immodest." She chewed on her lower lip.

"If he does, there will be no wedding, and you will never see him again, so what he thinks will be unimportant. But it is quite likely that he will be delighted, and it will be a pleasant surprise for both of you."

THE CHURCH BELL IN THE VILLAGE CHIMED EIGHT. Will could hardly fail to hear it, since the church was scarce a hundred yards from the inn. Unfortunately, he had awakened hours before, bathed, shaved, dressed, and breakfasted. That left him with little to do other than fret about whether or not Maria would accept his proposal. At least another hour remained before he could learn her answer. Much as he tried, he could not convince himself that eight was a reasonable hour at which to call upon her.

Miss Garland. It ought to be easier if he could remember to think of her as Miss Garland. He had no right to call her Maria, not yet. Not until she agreed to marry him . . . to be his.

A fierce rush of possessiveness swept over him. His! She would be his to protect. Even crippled as he was, he would be able to protect her. Once she was his, she would be safe.

He would wrap her in luxuries. He would drape her in jewels, dress her in the finest silks. He would undress her, wrap her in his arms . . .

He stomped over to the basin and splashed cold water on his face.

Nine o'clock: that would be a reasonable hour. She was always up and about long before that time. No frivolous, giddy creature she, to lie abed half the day. He paused, still leaning over the basin. Perhaps she had always been up and busy early in the morning only because she had to be. After all, the responsibility for the family had all been on her shoulders. Given a choice, perhaps she would like to lie abed in the morning.

He smiled slowly. He could picture her, rosy with slumber, lying there on smooth white sheets, plump pillows scattered around her, one of those reddish-brown curls falling across her cheek and tangling with her long lashes. He would trail a finger along her shoulder, up the graceful line of her neck, and . . .

He bent over and splashed more cold water on his face.

At nine o'clock precisely, the Claremont coach rolled up to the inn door and Will, hat folded under his arm, climbed aboard. Once seated, he stretched his neck uncomfortably. His fresh cravat was too starched for his liking, but the earlier one had gotten wet with all those splashes of cold water. This would have to do.

It was no distance at all to the Garland residence—a few minutes sufficed for the trip—but Will had no intention of limping along the streets for the entertainment of the village children. Bad enough that they could see him as he hobbled from the coach to the inn and back again, especially since he needed the assistance of a groom to make certain he did not fall on his face getting down from the coach.

The maid, Maddy, let him into the house and into the drawing room. Maria was already there, standing near the window. The morning sun—for once it wasn't raining—made a sort of halo around her, dancing over the reddish lights in her hair. But with the light behind her, he couldn't see her expression. He tightened his grip on his cane.

She raised her eyes to greet him. At least she didn't seem to look pitying. That was a good sign, wasn't it? But she did look uncertain. That was not so good.

"Miss Garland, have you made a decision?" *Damnation.* That sounded insultingly brusque, as if he were asking a midshipman if he had carried out his orders. He cleared his throat and tried to make his voice less gruff. "If you need more time . . ."

She licked her lips nervously. "My lord, please do not think me too forward . . ." She stopped and licked her lips again. Did she have any idea what that did to him? "My aunt suggested . . . My lord, before I give you my answer, would you be willing to kiss me?" The words came tumbling out in a rush. "Kiss me as if you mean to go on?"

He felt the blood rush to his head. Then it rushed further down. Would he be *willing*?

Any words he might have spoken stuck in his throat. For a second, he could not move. Then he discovered that he had closed the gap between them. His hand trembled as he reached out for her, and then steadied as he cupped her cheek, tilting her head to just the right angle as he lowered his mouth to hers. Gently he brushed her lips. He must go gently. He did not want to frighten her.

Gently. The thought fluttered in his mind as his mouth settled on hers. His tongue teased lightly along the seam of her lips. Then with a sigh, her lips parted, and her hands rose up to cling to his shoulders.

All thought took flight as waves of hunger and desire rolled over him. He was naught but sensation as he tasted her, devoured her, his hands and mouth feverishly exploring her. Her cheek, the lovely line of her jaw, the whorls of her delicate little ear—he licked and nibbled his way across and back and settled once more to delve into her mouth. His hands caressed her, tracing the long line of her spine, reaching around her to feel the soft weight of her breasts, and then, sliding down, he leaned against the wall for support and pulled her against him.

He heard a little gasp of surprise. Of shock? He began to pull out of the maelstrom that had engulfed him, but he was adrift in a sea of confusion. What was he doing? He had dropped his cane, and both his hands were clutching her buttocks, holding her against him so that his cock was pressed against her belly. Good God, what had he done? Did she know what that was?

As he loosened his hold on her, he could see that she was somewhat dazed. Had he completely terrified her? How had he lost control so completely?

"I'm sorry, Miss Garland." His voice was so hoarse he could barely speak. "I did not intend . . ." How could he possibly explain himself? "Please forgive me."

He forced himself to meet her eye. She was swaying slightly as her vision cleared, her hair tumbling about her shoulders. Her lips were parted slightly, and she seemed to be taking in his words. She stiffened and turned very pale. Then she lifted her hands to her mouth and turned bright scarlet.

"You're sorry?" The words came out as a croak. She spun away, turning her back to him, her arms wrapped around herself as more words tumbled out. "I had not thought—but of course, you would have wanted to know too. And now I have given you disgust of me with my forwardness, and you wish to withdraw your offer."

Withdraw his offer? What was she talking about?

She turned around to face him again, tilting her head up proudly. "I quite understand, my lord, and I apologize for my behavior. I assure you, you may consider your offer withdrawn. I thank you for the kindness that prompted it."

"Withdrawn?" he roared. "Woman, have you lost your mind? Why would I withdraw my offer? If you want to refuse me, just say so straight out."

"But you said you were sorry," she said, her confidence faltering as she stepped back and pressed her arms to herself again.

He took a deep breath and let it out slowly. Doing his best to keep his voice calm, he said, "I was afraid I had frightened you, that I had been too . . . . enthusiastic."

"Oh." After a long silence, a small smile began to tug at her mouth. "I've never been kissed like that," she said. "It was . . . I found it . . . quite exciting."

An answering smile found his mouth. "Exciting? Then you were not frightened?"

"Oh no." She was blushing. "Not frightened at all." She looked up to meet his eyes with a hesitant smile. "Should I have been?"

Exultation roared through him. He forced down the shout that wanted to escape and took a deep breath. When he decided he could speak like a gentleman and not roar like a captain, he said,

"In that case, Miss Garland, would you do me the very great honor of agreeing to be my wife?"

"I would be proud and happy to be your wife."

This time, their kiss was indeed gentle, but full of promises, and he stood there with his arms around her, holding her close and resting his cheek against her hair while he slowly absorbed the fact of his good fortune.

It was their last peaceful private moment for some time.

CHAPTER 6

It was perfectly obvious that her future husband had been the captain of a ship. Once they had announced their engagement—and once Aunt Sophia had stopped exclaiming and kissing and exclaiming and hugging—he had begun to chart their course. As soon as she and Aunt Sophia could get themselves packed up, he announced, they would repair to Ashgrove, the home of his Uncle Roderick and Aunt Beth—Sir Roderick and Lady Fortescue—in Oxfordshire, where they would stay until the wedding.

His announcement was met with silence.

She looked at him without speaking and waited for him to realize that his simple pronouncement was inadequate. She was not about to either agree or refuse until she had some notion what he was on about.

Aunt Sophia also looked at him, but pityingly. She did not keep silent for long. In her most gentle voice she said, "A lady generally has some say in the arrangements for her wedding."

He looked startled at that and turned to look at Maria. When she nodded, he flushed and began apologizing. It was a rather confused and stumbling apology, ending with, "I had not thought. You will doubtless wish to be married from your own home."

That pronouncement gave her pause.

Home. She rolled the thought around in her mind as she looked around the room. Most would call it a well-appointed drawing room, of decent size. The same could be said of all the rooms. However, it was not a house she had ever thought of as home. It was not a place filled with happy memories.

She realized that there was no place, no house, that she thought of as home. What an appalling thought. Everyone had a home, at least a place they thought of as home, didn't they? Why didn't she? Was it because they had rarely stayed in one place for more than a few years?

She had never really had a home. Her happy memories were tied to people, not to places. She had friends, certainly, friends in every place she had ever lived. They all corresponded regularly. But there was no place that came to mind when she tried to picture "home." Certainly not this place, where first her mother had sickened and died, and then her father had come to die.

"No," she said, "I have no wish to be married from here if there is some other place you would prefer."

He still looked embarrassed as he began his explanation. "Sir Roderick is my uncle, my mother's brother. After I was sent to sea, it was with him and his wife that I stayed when I came ashore. He is the one who found me in the hospital after I had been injured and took me home with him to recover." His mouth twisted in a mocking smile. "If one could call it recovery."

There was more at work here than she had realized. She had thought it was only his injuries that distressed him. But when she thought about it, she realized he always said he was *sent* to sea, not—as most men said—he *went* to sea. And when he was ashore, he went to his uncle's house, not to his own home. Yes, his mother had died when he was a child, and his father and brothers were dead, but that had just happened last year. There was much about her future husband and his family that she needed to learn, but not, perhaps, just now.

She smiled at him. "If your aunt and uncle do not object, their home seems an admirable place from which to marry."

She doubted it would always be so easy to bring such a look of relief to his face.

Aunt Sophia did not look entirely convinced, but she would understand as soon as Maria explained. As for the servants, Gibbs looked delighted by the news. Maddy, however, burst into tears.

That should have been expected, though the reaction terrified both Will and Gibbs. Maria held the girl while she sobbed. Maddy had only stayed for the meager wages they paid because her family lived nearby, as did Charlie Benton, the young man who was courting her. Maria made soothing noises and assured the girl that they were not at all angry that she could not accompany them to some foreign place. That on the contrary, they were very grateful to her for her service and loyalty, and that they wished her and Charlie nothing but happiness.

Then, remembering that she no longer needed to worry about coal and that she would not be paying the next quarter's rent, Maria said, "And Lady Pellew and I hope you will accept ten guineas as a wedding gift."

That produced more tears and exclamations. Eventually Gibbs led the girl off to the kitchen for a cup of tea. Their departure left the drawing room strangely quiet.

"If they're to wed," Will said gruffly, "fifty guineas will give them a better start."

IT DID NOT TAKE LONG TO PACK. The house, like every house in which she had ever lived, had been taken furnished. Their china, silver, linens, books, assorted ornaments and trinkets, and the portrait of Maria's mother had all been crated up to be dispatched to Belford Park after the wedding.

Still, it proved more difficult than Maria had expected. The house itself held no fond memories, but the things . . . That was another story. Her father's sword—she had gone to pack up his things and had found herself sobbing as she cradled the sword in her arms. The cutlass with its ivory grip and brass chasings on the scabbard had always fascinated her when she was a child. When her father was home, it would hang over the mantelpiece in their parlor until the time came for him to return to sea.

The last time when he returned, he had packed it away in his trunk.

It would travel with her, she decided, to Ashgrove or any other place where she might go.

The same was true of her mother's rosewood tea caddy. She ran her fingers over the polished wood. It felt as silky now as it had when she was a child, allowed to turn the key in the brass lock and carefully measure out the precious tea leaves. It had been empty for years now, but she vowed that once she had her own home, it would be filled once more . . . and with tea of the finest quality.

The caddy and the sword would go into her trunk. There was certainly enough room for them. Maria and Lady Pellew were barely able to fill a trunk apiece with their clothes and personal belongings.

Then it was over. Goodbyes were said to the neighbors, and thanks were made to the doctor and the vicar and his wife for their many kindnesses. She stepped out of the house that had been her home for the past six years and felt a strange mixture of nervousness at leaving a familiar place and relief that the years of illness and suffering were over.

It suddenly struck her that she was an orphan now. That meant she had no parents to turn to as well as no ties to bind her to any place. She had no home, and she did not really know what lay ahead. For all she knew, she was about to set sail toward that part of the ocean where the old maps showed serpents and monsters. She froze in momentary panic, her foot on the step of the carriage, one hand lifting her skirt, the other grasping the carriage door.

"Maria?" Aunt Sophia's voice, with its note of concern, prodded her into motion. She hastily climbed aboard.

Once she was actually seated next to her aunt, the change in her circumstances began to sink in. She had seen the coach before, of course. Lord Claremont—Will, she could think of him as Will now that they were betrothed—had regularly arrived at her door in it. But this was the first time she had ridden in it herself.

It was, without question, the most comfortable vehicle she had ever entered, with well-padded seats covered in wondrously smooth red calfskin and with thick woolen lap blankets in a matching shade of red piled in the corner.

A qualm assailed her as she sank into the seat. This was more than comfort. It was luxury. She caught sight of her feet and promptly tucked them back so they were hidden by her skirt. Her half-boots looked out of place here, their leather so much more worn than that of the seats.

Yet Lord Claremont's—Will's—clothing did not suit the coach any more than her old shoes did. His coats were respectable, certainly, but they were worn, ill-fitting, and certainly not of the latest fashion.

The coach swayed as Will clambered aboard and swung into the seat opposite. Gaunt he might be, but he was a big man with broad, powerful shoulders. She remembered how easily he had picked up Jeremy and dangled him in the air. The memory made her smile. She peered at him through the black veil draped over her bonnet.

Perhaps he was a bit less gaunt than the day he had arrived, but his coat still hung loose on him. Had it been made for him before he was injured? Probably, but why had it not been replaced? Could he not afford it?

She half hoped that was the case. If he had inherited an estate loaded with debt, well, title or no, that was something she could help with. She might not know how to deal with luxury, but she knew how to economize. Long experience had made her quite good at it. She could make Will's life comfortable even while watching the pennies.

The coach could be something that he inherited with the estate, a bit of ostentation to proclaim the owner's state, rather like the finery many wore to cover up the fact that they could not pay the grocer's bill. She hoped so. At best, her family had never lived more than comfortably. She had never moved in any but the most ordinary of respectable social circles, and these did not include members of the aristocracy.

How could she possibly become a viscountess? She had never even *seen* a viscountess and had no idea what a viscountess was supposed to do. Every time she thought about it, she began to worry her lower lip—as, she realized, she was doing now. Clamping her teeth closed, she forced her lips into a small smile.

The coachman started the horses, and the coach bounced a bit before settling into a steady, swaying motion. The town, the nearby farms, anything familiar soon slipped out of sight.

"You can remove your veil, dear," said Aunt Sophia. "You will be much more comfortable without it."

As Maria lifted the heavy black lace from her bonnet, her gaze met Will's. He was seated across from her, facing backwards, and smiling uncertainly. She impulsively leaned forward to lay her hand on his. Immediately it was enfolded in his grip, and he lifted it to his mouth for a kiss.

"We shall manage this, you and I," he said.

The prospect of becoming a viscountess was still unsettling her, and she had very little notion of what her future life would be. Despite his kindness and generosity over the past month, she barely knew her future husband. But she did know one thing. There was something very comforting about the prospect of marrying Will Claremont.

THEY SPENT A LONG DAY BEING TOSSED ABOUT in the coach, stopping for the night in Andover. It was a poor choice. The inn was well enough appointed, but it was a busy one on the main road. Horns and shouts echoed throughout the night as mail coaches, stagecoaches, and—Will was ready to swear—just about every private coach in England pulled in, changed horses, and pulled out.

He was also ready to swear that the landlord had given them the noisiest rooms he had. There had been no mistaking the look of distaste on the man's face when he caught sight of Will's face. Nor had Will missed the hint of sneer in the man's voice when he said, "My lord."

They would make the rest of the trip in a single day, Will swore to himself. He would not allow Maria to be insulted by the poor service offered because he did not look worthy of being a viscount.

Over breakfast in a private parlor the next morning he tried to apologize to the ladies, who were trying to be cheerful as they yawned. Lady Pellew smiled and told him not to worry about it. Maria said the inn was so crowded that they were fortunate to get a private parlor for their meals.

They didn't realize that they had been given the private parlor only because even the landlord could recognize that the women were ladies.

The horses, at least, were well rested, and the roads were not too terrible, so for the remainder of the journey the ladies were able to doze in the coach while Will fretted in silence. It seemed to him that he had not shown himself to good advantage as an escort and protector so far.

It was twilight by the time they turned into the drive of Ashgrove, and he could feel the peace of the place settle over him. The tension left his shoulders, and he could feel his face relax into a smile. If he had a home on this earth, it was here. But even as he began to feel easy, a sudden qualm struck him.

What if Maria did not like it?

The swing of the carriage startled her from her doze, and she seemed momentarily lost until her eyes found Will and she smiled.

"We should be there in a few minutes," he said.

Her eyes widened and she turned to peer out the window. Ash trees lined the drive, their fissured trunks standing straight as sentinels. As they rounded a curve, there was a break in the trees and Ashford itself appeared, a simple brick house glowing in the last rays of the setting sun. It was of no great antiquity, perhaps seventy years old, but it sat comfortably in its park, surrounded by gently rolling fields and enclosed by woodlands. Its unadorned lines were softened by tendrils of ivy reaching up around the windows.

"How lovely," she said softly.

Will began to breathe more easily.

CHAPTER 7

THIS DID NOT LOOK TOO DREADFUL, Maria thought as she stood beside the carriage looking up at the house. It was much larger than any house she had ever lived in, true enough, but it was a far cry from an intimidating palace like Blenheim, which she had visited once as a child.

Black paint gleamed on a front door that was surrounded by a simple stone pediment, and the three broad steps leading to the door were equally simple. Its pristine condition—every window sparkling, every bit of paint fresh and unmarked, every inch of the gravel forecourt neatly raked—betokened wealth but not ostentation.

She could do this. She could enter this house and not feel an unworthy intruder. She took a deep breath, laid her hand on the arm Will offered, and arranged her face to display polite pleasure as they mounted the steps to the now-open door.

She needn't have bothered.

The older couple hurrying into the hall fell on Will with cries of delight, and Maria and her aunt might as well have been invisible.

It was Jack Sprat and his wife, she thought. Neither one was very tall—Will topped the man by a good half foot, and the woman was a round little creature, twice as wide as her husband. Their focus on Will gave her a chance to look around, but what she noticed first was not the hall itself. It was the servants—it looked like a butler, two footmen, and a woman who must be the housekeeper—all as pleased to see Will as the elderly couple was.

The delay was just long enough to give her time to start worrying again. It was taking all her effort to keep her hands still at her side and not twist her shawl into a rope. If only she had thought to put her veil down so she would not be exposed before she had a chance to observe their expressions when they looked at her.

When they eventually turned to her, it was not as bad as it might have been. There was a welcome, even if it was merely courteous and tempered with distrust. She could not fault Will's introduction. He presented her not simply as his betrothed, but as if she were a prize he was proud to have won. That should have made her feel encouraged. What it did was make her feel inadequate.

She smiled as courteously as her hosts and dipped into her most elegant curtsey. Next to her, Aunt Sophia, being of higher rank than the Fortescues, merely inclined her head. Thank goodness for Aunt Sophia. Maria often forgot that there was actually a title in her family. She felt a little better.

A flurry of practicalities then swept over them, with Lady Fortescue exclaiming that they must be exhausted from their journey and sending the ladies off with the housekeeper while footmen carried in their trunks. Maria did not protest. She was not precisely tired, but she was worn and achy from the long carriage ride, and she could see the lines of strain in Aunt Sophia's face. The housekeeper, Mrs. Biddle, was pleasant enough, but did not seem to be the gossipy sort. That was no doubt admirable, though Maria would not have objected to a bit of information about the family.

Far better than gossip, she decided, was the smooth efficiency of the household. Almost before she had removed her bonnet, gloves, and outer garments, a large tub had been placed before the fire in the dressing room and filled with steaming water. The maid assigned to assist her helped her undress, and Maria sank blissfully into the herb-scented water. She could smell rosemary and mint. Leaning back with her eyes closed, she let the warmth soothe her aching body. The gentle thumps and rustles from the bed chamber were the sounds of the maid unpacking her trunk and putting things away. She lifted some water in her hands and let it pour over her face and down her neck.

Luxury had much to recommend it. She suspected that the Fortescues would be glad to send her packing once they found out who she was, and they should be able to convince Will that he could do far better. She might as well enjoy this while she could.

WILL WAS GIVEN NO OPPORTUNITY TO REST. The moment Maria and Lady Pellew were out of sight, Aunt Beth seized hold of his arm and steered him into the drawing room. As soon as the door was closed on the servants, she began, "What on earth is going on, Will? Your message said that you were bringing your betrothed to us. Who is she, and why is she in mourning?"

Will held up his hands to calm her. "Miss Garland is the daughter of Captain Robert Garland. She is in mourning because he died only weeks ago."

Uncle Roderick frowned. "Captain Garland? I am sorry to hear that. I never met him, but you always spoke well of him."

"You did not, however, speak of his daughter." Lady Fortescue was also frowning. "I am, of course, sorry to hear of his death, but I did not even know he had a daughter, no less that you had some sort of understanding with her."

Perhaps coming here had not been such a good idea after all. He should have realized that his aunt and uncle would expect an explanation. They would not be content to simply be presented with his bride-to-be. He should have married Maria first and then come here. Now it was too late for that. Explanations would have to be made.

He kept it simple. After all, now that he had come into the title, there were social obligations, he needed a wife, he needed an heir, that sort of thing. No need to be more specific, and certainly no need to mention Frederick's hopes of inheritance, or the woman who had shrieked at the sight of him.

Judging from the look on his aunt's face, simple was not enough. His words did nothing to dispel her worried look. When he came to an end, she eased her worried frown into a gentle smile.

"Of course, you need to marry," she said, "but you have time to think about that. Why choose a young woman of no background? There are any number of girls of good family who would be eager to marry you."

Uncle Roderick had looked as disturbed as Aunt Beth ever since the door closed on Maria and her aunt. Now he nodded in agreement with his wife. "Not as if this one's any great beauty," he grumbled.

Will swung around in outrage at that comment. "I beg to differ," he said stiffly.

Ignoring this exchange, Aunt Beth continued, "I simply do not see what the great hurry is. You could at least wait until the young woman is out of mourning." She paused and looked sharply at Will. "There isn't any reason to hurry, is there?"

"Certainly not." He stood stiffly, reminding himself that their doubts rose out of concern for him. "Miss Garland is a lady of respectable family and impeccable reputation. She is all any gentleman could look for in a wife. If you feel for any reason that you cannot welcome her and her aunt here, we will leave as soon as possible. However, since it is late in the day, I trust you will allow us to spend the night."

"Oh Will!" Aunt Beth burst into tears and threw herself on Will to sob into his waistcoat. "How can you say such a thing?"

"Now, now, lad," Uncle Roderick said gruffly, "just worried about you, that's all."

Aunt Beth subsided into snuffles as Will patted her on the back. "It's just that we want you to be happy."

He continued to pat her back to soothe her. "You're just upset because I found her on my own, without asking for your help. I'll wager you had a number of candidates in mind yourself."

"And if I did?" She drew herself up and thumped his shoulder. "It's no more than your mother would have done if she were still with us. And Georgina Cowell is a lovely girl. I'm only glad I never said anything about you to her—or to her mother."

"I'm sure she is delightful, but I have made my choice."

With a final sniff, Aunt Beth nodded and accepted her husband's handkerchief to blot her eyes. "I must look a sight. I had best go repair myself before our guests come down."

Uncle Roderick watched his wife depart before he turned to Will. "You're set on this young women, then?"

"I am. This marriage will benefit us both."

His uncle shook his head. "Sounds a bit cold-blooded to me, but if this is what you want."

Will hesitated. "You do not know her. She is strong and brave and . . . and when you see her smile, you will know that she is beautiful as well. You and Aunt Beth have been talking as if the benefit from this marriage will be all on her side, but that is because you don't know her yet. She could do better than a one-eyed cripple. No," he insisted when his uncle tried to protest, "let us not pretend. I know what I am, and I am the one who will gain."

DINNER WENT AS WELL AS MIGHT BE EXPECTED from a meal at which everyone was on his best behavior and trying not to allow any misgivings to appear. Sir Roderick and Lady Fortescue offered sympathy on the death of Captain Garland, asked about their visitors' journey, and commiserated on the discomfort of the inn at Andover. Maria and Aunt Sophia praised their rooms and admired the scenery they had passed through. Will watched everyone uneasily. And they all talked about the weather, the cold, wet spring that had only recently turned pleasant.

Maria choked down as much food as she could manage in an

effort to be polite. What had actually been served, she would have been hard-pressed to say. Aunt Sophia managed to communicate that her late husband, Lord Pellew, had been a baron. Will's aunt and uncle did not appear particularly impressed by this information.

Pleading fatigue, Maria excused herself shortly after dinner and sought her bed. She lay there, looking up at the canopy, the clean, white canopy. It looked pristine—not just clean, but not even worn, not a mend or a darn in sight. She was quite good at mending herself, and her repairs were always inconspicuous. This canopy, however, had no repairs at all.

It was pristine.

Maria was not sure she was going to be able to manage this.

She had dressed for dinner in the best mourning gown she had, the one she had worn to greet the guests after Papa's funeral. A maid had pressed it, but it was still a four-year-old dress that had never had any aspirations toward fashion in the first place. Lady Fortescue's costume had not been wildly elaborate or extreme in any way, but her lilac silk dress was beautifully cut and sewn, the lace ruffles at the neckline were very fine, and her cap of darker silk trimmed with bows was charming.

Maria closed her eyes. Perhaps in the morning when she talked to Will it would all seem less impossible.

The next morning, when she went down to breakfast, she found Will looking happy and contented. He was finishing off a plate of beef along with fresh rolls slathered with butter and was draining cup after cup of tea.

Since she had spent the night worrying rather than sleeping, she felt anything but happy and contented. Her stomach churned at the mere sight of all the food piled on the sideboard. She poured herself a cup of tea, weakened with additional water and sweetened with honey. She hesitated to actually swallow it, but she held it under her nose to enjoy the soothing fragrance.

"We need to speak when you have finished," he said, smiling cheerfully.

She glared at him. "Indeed." She stood up. "I am quite finished."

That made him look uncertain as he politely rose. "But you have not eaten."

"I am quite finished," she repeated.

Still looking uncertain, he offered his arm to lead her from the breakfast room to a small sitting room nearby. How many sitting rooms were there in this place, she wondered.

"I have had a letter from Lieutenant Sinclair. Hal." He looked at her as if she ought to know the name. "He was my second in command on the *Hector*."

Oh, his ship in the battle at Copenhagen. She nodded in understanding.

Will looked easier. "He has invited me to stay with his family while I am in London."

She was not at all clear on the point of this. What was he talking about?

"While you are in London?" She hoped he understood that that was a question and not a statement.

He seemed to think he was making sense. "Yes. There's a house there that goes with the viscountcy, of course, but I have no idea what sort of condition it's in, and it makes no sense to open it for a stay of a week or so. I could stay in a hotel"—a shadow crossed his face at that prospect—"but this will be much easier."

No, he would not want to stay in a hotel if that could be avoided, certainly not one in London. She understood that, but his discomfort was beside the point.

He had brought her here to stay with strangers—strangers who did not particularly care for her—and now he was going to leave her? She was trying to remain calm, but it was not easy. She did not seize hold of his coat to shake him, but simply asked, "Oh?"

"I must get the license," he explained.

"Of course. I had not thought of that."

It made sense, she supposed. Since neither of them lived in this parish, they could not ask for the banns to be read. Even if they could, that would mean waiting for a month before they married. This way, he could be back in a few days, and it would all be settled.

But in the meanwhile, she would be here under the eyes of his aunt and uncle—strangers to her, and strangers with disapproving eyes at that. She pursed her lips.

Appearing oblivious to her concern, he continued, "Since I will be in town, I thought to ask some friends for advice about the management of the estate. The steward does not inspire me with confidence, but it could be that is simply my ignorance."

That had to be done now? She took a deep breath to calm herself. Yes, of course. It needed to be done, and if his friends were in London, it was only sensible to confer with them when he needed to be in London anyway. After all, the reason for this marriage— his reason, at least—was his concern for the estate. It was not as if he was passionately in love with her.

He looked at her with some concern. "Does it distress you to stay here? I should have realized that I would have to leave you and your aunt behind. You might have preferred to stay in Widham."

"It's not that I wished to stay in Widham," she said carefully. "It's only that I had not expected you to depart so quickly."

"Ah. I should have explained my plans before uprooting you, shouldn't I?" He had the grace to look embarrassed. "I apologize for that. I'm unaccustomed to owing anyone an explanation. But I didn't want to leave you anyplace where that Cuttlebush creature could come sniffing around."

She smiled slightly at that.

Will looked at her intently and closed the distance between them. Before she realized what was happening, he wrapped an arm around her to pull her close, and kissed her fiercely. She felt herself melting against him and clutched at his shoulders to keep from falling.

Eventually he broke the connection and rested his forehead on hers as they both recovered their breath.

"Just remember," he said hoarsely, "if any of the local sprigs come offering for you, you are promised to me."

"I could never forget that." She reached up to caress his scarred cheek, but he caught her hand before she could touch him and pressed a kiss into the palm. Then, he let go of her and stepped away.

As he turned to leave, they realized that Lady Fortescue was standing in the doorway, an odd expression on her face.

"Take good care of my lady, Aunt Beth," he said.

"I will do that." The odd expression was softened by a smile.

Left alone with Lady Fortescue, Maria did not know quite what to say. So she said, "My lady, I don't know what you must think of me . . ."

But Lady Fortescue just smiled and took Maria's arm. "There is no need for you to worry, my dear. You have done much to ease my mind."

CHAPTER 8

IT BEGAN THE NEXT DAY. Lady Fortescue joined with Aunt Sophia in insisting on a course of instruction in the running of a household. When Maria protested that she had been running a household for the past six years, they looked at her with pity and seated her between them in the morning room.

"And you did it marvelously well," said Aunt Sophia, "but running a large establishment is something very different."

"You know how various tasks should be done, which is all to the good." Lady Fortescue smiled kindly at her, with only a small amount of condescension. "That means you will know when the servants are doing their jobs properly. But supervising is different from doing."

"Now, a good housekeeper can make all the difference." Aunt Sophia looked at Lady Fortescue and asked, "Do you have any idea what the situation is at Belford?"

Lady Fortescue shook her head regretfully. "I'm afraid I have no idea. We haven't been there in more than twenty years. However, it has been a largely masculine household for much of that time, so I suspect things have been a bit lax."

The two older women looked at each other, considering.

"Your housekeeper?" asked Aunt Sophia tentatively.

Lady Fortescue nodded. "Yes. We had best confer with Mrs. Biddle." She rang the bell, and when a footman appeared, said, "John, please tell Mrs. Biddle that we are in need of her expertise and would like to join her in her parlor in about half an hour."

They seemed to be making a ridiculous fuss about nothing. Yes, Maria could see that there were more servants and more rooms to be cared for here at Ashford than there had been in any home she had ever had, but really, how different could it be? She had always maintained a schedule of the tasks to be done. It was simply a question of seeing to it that the servants were assigned to those tasks and given a schedule on which to do them.

This room was one example. She looked around. The daily maintenance would be more or less the same as in any room in any house she had ever inhabited. First thing in the morning the curtains would be drawn. If the fireplace had been used, the hearth rug would need to be taken outdoors to be brushed and shaken and a cloth laid so that the ashes could be swept out and the fireplace cleaned before a fresh fire could be laid. With a coal fire, the hearth and chimney piece probably needed to be washed several times a week if not every day. And that chimney piece—it looked like marble. She was not sure she knew how to deal with marble. Did you just wash it with soap and water or was some special treatment needed?

Then everything needed to be dusted—were all those ornaments trusted to the servants? There were a great many of them, scattered about the place, and some of them looked delicate and expensive. Did Lady Fortescue wash them herself? She knew that some ladies did. The carpet needed to be swept—were there enough tea leaves for all the carpets in this house? Did they use something else? And all the candles—she looked around. Each candlestick, each wall sconce, held a fresh new wax candle. Were they replaced every day? Surely that would be an insane extravagance. And she had noticed that some of the other rooms had the new Argand lamps. She had no idea what sort of attention they needed.

The ceiling moldings. She tilted her head back to look up at them. They were much too high to reach with a duster. They looked pristine, so they must be cleaned regularly, but how? Did someone have to go up there on a ladder?

How many servants were needed in a house this size? She began to think that perhaps she did need at least a bit of information about the running of a large household. While she was pondering this revelation, she noticed that Lady Fortescue and Aunt Sophia were looking at her patiently and she realized one of them had asked her a question.

"I'm sorry. I must have been wool-gathering," she said.

"We were talking about your wardrobe, my dear," Aunt Sophia said. She looked rather uncertain.

"My wardrobe?" Maria blinked.

Lady Fortescue nodded. "You need a good many things. Ideally, we would send for a mantua-maker from London, but I am afraid there may not really be time enough for that."

Saying that she needed instruction in how to run a household was one thing. This was something else, and she couldn't understand why Aunt Sophia was abetting the women. She looked coldly at them. "You seem to have forgotten, Lady Fortescue, that I am in mourning. My father died not even a month ago."

"Oh, my dear, I assure you no one has forgotten, and I do not in any way wish to minimize your grief." Lady Fortescue reached over to squeeze Maria's hand sympathetically. "I am thinking only of the impression you must make when you arrive at Belford Park."

"I hardly think the staff at Belford Park will be expecting some grand lady! And really, I don't think we should be wasting Lord Claremont's money on nonessentials. I have no idea what the condition of the house and the estate are, but any money there is should surely be devoted to necessary repairs and improvements, not fripperies." Maria felt exasperated. Lady Fortescue was a dear, sweet woman, but she had obviously never needed to think about economy.

That lady sat back in her chair, looking at Maria in astonishment. "Fripperies?" she asked eventually.

"Yes," Maria said firmly. "Now there are obviously things I need to know. The Argand lamps, for example. I don't know if there are any at Lord Claremont's home, but in case there are, I need to know how they work. And marble. I'm not quite sure how one cleans it. But I'm sure that when I get to Bedford Park, I will be able to find ways to economize." She looked at her hostess expectantly.

But Lady Fortescue was still staring, though her face was now beginning to relax into a quizzical smile. "My dear," she said eventually, "what makes you think you will need to economize?"

"Why, why surely that's obvious." Now it was Maria's turn to sit back in surprise. "Look at Lord Claremont's clothes. If he cannot afford a new coat . . . and his linen is almost threadbare . . ."

Lady Fortescue dissolved into whoops of laughter. So much so that her husband, who had been walking past, came in to see what the matter was. He stood in front of his wife, waiting patiently.

"She . . . she . . ." Lady Fortescue waved a hand in Maria's direction. "She thinks Will is poor!"

"Poor?" Sir Roderick began to laugh as well. "Our Will? Poor?" He turned to Maria. "Wherever did you get a fool idea like that?"

Recovered sufficiently to speak, Lady Fortescue managed to say, "His clothes."

"His clothes?" Sir Roderick paused, and then chuckled. "Well, I admit that makes a bit of sense."

"I told him that the first thing he needed to do when he got to London was visit a decent tailor." Lady Fortescue got her whoops under control. "His appearance is quite disgraceful. He could hardly expect the Archbishop to go granting a special license to someone who looks like a beggar."

"No need to worry, my dear," Sir Roderick said, patting Maria's hand. "What with his prize money and his inheritance from his grandfather, all of it sensibly invested, he was a wealthy man even before he inherited the title. The estate that goes with it may not be in the best of condition after his father's indulgences, but at least it isn't burdened with debts and mortgages. No, Will can stand any nonsense you care to name."

Aunt Sophia, who had been looking a trifle nervous, resumed her cheerful smile, but Maria was now worried. She had better ask, since the Fortescues seemed to assume she knew. "Then Claremont's home is not a simple manor? Is it as large as this?"

The looks of shocked amusement returned to the Fortescues faces and Sir Roderick's laughter resumed.

"As large as this?" Sir Roderick started to speak but his words were choked once more with laughter.

"My dear child," said Lady Fortescue, close to laughter herself, "this house is nothing compared to Belford Park. Why, Belford is one of the great houses of England, built during the reign of Queen Elizabeth."

"And added to by every Claremont since," said Sir Roderick, wiping his eyes with one of his enormous handkerchiefs.

Aunt Sophia was now looking as startled as Maria felt. "But he is only a viscount," she began and then stopped, flushing with embarrassment. "What an utterly idiotish thing for me to say."

"No, no," said Sir Roderick. "You're perfectly right. It's the sort of estate you would expect a duke to have. But the Dormers have always been practical sorts, and chased after land instead of titles. Kept their heads down when others wanted to chase after glory. Others may have gotten the glory, but Dormers got the land. Will must have inherited something over a hundred thousand acres. A large piece of it's in Somerset, but there's the coal mines in Durham and several other estates scattered about as well."

"I don't understand," said Maria, wishing she were someone who could faint at will. This was not at all what she had expected, and perhaps if she could faint, it would all be different when she awoke. "Any time he's mentioned Belford Park, it's sounded as if he dislikes it. I assumed it was something small and rundown. A burden. Something that would need repair, refurbishment to make it a home."

"Ah, well . . ." Sir Roderick's voice trailed off.

"The house certainly isn't small," said Lady Fortescue, "though with three men living in it for the past twenty years without a woman in charge, it may well need refurbishment."

Sir Roderick frowned in concentration. "Didn't George have a wife?"

"That ninny Isabella Blackwell?" His wife sniffed. "The phrase 'more hair than wit' was invented with her in mind." She turned to Maria with a smile. "I'm sure there will be plenty for you to do to get the house in order. It's an enormous warren of a place with at least twenty bedrooms and heaven only knows how many reception rooms. The kitchen was old-fashioned in my sister-in-law's day, and they are probably still drawing water from the well outside."

"Twenty bedrooms?" Maria gasped. "How will I manage the laundry?"

Lady Fortescue looked startled once more, and then smiled and patted Maria on the arm. "Don't worry too much about it. The housekeeper will have been managing everything for years. I'll go over the things you'll need to take note of, and if she isn't up to snuff, you can always get a new housekeeper."

Maria was speechless.

Aunt Sophia also seemed confused. "I would have thought Claremont would be proud of an estate like that. But he seems to actually dislike it."

The Fortescues exchanged glances.

"As to that," Sir Roderick began hesitantly. "Ah me, I suppose you'd best know. My sister did not have a happy marriage." His mouth twisted wryly. "Hard to know when you're courting. Not everyone is as lucky as my Bess and I are." He smiled fondly at his wife, who smiled back. "But my sister and Claremont—well, we didn't know it at first, but they were a bad match, and it got worse as the years went on."

"Will is a good bit younger than his brothers," Lady Fortescue put in, "and we thought that when he came along it meant a reconciliation. We were wrong."

"Will was his mother's favorite, but his father seemed to resent him, and his brothers—less said the better there. Anyway, my sister was barely in her grave before Claremont shoved Will into the Navy." Sir Roderick shook his head. "Nothing I could do to get him out, though I'd have been glad to have him here. At least there was a home for him here when he was on leave, and a place for him while he was recovering."

Something about that made Sir Roderick grin suddenly. "Must tell you. When his father and brothers were killed, Will was still in no condition to go to the funeral. Couldn't even get out of bed yet. So I went, and what do you think! They all thought Will was dead. There'd been a mistake in the first list of casualties, and they never bothered to check."

He had to pause while he broke out in laughter, but managed to continue. "And there was that cousin of his, lording it over everyone, thinking he was the new viscount. You should have seen his face when I told him Will was still alive."

Belford Park

SEATED BEHIND THE BROAD LIBRARY DESK, Dormer regarded Hopworth through narrowed eyes. "What do you mean, there have been no evictions?"

The steward bent forward in an apologetic bow. "Lord Claremont said there were to be no evictions before he left. He said it before he left, I mean."

Dormer sighed. It was so difficult to work with fools. "The evictions were decided long before he even arrived here. How did they even come to his attention?"

Hopworth cringed a bit more. "I happened to mention Parsons to him." There was a pause while Dormer waited in silence until the steward felt obliged to continue in a rush of words. "And then he asked if there were any others."

Another sigh. The steward's idiocy was giving Dormer a head-ache. He pinched the bridge of his nose. It didn't help. "Very well. You may go."

Hopworth scurried out, failing to close the door properly behind him so it creaked on its hinges—another sign of neglect—in a well-run household . . .

Dormer closed his eyes and leaned back in his chair. This would be another requirement for his future wife. In addition to a large dowry, she needed to be sufficiently intelligent to main-tain a household—unlike Isabella and her fool of a mother. Lady Blackwell didn't even notice that the servants weren't doing their jobs so long as they treated her with deference.

Well, that was Will's problem for the time being. Or was it?

It had been well over a month since Will had taken off to visit "a friend." There had been no word from him and no indication of where he was, or when he could be expected to return. If any-thing had happened to him, they would surely have heard about it. Unless . . .

Unless he had been attacked by thieves. Crippled as he was, he would be unable to defend himself, and thieves might not have left anything that would identify the body.

Of course, a month wasn't that long, and it was unlikely that Will would feel obliged to write to anyone at Belford. Still . . .

Dormer settled more comfortably into the chair. It was never too early to start making plans, plans to cover all contingencies.

CHAPTER 9

WILL HAD NOT EXPECTED TO BE the guest of the Earl of Newbury. He knew Hal was one of the earl's sons, but somehow he assumed that Hal's invitation meant that the earl would not himself be in residence. And even if he had known the earl would be in residence, he would have expected him to be, somehow, more earl-like than he turned out to be.

Riding through the London crowds, Will had been grateful for the privacy afforded him by his carriage. He had been able to lean back, his scars hidden from view, able to see without being seen. He had expected Newbury House to offer similar shelter so that he would be able to conduct his business from the house in private. Even if he did need to call on attorneys or go to Doctors Commons for the special license, he could travel by carriage and avoid the stares of crowds.

Will had not realized that Hal's entire family would be in London—well, not his entire family—just his father, three brothers, and a few cousins, all of them male.

"We're a bachelor party at the moment," said Hal, welcoming him with a beaming smile. "Mother and the girls are off visiting the Mertons down in Sussex, so this is Liberty-hall. No kickshaws for dinner and no morning callers. Come meet my father."

Will limped as closely to a march as he could manage. Hal, sensible fellow that he was, made no effort to slow his pace to something suitable for an invalid, and Will managed to keep up with him, only slightly out of breath by the time they reached their destination at the rear of the house.

In front of them was a massive oak door high and broad enough for a giant to pass through. It reduced Hal, the largest officer on the *Hector*, to merely ordinary size as he hammered on it.

In response to a mutter from within, Hal opened the door. "Here we are, Father. Captain Dormer—Lord Claremont—has arrived."

The man behind the desk dropped the jeweler's loupe from his eye and jumped to his feet. "Captain—no, Claremont!" He hurried across the room to clasp Will's hand. "Delighted! Delighted to finally meet you."

"My lord," said Will, doing his best to keep his composure. This scarecrow was the Earl of Newbury? As tall as his son, the earl was at most half of Hal's width. He was wearing a tasseled cap on his shaved head, an ancient banyan flapped loose over his shirt and breeches, and on his feet were a pair of bright red slippers with turned-up toes. But his eyes were as bright and eager as Hal's, and his grip on Will's hand was strong.

"Come in, come in," Newbury said, drawing Will over to the desk. "Can never thank you enough for getting Hal back to us safe and sound."

Then his attention switched to the conglomeration of springs and wheels covering the surface of the desk. "This may interest you. Clockworks. You've used Harrison's marine chronometer, no doubt."

"I've seen it used," Will said cautiously. The clock could keep accurate time despite the rolling of the sea, making determination of longitude far more reliable, but it was far too expensive for widespread use.

The earl nodded in satisfaction. "Marvelous invention, that. Can't believe it took Parliament so long to award him the prize.

Bunch of penny-pinching pettifoggers, eh? But look at this. What do you think of it?"

Will looked, not entirely sure what he was looking at. "The parts of a clock?" he guessed.

"Right you are." The earl clapped him on the back. "But not just any clock. Or clocks, in this case. There are two of Christopher Polhem's clocks there."

"My father's always fascinated by new inventions," said Hal with the affectionate tolerance of a child for a parent's oddities.

"Not quite new," his father corrected. "These clocks are about seventy years old now, but people are just beginning to see the beauty of the notion."

Will was still frowning at the assortment of metal bits and pieces. "What *is* the notion?"

"Machine-made parts, and all interchangeable!" The earl beamed with delight. "Polhem built a factory up in Sweden to make them. The clocks are made much more quickly, and repairs are easy. If something happens and a spring on one of the clocks breaks, or if one of the gears is bent, you don't need a craftsman to make a new one. You just pick a spare out of a drawer and pop it into place."

"Really?" Will was intrigued in spite of himself. "Does it actually work?"

"See for yourself." The earl quickly put a section of the mechanism together, demonstrating the way the wheels meshed. After giving Will a chance to observe it, he removed one of the wheels and replaced it with a new one. "You see? They're exactly alike."

"Impressive." Will picked up a pair of springs and held them side by side. "I can't see any difference."

"There is none. Just think of the possibilities. Soon all sorts of goods will be cheap enough for the ordinary workman to afford them." Newbury beamed, but then a shadow passed over his face. "I hear the French are doing something like this with the manufacture of muskets."

Hal laughed. "Does that mean every poacher will be able to own one?"

Will wasn't laughing. "It might mean the French army will be a damned sight better armed than ours."

"And it would be a damned sight cheaper to arm the soldiers," added the earl. "But it may come to nothing." He stood still for a moment and then recovered his good cheer. "But come, sit down and tell us what brings you to London."

Although Will did not enjoy talking about his own affairs, it never occurred to him to decline. The earl, for all his bizarre costume and almost childish enthusiasm, radiated authority. He was comfortable in his position. Perhaps Will ought to study him for pointers on how a lord should behave.

Unfortunately, at the moment Will was anything but comfortable. There was no desk for him to sit behind—since this was Newbury's library, that spot was Newbury's prerogative. Nor was there a table. They were sitting down for conversation, not a meal. That meant that his wooden leg would stick out at its grotesque angle with no way to hide it. Once seated, he leaned forward, his hands on his cane erect in front of him, like a standard to distract the eye.

"You must excuse my father," said Hal, seated with his legs stretched out in front of him, and his feet crossed at the ankles. "If my mother were home, she would never allow him to appear in such dishabille. It would be breeches and wig and cravat for him!"

"And you would never be allowed to sit in such a disgracefully casual pose," retorted the earl with a grin.

The ease and fondness between the earl and his son were obvious. Will could not deny a pang of envy at the sight, and at the realization that he did not know how to be a father any more than he knew how to be a viscount. Or a husband. Was it even possible to learn such things?

"But we need to talk about you." Newbury turned to Will with a smile. "I gather you have found yourself unexpectedly turned into a viscount."

Will grimaced. He couldn't help it, and the earl immediately noticed.

"Ah. You're not best pleased by your elevation, I see. Any particular reason? Grief at the deaths of your father and brothers? Sometimes makes men feel guilty, profiting by others' misfortune."

"Neither grief nor guilt. I'd not so much as seen them in twenty years." Will noticed the earl's gaze sharpening at that and realized he needed to be careful what he revealed. "No, it's more annoyance at being thrust into a role I've no idea how to fulfill. I'm sure there are duties and obligations that are being neglected, and I don't even know what they are."

Newbury tilted his head and looked at Will through half-closed eyes. "Hmm. A good steward or agent can help with that. Have you got one?"

"Well, there's one in place, but whether he's good or not I couldn't say. I'm not sure he's honest and I don't think I can trust him."

"Anyone who commanded a ship as effectively as you did has learned how to sum up his men quickly. If you're uncertain, then you can't trust him. Replace him." Newbury spoke as if such a replacement were the easiest thing in the world. He must have seen Will's discomfort because he said, "If you like, I'll see if I can think of anyone who might suit."

"Very kind of you, my lord," said Will, feeling slightly overrun.

But the earl wasn't finished. "You'll probably also need a wife," he continued. "They can be damned useful when it comes to settling in."

Will could feel the heat flushing his face. "As a matter of fact, I am planning to marry. One of the reasons I came to London was to get a special license."

He had expected mild surprise, either courteous congratulations or less courteous raised eyebrows. What he got was an explosion of enthusiasm. Of course, that came mainly from Hal, who leaped to his feet, clapped Will on the shoulder, and poured out a river of exclamations and praise.

Even the earl beamed at him. "Splendid. And who is the young lady? Might I know her?"

"That is unlikely," Will said, rescuing his hand from Hal's grip. "She is the daughter of Captain Garland and has been living quietly near Portsmouth."

"Garland? Is he not, like you, one of Nelson's band of brothers?" Newbury asked.

"Indeed he is!" Hal clapped Will on the shoulder again. "At the Nile he was absolutely brilliant and fearless." Hal stopped abruptly, his hand in midair. "But did I not hear . . .? There was notice of . . ."

Will nodded. "Yes. He died quite recently. That is the reason for the special license. Miss Garland and I hope to wed quietly at the home of my aunt and uncle, Sir Reginald and Lady Fortescue."

"Ah," said the earl, nodding solemnly. "That would doubtless be best. And I am sure that the daughter of such a brave naval hero will make you a splendid wife." The solemnity vanished before a return of enthusiasm. "And now we must have a splendid dinner to celebrate. Hal, you must go and warn the cook after you show Claremont to his chambers."

DINNER WAS, AS HAL HAD PROMISED, free of kickshaws, but, as his father had promised, splendid in the quality and quantity of the dishes—roasts and stews and vegetables all blessedly free of the disguising sauces Lady Blackwell insisted on. Perhaps when he returned to Belford, he could insist on plain dishes for dinner. He started to smile at the thought until he realized that Maria would be the one planning the meals, and he had no idea what she would choose. Would a wife ask her husband what he liked? Or would she order what she considered suitable?

The cheerful noise around the table recalled him to his surroundings. It was, as Hal had said, a bachelor party, but while the talk was lively and full of high spirits and humor, it never tumbled over the line into bawdiness. Having experienced many years of masculine chatter in mess rooms and taverns, Will found this unexpected but surprisingly pleasant. This was the earl's influence, no doubt.

It was the kind of comfortable camaraderie he had found in the officers' mess aboard ship. Most of the time, at least. He had been fortunate, he supposed, in that he had rarely been encumbered with officers whose envy and malice could endanger the entire ship. He had felt far more at home there with his fellow officers than he had ever felt at Belford Park.

But he had also felt at home in the Garlands' kitchen. Smiling at the memory, he wondered if perhaps he and Maria could take their meals in the kitchen once they were married. Would the walls of the building collapse in horror?

A shout of laughter recalled him to his surroundings.

Lord Kennet, Hal's oldest brother and the heir, a clever mimic, was regaling them with an impression of St. Vincent, now the First Lord of the Admiralty, trying to force reform on the lords of the Navy Board. He hit off the stern and rigid admiral perfectly, and Will feared that his portrayal of the smarmy, venal lords was equally accurate.

"Have I got them right, James?" Kennet asked his cousin.

James Sinclair was laughing along with the rest. "Only too right," he said, sounding a trifle bitter. "St. Vincent is having the devil of a time trying to pin them down. Every time he discovers something egregious, there is someone ready to explain it away."

Newbury broke in to ask Will, "Aside from a trip to Doctor's Commons for the license, is there anything else you're planning to do while you're in town?"

Before Will could answer, one of the other cousins called out, "Rundell and Bridges! Must get a ring and a gift for the bride!"

Of course that was necessary, and Will was embarrassed that he had not even thought of it. He nodded in agreement, however, and added, "And my aunt tells me I must pay a visit to a tailor. Perhaps you can recommend one?"

"I'm your man for that," Hal said. "And we'll fix you up with a barber and linens and hats and boots . . ." His voice trailed off.

"One, at least," Will said with a crooked smile.

"As to that . . ." The earl hesitated but went on. "I know I am interfering, but there's a fellow, name of Potts, who's just acquired a patent for an artificial leg. It sounds quite promising."

Will flushed with anger this time. No one could fail to notice that he was missing a leg, but they might have the decency not to mention it.

Hal's grin returned. "I told you my father was always going on about new inventions."

"And the ones that catch his fancy are often the successful ones." James Sinclair broke in and shrugged at Will. "It can't hurt to look into it."

CHAPTER 10

IT WAS JAMES SINCLAIR, RATHER THAN THE EARL himself, who accompanied Will to the shop of Mr. Potts. The inventor was a man of middle years, on the small side, who carried a stick and moved about with only a slight limp as he went between his benches and tools and piles of wood. Will could not quite believe that Potts was actually missing a limb, whole as he appeared to be.

The contrivance, an ingenious arrangement of wood and steel with artificial tendons of catgut to enable the knee and ankle to bend in a way that appeared normal, was a source of great pride to Potts, who insisted that he could walk ten miles on it with no difficulty.

Will, though not quite convinced, was most certainly intrigued, perhaps by the appearance even more than by the operation of the thing. He had never thought of himself as a vain man, but the prospect of being able to stand beside Maria on two feet, of not looking like a grotesque abomination when they were wed—

"How long . . . how long will it take?"

Potts rubbed his cheek thoughtfully. "Well now, my lord, it's not that easy to say. If you're asking how long it will take for me to make you a leg, I expect I could have it fitted and finished within the week. If you're asking how long it will take you to learn to walk comfortably on it, that all depends."

Will waited.

"It'll be uncomfortable to start with, I won't deny that, but I expect that peg you have now was uncomfortable to start with as well. And maybe is less than comfortable to this day?"

Will nodded.

"It's mostly a matter of practice. You need to get used to having it there, and you need to get used to moving about with it. Getting about on the level, like this,"—Potts waved at his shop—"is easy enough. Stairs, now, and climbing hills, that takes a bit more practice."

"What sort of time are we talking about?" Will's mouth felt dry. "A week, a month, a year?"

"It's partly up to you." The inventor gave a quick grin. "I'm thinking that if you were a naval man, you won't be an idler. In three or four weeks you should be able to walk about passably, though it will take longer to go any great distance. And you'll be slow to start with."

Will took a deep breath and let it out slowly. "I'll do it." It was only then that he realized Sinclair had been looking on approvingly. "Am I being a fool?"

Sinclair shook his head. "It's never foolish to take a chance at improvement. It's only giving up that's foolish."

CHAPTER 11

Maria couldn't help worrying. Will should have been back by now. A day's journey to London, three days at most to obtain a special license, and another day back. But those few days had stretched into more than a week. He should have been here by now.

That was if he was going to return.

He was in London, where all the most fashionable and elegant ladies were to be found. Ladies far more suited to be a viscountess than she was. It was certainly not beyond the realm of possibility that he was regretting the charitable impulse that had prompted his proposal.

Perhaps that impulse had not been entirely charitable. She remembered the kiss—both kisses. At the memory, her toes curled, her face flushed, and everything in between warmed and softened.

Unfortunately, a man in Lord Claremont's position could easily find another woman he would enjoy kissing, a woman who possessed both fortune and family, the twin pillars of aristocratic marriage, the twin pillars she lacked.

She straightened her spine. Not that it needed stiffening, but she had no intention of falling into self-pity. If she lacked those two pillars, there were two others she did possess: good sense and practicality. Everyone had always said so. And both good sense and practicality told her that she could manage without him.

If she had to, she could.

With her head held high, she went down to breakfast to discover that there was a letter for her. She quickly slid it into her lap, hiding it under her napkin. It was almost certainly from Will—who else would be writing to her?—but she didn't want to mention it until she knew what it said.

She managed to greet the others politely as they came into the breakfast room and drink a bit of tea before she excused herself to hurry into the library. There she went to the window, broke the seal—a rather ornate C—and read the letter.

October 2, 1802
Dear Miss Garland,
I fear I will not return to you as quickly as I had hoped. Do not be concerned—It is nothing dreadful that keeps me here in London. On the contrary, it is something that may prove to be an improvement to my current situation. Yet it may do nothing of the sort. I would not even mention it, but that I do not wish you to think I break my promise to return promptly because of some trifle.

First, I must tell you about my host. I am staying not simply with Lieutenant Sinclair but with his father, the Earl of Newbury. The earl is an enthusiastic gentleman of a scientific bent and wide-ranging interests. His son swears there is not a mechanical novelty that he does not know about, and I do not find that difficult to believe.

It is difficult to resist the earl when an idea has taken hold of his mind. As a result, I found myself in the shop of a carpenter here in London by the name of James Potts. Mr. Potts has himself lost a leg and put his ingenuity to work to create an artificial limb that would restore some of his lost mobility.

I confess that I was dubious when the earl told me about it—more than dubious. Incredulous would better describe my thoughts. However, when we entered the shop, I did not realize that the fellow greeting us was indeed the fellow with the missing limb. When he began to move about, I could see that he had a limp, even when using a walking stick. However, when he stood before us with the false limb covered by his garments, he appeared to be a whole man.

The thing is made of wood and steel, which he has arranged in an ingenious contrivance that gives the illusion of natural movement.

Mr. Potts is, of course, enthusiastic about his invention, and swears he can walk ten miles on it with no difficulty. However, there is no guarantee that for someone else the device will perform as well as it does for the inventor. I do not wish to raise your expectations too much and I must ask that you not divulge this to my aunt and uncle just yet. I know them too well to think that they will be able to restrain their hopes.

Although I am not convinced of success myself, I have placed an order with Mr. Potts. This will, unfortunately, delay my return since the leg must be constructed and fitted, and I will require a bit of time to grow accustomed to it. Will it distress you too much if we must delay our wedding until November?

Yours,
Claremont

She collapsed into a chair with relief. He hadn't changed his mind. And what was this device, this artificial limb? She had no idea if it was something practical or just the sort of wicked fantasy that gave deluded hope to invalids. Will was not a fool, but she had no idea how gullible the earl might be. Yet she did not want to sound discouraging when she replied.

Yes, she would be careful not to sound disbelieving, but she would not say anything to the Fortescues lest she raise false hopes.

Just then, Lady Fortescue came in. "Was that by any chance a letter from Will? I don't want to pry, but Sir Roderick and I have been unable to keep from worrying . . ."

"Yes, it is from Will." Maria hoped her smile looked reassuring. "He apologizes for the delay, but apparently problems to do with the estate have come up, details he had not expected. He would like to get them settled and done with before the wedding, so he will not be returning until next month."

"Oh." Lady Roderick's face fell, but then transformed into a broad smile. "In that case we will have plenty of time for your lessons."

October 5
My dear Lord Claremont,
What astonishing news! If there is any hope at all that this device of Mr. Potts will make your life more comfortable, then you must of course attempt it. I have explained the delay in your return as resulting from the discovery of ever more problems regarding the viscountcy that you must deal with.

I shall, of course, regret the delay, but you need not feel that I will be sitting here with nothing to do. Your aunt and mine have decided between them that there is much that I must learn before I am prepared to run your household. It seems that it is a much larger household than you had led me to expect! From the way you spoke of it, I thought it to be a broken-down ruin of a place.

I am now receiving daily lessons about the duties of the various ranks of servants. Apparently I would bring the entire household crashing down were I to ask a footman to lay the fire in the sitting room when that is properly the housemaid's task.

I no longer blanche at the amount of bed linen needed for a house with twenty bed chambers, and I can distinguish in a blink (or a pinch!) between table linen suitable only for the servants' hall and the fine damask cloth that will cover the master's table.

In addition, I am learning about the various ways to clean and preserve the household furnishings—not that I should ever do these tasks myself, but so that I know how they should be done. Did you know that the best way to clean marble is with a combination of verdigris, pumice, and lime?

I am keeping a notebook with all these instructions and recipes, for I will never be able to keep them all straight in my head. I begin to hope that with my notebook at hand, I may be able to maintain your house in reasonable comfort.

Meanwhile, I shall be eagerly awaiting your news.

Yours,
Maria Garland

Had he misled her about Belford Park? Will didn't think he had said much about it at all. He didn't want to intimidate her, but he doubted he had been able to hide his dislike of the place. That in itself may have led her to dismiss it.

It had never occurred to him that there was any kind of preparation needed for running the household. She had been managing perfectly well in her father's house. He had assumed it would be much easier for her at Belford, with more servants to do whatever needed doing.

Well, at least it sounded as if she was reasonably comfortable with Aunt Bess and Uncle Roderick. He had begun to worry. If she feared he had abandoned her there, she might have changed her mind.

October 11
My dearest Miss Garland,
If all goes well, after what seems to me to be an excessive number of fittings, Mr. Potts will have the device ready for me

tomorrow. He warns me that it will take at least four weeks of practice before I will be able to navigate comfortably with it, so I am hoping to return to you by the week of November 15.

Lt. Sinclair has taken me in hand as well and has steered me to tailors and haberdashers and barbers. Final fittings from the tailor and a visit to the bootmaker await the final fitting of the device. I had never thought it required so many people to get oneself ready to face the world. There seem to be a dozen different ways to tie a cravat, and the dandies spend hours getting the creases just so! People also read all sorts of meaning into the color of a waistcoat. Ah, for the days when all I needed to do was brush my uniform!

Lt. Sinclair is taking far too much pleasure in ordering around his former captain. At least he agrees that I do not need to wear a wig.

I must also tell you about another Sinclair—James Sinclair, who is some sort of cousin to the earl. I don't know if I even mentioned to you my misgivings about the current steward at Belford. Whether he is competent or not I cannot say, but I am dubious about his honesty in dealing with the tenants. I feel guilty leaving the administration of the estate in the hands of a man I do not trust, but I do not know enough about the matter myself to determine if there is actually anything wrong.

The earl recommends his cousin for this very reason. Sinclair, the earl says, is very good at uncovering chicanery, too good for his own good. It seems that in his last position at the Naval Boards, he uncovered more chicanery than he was supposed to notice. This created much embarrassment for his superiors, and he was asked to leave.

He is willing to come to us at least for a while, though I do not know how long he will stay. Lord St. Vincent, the First Lord of the Admiralty, came to dine with Lord Newbury the other day. He is endeavoring to combat the corruption in the

shipyards and supplies for the navy, and he was most interested in what Sinclair had to say.

To prepare myself, I spend my leisure hours reading books
about estate management, farming practices, and orchard
management. It seems that those apples I was sneering at are
actually a very profitable crop, not for pies but for cider! One
of the many things I admit I have never thought about.

I wish you were here with me, for I would value your comments and insight. I know that propriety would not permit it
until we are married, but that does not keep me from missing
your company.

In hopes that I can be with you before another month
passes, I am

Yours faithfully,
Claremont

Maria sat there with the letter on her lap for a long moment,
staring at the last few sentences. He missed her? Oh, how she hoped
that was true. Reading his words made her realize how much she
missed him, and how eagerly she awaited his letters.

Yes, a dishonest steward was a serious problem, and it was good
of the earl to find a replacement. That thought made her laugh at
herself. She was feeling grateful to an earl! Never had she expected
to come near to an earl, no less to be in a position to receive favors
from one. Staying with the Fortescues, was she actually becoming
accustomed to this life?

Perhaps not quite accustomed. She still had to force herself
to leave the bed unmade every morning so that the maid could
straighten it when she could perfectly well have done the job herself.

October 16
My dear Lord Claremont,
I hope that by this time you and the device have made each
other's acquaintance and that it will be smooth sailing from

now on. I cannot help hoping for success, knowing how much easier it could make your life.

My life here is under the control of The Aunts—I now think of them that way. There may be only two of them, but I would swear they have the power of a Fleet! At any rate, they are determined that I shall not disgrace you, and they insist that I need an entire wardrobe if I am to be considered presentable as your wife. When I protest at the cost, they tell me that if I am not fashionable, the neighbors will scorn me, to say nothing of the servants! So, a seamstress has come from Oxford, patterns have been chosen, and fabrics have been ordered from London. Dark colors, or very pale ones, to honor my father, though not black because a bride does not wear black.

One problem is that I shall need a lady's maid, since I cannot get in and out of the new garments on my own. And The Aunts tell me that I must have someone to do my hair. Soon I shall have to begin interviewing candidates, and I confess to nervousness. Can I possibly live up to the standards of a lady's maid?

Believe that you are ever in my thoughts,
Maria Garland

Will smiled at the letter. A new wardrobe? She probably needed it as much as he did. He hoped that at least some of the dresses would be made of silk. He had been longing to wrap her in silken luxury.

A lady's maid?

Now that gave him an idea.

CHAPTER 12

Oxfordshire

MARIA WAS NOT DRESSED IN ANY of the new garments that were accumulating in her dressing room. That was only partly because she did not yet have a lady's maid. More importantly, those dresses were making her nervous. They belonged to a life that was not yet hers, a life she was still not able to believe would soon be hers.

Instead, she wore one of her old mourning gowns. It ought to make her feel comfortable, but it did not. It now belonged to a life that was no longer hers. At the moment, she felt as if she did not belong anywhere. She kept looking backwards and forwards until she was dizzy.

Even the needlework she was engaged in at the moment was a compromise—neither the fancy but useless needlework The Aunts said was suitable for a viscountess, nor the mending she was accustomed to doing. Instead, she was hemming fine lawn handkerchiefs that would be for Will. They would not, unfortunately, be embroidered with an elaborate initial. She did not think he would mind.

A footman appeared in the doorway. "Excuse me, madam, but a letter for you has arrived by messenger."

"A letter?"

Moving silently over the thick carpet, he offered it to her, on a gleaming silver salver carried in his impeccably gloved hands. She wondered if it had been equally protected from human touch ever since it left the sender.

It was from Lord Claremont. She recognized his hand and his new seal, a highly decorative C that she wished she could copy on the handkerchiefs. But why send this letter by messenger? She used the scissors from her sewing basket to break the seal and unfold the letter.

October 21

My dearest Maria,

Do not be alarmed that this letter comes to you by hand rather than by His Majesty's mail service. I ask your indulgence to introduce the messenger. She is Rebecca Chapman, the sister of my manservant, and Gibbs assures me that she is an experienced lady's maid. You mentioned that you are in need of such, but I know that it is most certainly your prerogative to choose your own maid.

If you would not care for her in that position, do not distress yourself, but I would ask that you keep her with you at least for the time being. She can tell you her story herself. If you decide she does not suit, another position can be found for her. In the meantime, she may serve as an ally when we reach Belford.

For that matter, I am informed by Gibbs and Lt. Sinclair that I need a valet. Gibbs tells me that it may be all very well for him to brush my uniform coat, but he knows nothing of the fashions in coats and cravats.

Lord Newbury suggested that Gibbs would be of far more use in the position of house steward. This position, I am told, is the equivalent of captain on the admiral's flagship, with my humble self being admiral. As this is in fact the way Gibbs has

*been serving, the change will be minimal. Except, of course,
to me as I will be expected to accustom myself to someone
needed to get me in and out of my coat, etc.*

*I fear I am writing a good deal of nonsense, but I trust that
together we will be able to make sense of it all. And I hope that
we will be together soon. If it is acceptable to you, I will write
to my aunt and uncle asking them to arrange for us to be married in the village church on November 16. If you would prefer
another date, please make your wishes known. Meanwhile, I
await most fervently the day when you shall be mine.*

Yours with longing,
Will

Staring at the letter, she traced her finger over that last sen-
tence— *I await most fervently the day when you shall be mine.* "Oh,
Will, I fear I feel just that way," she whispered.

Pulling herself out of her daydream, she realized that she was
crumpling the letter and still had to deal with the woman Will had
sent to be her lady's maid.

A lady's maid. The problem was not simply that she had never
had one. It was more that she did not really feel adequate to having
one. She looked down at the skirt of her black dress, which was
looking rather rusty and faded. Would a lady's maid turn up her
nose at it and sniff in dismissal? She didn't want to have to deal
every day with someone who considered her inadequate to her
position. Especially since she felt that way herself.

But Gibbs' sister might not feel that way. She might feel the
same loyalty her brother felt and be unlikely to go gossiping about
her inadequate mistress.

If this woman was experienced, at least she would know what
she was supposed to do, because Maria didn't. Fix hair, she supposed, and make sure there were no ripped seams or trailing hems.
More importantly, she would know what was fashionable and what
was suitable for whatever occasions arose.

In addition, this particular lady's maid was also to be an ally at Belford. She was going to need an ally? She gathered from what Lady Fortescue said that the house had probably been rather carelessly run, but she had not thought that there was likely to be open warfare between the staff and the lady of the house. Of course, if the servants had grown lax in their duties with no supervision, they might resent being called to order.

Perhaps there were even more problems to face than she had realized.

She roused herself from her thoughts and asked the footman to show the messenger in.

The messenger, Rebecca Chapman, proved to be a woman in her forties, looking very much like her brother but in a slimmer, more quietly fashionable package. She paused in the doorway, looking slightly hesitant.

"Mrs. Chapman? Do come in please, and be seated." Maria indicated a chair beside her.

"Thank you, miss." She sat with hands folded in her lap and waited.

Maria waited as well, but her pause was because she didn't quite know what to say. She had interviewed servants as maids before and even, a few times, as cooks, but she didn't quite know what to ask a prospective lady's maid—especially one who looked as elegant as this one did. But she took a deep breath and plunged in. "Lord Claremont has recommended you to me as a lady's maid. Have you much experience?"

"For the past ten years I was lady's maid to Lord Biddlesford's daughters. The youngest was married just recently." There was a slight hesitation in her voice. "Perhaps you heard about it?"

Maria managed not to laugh. "I'm afraid I am not privy to the latest social *on dits*."

"I ask because it was something of a scandal, and the reason I am applying for this position." Mrs. Chapman hesitated again. "And the reason I am applying without a letter of recommendation.

You are sure to hear about it soon enough. My young lady ran off with a young man to whom her parents objected. They accused me of knowing about it and helping her, and they turned me off without a character."

Interesting. "And did you? Help her, that is."

"Not exactly." A wry smile appeared. "I did not precisely know, but then I did not inquire, and on what I suspected was the day, I made certain neither I nor any other servants were in a position to interfere."

Maria tilted her head. "Why? Are you of a romantic turn of mind?"

"No, not that. But the man her parents had chosen—he was well born enough and wealthy enough, but he was not a good man. Her parents may have been ignorant, but servants know. I thought it only right to allow her to make her own choice."

Mrs. Chapman sat a trifle stiffly. Did she really think that Maria would turn her away after Will had sent her? Maria almost laughed, but instead she smiled an encouraging smile. "Fair enough. Well, Mrs. Chapman, with Lord Claremont and your brother recommending you, I am sure you will do splendidly. However, I feel I ought to warn you that I have never had a lady's maid, and don't entirely know what you ought to be doing."

"That's all right, miss," the new lady's maid said, relaxing slightly and casting a critical eye over Maria's dress. "I do know. And you'd best call me Chapman."

CHAPTER 13

London

NEWBURY SEEMED DETERMINED TO TAKE DIRECTION of Will's estate and finances as well as his anatomy.

He was indirect about it, of course. He merely commented that he had difficulty understanding the position of Frederick Dormer in the household. Had that been some provision in the late viscount's will?

Will managed to avoid answering that one, at least for the moment.

Then Newbury asked about Mrs. Dormer—Isabella—and her mother. Surely it was unusual for a widow and her mother to remain in her brother-in-law's house after her own husband's death. Had Will's brother made no provision for his wife?

At that point, Will confessed that he simply didn't know. He had never actually seen his father's will or any other documents concerning the estate. The attorney, a Mr. Cruickshank, had appeared while Will was still recuperating from his injuries to tell him of the deaths of his father and brothers and to inform him of his inheritance.

"Yes, but that must have been some months ago," the earl said. Will nodded.

"And since then? What have you learned of the estate? Is it in good health?"

Will resisted the urge to wriggle uncomfortably like a schoolboy unprepared for the lesson. "The steward comes in and tells me about things, like the apple harvest." That sounded inadequate even to Will's own ears, especially since he remembered being told about evictions and doing nothing about them.

The earl sat back and peered at Will. "Dear me, that will not do. That will not do at all. You can't even send James down to look into things until you have a much better picture of the situation. You had best look into it."

Will had no idea how he was supposed to "look into" the situation. His confusion must have shown in his face because the earl took pity on him.

"You should begin by conferring with the attorney for the estate. He should be able to answer many of your questions," Newbury said kindly.

However kindly the earl meant his advice, it did not seem so to Will. Instead, it sounded humiliating. Confer with the attorney? His new leg had been fitted only the day before. So far, he had managed to take all of two steps at a time, holding himself erect only with the help of crutches.

"I do not think I am quite prepared to visit anyone just yet."

"Oh my dear boy, I didn't mean . . . you must think me shockingly insensitive." The earl sat up abruptly, his odd tasseled cap slipping to one side. It was apparently his normal headgear in the house when he did not feel obliged to wear his wig for guests. "I forget that you are still unused to your position. Visit your attorney—tsk, tsk. You may have done such things in the past, when you were only an officer, but as a viscount, you summon your attorney to call on you."

So it was that two days later, it was Will behind the massive oak door, seated at the broad desk. He tried to make himself comfortable though it wasn't easy. Still, he appreciated Newbury's offer of his library for this meeting, and it was certainly an impressive setting.

It hadn't seemed quite so intimidating when he first saw it, but that was when the desk had been covered with springs and gears and the room itself seemed to vibrate with the earl's enthusiasm.

Now the desk was empty, nothing but a broad expanse of highly polished mahogany . . . waiting, just waiting.

He was being ridiculous, he knew. The desktop was empty because it wasn't his own desk. It had been cleared off so that when Cruickshank appeared, he would be able to spread out whatever papers Will needed to see. It was simply courtesy on Newbury's part. The intimidation was all in Will's mind.

He settled back in the chair. To his surprise, it fit him quite comfortably. He hesitated to put his hands on the gleaming desktop, but they settled easily on the arms of the chair.

From this vantage point, the room as a whole did not seem at all intimidating. Indeed, it looked quite comfortable. There was a fire burning comfortably on the hearth, the shelves of books covered no more than half of the walls, and there were half a dozen chairs and tables in groups around the room, for reading or for conversation, he supposed.

In size, it wasn't much different from the library at Belford. He'd never felt comfortable there, though it was the room where he spent most of his time. The room where he had hidden, he admitted to himself. But it could be a comfortable room like this one. Perhaps with a pair of chairs by the fireside, where he and Maria could sit of an evening, reading or talking over the day's activities, a pleasing picture.

He frowned slightly. What was missing from the Belford library—aside from Maria—was books. Oh, there were a few, some books about horses and racing and a collection of sermons that he doubted had ever been read, but there weren't many.

He could hardly blame his father and brothers for not reading. He was no great reader himself. There was little space on a warship for nonessentials, and the schooling he received there was of a largely practical bent. He had never thought of reading for pleasure. Perhaps he should.

He recalled seeing quite a few books in the Garland home, so perhaps Maria did enjoy reading. Novels? That was the preferred reading for young ladies, he'd been told. But then, Maria was no ordinary young lady—not at all.

Lost in thoughts of Maria and the future, he almost failed to notice the knock at the door that preceded the entrance of a footman announcing Cruickshank. The attorney was a small man, to Will's surprise. He had seemed much larger the last time Will saw him. Of course, Will had still been lying in a bed in the Yarmouth naval hospital at the time, so the view was rather different now.

Cruickshank seemed much more cheerful this time. He still wore a wig, and his coat flared out in a manner even Will knew to be dreadfully old-fashioned, but he was practically bouncing in his buckled shoes.

"My lord, I am delighted to see you in such good health. A far cry from our meeting in the hospital, eh?"

Will didn't quite know what to say to this, but his failure to respond was unimportant. Cruickshank burbled on. "Of course, that was a sorry time, with your father and brothers wiped out just like that! It must have been a shock to you."

"Er, yes. A shock," Will acknowledged.

"I confess, I was surprised to learn that the viscount—your father, that is—hadn't been in touch with you. He thought you were dead at first. You were listed among the casualties in the North Sea battle. But I investigated and assured him that you had survived."

"I'm sure that was a great relief to him," Will said dryly, waving the attorney to a seat.

Cruickshank perched on the edge of the visitor's chair, a thick folder of papers on his lap, and put on a pair of spectacles. "It must have been. Yes, I'm sure it must have been. But then he kept it to himself. I really don't understand, but then I never did quite understand your father. Why did he keep it to himself?"

"He never told my brothers?"

"Well, he may have told them. It was hardly possible to ask since they died with him in the accident. But he didn't tell your cousin, Mr. Frederick Dormer."

Cruickshank looked uncomfortable. "It was actually rather embarrassing. When I went down for the funeral, your cousin was under the assumption that he had inherited the title. He was quite shocked when I told him that not only were you alive but that you had inherited everything. Quite shocked."

"I daresay," said Will. "But I wanted to ask you about my father's will. Just what provisions were made for my cousin? And for my brother's widow?"

The attorney started, almost dislodging his papers. "But that was just the problem! He never made a will. Not in all the years I've known him. Not when his children were born, not when his wife died. He absolutely refused to do so."

"No will? But that's absurd."

"Indeed it is. Absurd and irresponsible. He said that those who came after could clear it all up. No need for him to make it easy for them. Now I ask you, what kind of attitude is that?"

"But . . . but . . ." Will couldn't begin to think of all the problems. "But George's widow—there must have been marriage settlements of some sort."

Cruickshank shook his head in disapproval. "Nothing. It seems she had no dowry and George just up and married her. Your father did not approve and refused to increase George's allowance."

"So that is why they are all at Belford." At least it was an explanation, and Will could see that he was going to have to continue supporting them.

"While we are at it," Cruickshank said, "what of you? Have you made your will?"

"That was one of the things I wished to speak to you about. But to go back to my father's will, or lack thereof, do you mean to tell me that the only reason I inherited is because my father couldn't be bothered to make a will?"

"Well, as the oldest surviving son, you of course inherited the title and the entailed estates, but yes, the unentailed properties and investments came to you for that reason."

"He must be turning in his grave to see me in his place!" The attorney looked slightly shocked, so Will continued, "You do realize that I hadn't seen my father or brothers since I was ten years old? The day after my mother's funeral he shipped me off to the navy and I never saw or heard from any of them again."

"My goodness gracious!" It was the attorney's turn to sit gaping, but he recovered from his embarrassment quickly enough. "Well, then, we'd best get down to business."

The desk was soon covered with papers—lists, accounts, leases, and maps— and Cruickshank was in his element, explaining the flourishing state of Will's inheritance. This was actually something of a surprise to Will. While staying at the earl's home, he had not failed to recognize the difference from Belford Park. He had assumed that Belford's shabbiness and lack of servants had been because the estate was pinched for money.

Not at all, Cruickshank insisted. It was true that in recent years the main estate had not been producing anything like the level of income one might expect, and that was puzzling, but the other properties—especially the coal mines—were flourishing.

As for the general air of neglect at Belford, that was really all it was—neglect. The old viscount had cared for nothing but his horses and his hunting. As long as the roof didn't leak and his dinner appeared on time, he was indifferent.

But still, there was that curious failure of the home estate to flourish. Cruickshank frowned. The old viscount had never wanted to be bothered, and for some years now he had left the administration of the estate to his nephew, Frederick Dormer.

Will perked up when he heard that. "Are you telling me that my cousin Frederick has been running things at Belford?"

"Hmm, yes, though I don't know how much he has actually had to do with the running of things." Cruickshank shook the paper he was holding. "That steward he hired doesn't seem to be quite up to the job. Even if there have been a few bad years for farmers, the rent rolls seem surprisingly low."

Will leaned back and thought for a bit. "Would you by any chance know anything about Frederick's own estate? I assume he inherited from his own father."

The attorney frowned over his spectacles at Will. "You understand that I do not act for Mr. Dormer and could not comment on his affairs if I did."

Will nodded his understanding and waited.

"Well, my impression—and you must understand that it is only an impression—is that it is a pleasant little estate, suitable for a gentleman, but not producing any great wealth. Nothing like Belford Park. That may be one reason for the falling out between your father and his brother."

"I never really knew anything about it," Will confessed. "I only knew that I almost never saw my uncle, though Frederick was almost constantly present."

"Nor do I know anything, anything at all, and I fear I should not be speculating." Looking rather embarrassed, Cruickshank turned back to his papers.

By the time they finished, Will was beginning to grasp that he was actually a wealthy man. He ordered Cruickshank to provide a list of the servants and their length of service to see who should be pensioned off and how liberally. Cruickshank would also prepare marriage settlements, providing liberally for Maria.

As for Isabella and her mother, Will could not envisage sharing a home with them permanently and charged Cruickshank with the task of devising some possible solutions for them—an annuity or an allowance perhaps, as well as various places they might live.

Frederick, however, had a residence of his own and there was no reason why he should live in Will's house. That had to change.

As did Frederick's supervision of the Belford estate. Will needed to talk to Sinclair about taking over as steward as soon as possible.

Oxfordshire

LADY FORTESCUE RECEIVED CLAREMONT'S LETTER setting a date for the wedding with exclamations of delight, echoed by Lady Pellew. The two aunts set to work preparing the house for the wedding and Maria for her elevation to viscountess.

To that end, Lady Fortescue planned some entertainments, beginning with a small dinner party for some neighbors. The most difficult part, from Maria's point of view, was overcoming what she thought of as good sense and what Lady Fortescue and Lady Pellew called cheese-paring parsimony.

Yes, Aunt Sophia said, a "simple" dinner for neighbors, not above twenty people, would call for two soups, two fish courses, three different roasts, four entrees, a dozen different side dishes, plus pastries and creams and cakes.

"Twenty people to dinner?" Maria was having trouble getting over that first hurdle. Her family had never had a table large enough to seat that many.

"And on occasion far more," Lady Fortescue assured her, and produced the guest list and menu for a dinner she was having in three days' time.

Maria looked at the menu in horror. "*Galantine de perdreaux à la gelée?* I don't even know what that is!"

Aunt Sophia looked over her shoulder. "Oh, that's just cold boned partridge. And *timbale de macaroni* à *la Napolitaine* is plain old macaroni pudding that you've had dozens of times. It all sounds more impressive when it's written out in French."

"Very true," Lady Fortescue said with a smile. "And what's important is to find out what dishes your cook does well. You'll have to talk to her to find out. There's no point in calling for elaborate dishes beyond her skills. Our cook's best dish is roast beef with onions, so for guests—especially guests who aren't close friends—I call it *côte de boeuf aux oignons glacés.*" She pointed to it on the menu.

Maria looked at it with a frown. "I don't know. I fear I will feel as if I am pretending to be someone I'm not."

"But you will be Viscountess Claremont. There's no pretense about it. If you don't provide all this fuss," Lady Fortescue waved the menu, "your guests will be insulted. They will think that you consider them too unimportant to be treated with courtesy."

"I know you don't like to think so, my dear, but appearances are important." Aunt Sophia put her arm around Maria's shoulders and gave her a hug. "It is just as well that some of your new dresses are ready."

"I thought those were for after the wedding, when I actually am a viscountess. Not while I am still in mourning for my father." Maria planned to dig her heels in. "After all, we will be living in Somerset. It is unlikely that these people will ever see me again."

Lady Fortescue sighed. She took hold of Maria's hand, led her over to the settee, and sat down beside her. "Try to understand, my dear. It is quite true that you may never meet these particular people again. However, they have known Will over the years, and have followed his career. He is quite famous hereabouts—one of Nelson's band of brothers. Naturally, they are curious about his bride."

The rebuke stung. "I do not wish to give offense," Maria said stiffly.

Lady Fortescue continued, "You must also remember that our world is actually very small. Although you may not meet these particular people again, they have friends and relations all over the country, and they are all inveterate letter writers. By next week, their impression of you will have been dispersed all over the country."

Maria could feel the color draining from her face.

"Now I am sure their impression will be most favorable, but the first thing they will notice, the first thing anyone anywhere notices, is your appearance and, more particularly, what you are wearing. Think of it this way. There is a reason that the higher an officer's rank, the more resplendent his uniform. What you wear signals your status in the same way."

"Yes, I see what you mean," Maria said weakly.

"There is no need to worry." Lady Fortescue patted Maria's hand. "You will do very well."

CHAPTER 14

IT WAS NOTHING BUT BRIDAL NERVES, which was perfectly understandable. All brides were nervous, unless they were utter fools. Marriage meant an overwhelming change, an irreversible change. A bride stepped through a door into her future and she had no way to be certain what lay on the other side. Nerves were only to be expected.

She sat in the morning room with Aunt Sophia and Aunt Bess—Lady Fortescue had insisted on being called that—all of them close by the window to make use of what little sun there was, busy with their needlework. While the older women were engaged in delicate embroidery, she hemmed a handkerchief. It was a handkerchief of fine lawn, but nonetheless it remained a plain, unadorned handkerchief because her skill with a needle did not extend to delicate embroidery. Instead, the handkerchief was sensible and practical.

The white of the handkerchief almost glowed against the dark blue of her muslin gown, which was neither sensible nor practical. It was one of her new dresses, almost dark enough for true mourning but fashionably styled in case visitors should appear. Her hair was also fashionably styled, thanks to Chapman, with a little scrap of lace serving as a cap. She felt like a doll, dressed and posed to suit the expectations of others.

It would not be so bad if only she had heard from Will. Here it was, only three days before the wedding—a date *he* had chosen in his last letter—and there had been no word from him since then—no letters, no messages . . . nothing.

Had something happened to him? Had some disaster befallen? Surely they would have been notified in such a case. And if he had changed his mind about the marriage, he would have let her know. He would have let his aunt and uncle know. He would never simply run off, deserting them.

But she could not help worrying.

A bustle in the hall drew the attention of the three women, and an unannounced stranger came into the room, limping slightly. He was a very well-dressed stranger in a beautifully tailored blue tailcoat, striped waistcoat, buff breeches, and highly polished boots, and he carried a walking stick with a silver knob. His hair was cropped short with a few curls dangling over his forehead, and a patch covered one eye. He smiled tentatively at Maria.

She stood up, the half-hemmed handkerchief falling unnoticed to the floor. "Will?" she whispered incredulously. "Will?"

He smiled then and stepped to her until he was close enough to take her hand. He raised it to his mouth for a long kiss before holding it to his heart. Neither of them seemed to notice the tide of excitement that rose and ebbed around them as The Aunts fluttered about, drowning each other out with their exclamations and questions. Moments later, Sir Roderick came hurrying in to add to the clamor.

Maria tore her eyes from Will's face to take in the whole of him. "You look simply splendid!" she said. "And the leg"—she glanced down before returning her gaze to his face—"it worked?"

Before he could reply, Sir Roderick burst in. "Dammit, boy, your leg! What's going on?"

"Your leg? Mercy me!" Aunt Beth clapped her hands to her

cheeks. "I was so excited to see you wearing proper clothes that I didn't even realize . . . What on earth has happened?"

HE DIDN'T EVEN REALIZE HE HAD BEEN HOLDING his breath until he saw her smile. She smiled that glorious smile of hers. It was going to be all right.

As he clasped her hand, he realized that The Aunts—he liked her name for them—and his uncle were swarming around them, buzzing with questions and comments. He would have to answer them sooner or later, so it might as well be now. With a regretful smile he stepped back from Maria, though he kept hold of her hand, and turned to his aunt and uncle.

"There has to be an explanation," Sir Roderick said gruffly. "I'm not about to start believing in miracles."

The Aunts weren't saying anything. They just stood there wide-eyed and silent, their hands to their cheeks in identical poses.

He could feel the flush rising in his face. He had become inured to stares of disgust at his scars, but stares of amazement were something new. Not something he enjoyed.

"It's all because of Newbury," he blurted out. "The earl, I mean."

His uncle and The Aunts were too astonished to interrupt, so he got through the tale quickly enough, all the while holding tight to Maria's hand.

Sir Roderick harrumphed. "The Earl of Newbury, you say? Well, that was very civil of him, very civil indeed. I don't suppose I'll ever run into him, but if I do, I'll be sure to thank him."

Will smiled. "Oh, you'll run into him. He's come down for the wedding."

"What?" Aunt Bess shrieked in horror. "Oh good heavens—where have you put him? Where am I going to put him? We have no rooms prepared—no meals—nothing planned—oh my goodness gracious—whatever am I going to do?"

She was spinning about, darting first in one direction and then in another. Will caught hold of her to bring her to a halt. "Calm down, Aunt Bess. There's no need to make a fuss."

"No need? *No need?* Will Dormer, are you out of your mind? Of course there's a need. You tell me you've brought an earl along with you and there's nothing prepared. *Nothing!*"

"Honestly, Will!" Maria was no longer looking at him with delight.

He began to think that maybe there was some sort of problem. "He's not exactly *here*." Will tried to explain. "He and his family have taken rooms in the village at the Crown."

"Is that supposed to be better?" Aunt Bess was not at all appeased. "An earl comes to visit, and you shove him into a village tavern? What will he think of us?"

"No, no. Lady Newbury insisted," Will said. "She said it was bad enough that he invited himself to the wedding and he was under no circumstances to foist himself on you as a house guest."

Aunt Bess moaned.

"And he's having a grand time at the Crown. When I left him, he was telling Pritchard about a new type of spigot for drawing ale from a cask."

Aunt Bess glared at him. She turned to Aunt Sophia and Maria and started to lead them away. "We'll have to talk to Cook right away." She stopped abruptly and turned back to Will. "How many of them are there?"

"Only three. The earl, Lieutenant Sinclair, and James Sinclair."

"Only three." Aunt Bess sniffed. "Roddy, you'd best talk to the butler about bringing up more port and brandy. And wine."

The women vanished out the door, leaving behind fragments of worry—menus, flowers, breakfasts. Will looked after them in bemusement, then turned to his uncle. "I don't understand. What did I do?"

Lord Roderick grinned. "You just learned a very important lesson about marriage. Don't ever bring home unexpected guests, especially guests with titles."

THE WEDDING TOOK PLACE in the village church. Sir Roderick had overcome Will's initial desire for privacy.

"People in the village have known you since you were a lad," he said. "They've seen you every time you came home on leave, and they're proud of you. You'll insult them if you don't let them see you wed."

Lord Newbury added his voice as well. "You're a viscount now, my boy. That means every man and his brother is interested in everything you do. So long as you perform your public actions for all the world to see, you'll find it easier to keep the rest of your life private." He grinned suddenly. "Fruit of my experience."

The ceremony was followed by a wedding breakfast at Ashgrove. Hal made a very pretty speech of congratulations and good wishes, Lady Pellew and Lady Fortescue shed tears, and Lord Newbury and Sir Roderick reminisced about the way things were done in their day. Will and Maria bore it all with blushes until they finally escaped to the cottage the Fortescues had offered to give them some privacy on their wedding night.

Maria went to put away her bonnet and pelisse. Will waited for her in the parlor and began to panic.

He hadn't really thought this through—the logistics of it.

He could get himself undressed well enough, and he was more than willing to help Maria if she needed help. But all the things that he had been dreaming about since he first saw her, all that would take place once they were in bed . . . and he hadn't thought of how to manage it while missing a leg.

On the wedding night, the husband was supposed to go to his wife's bed. He supposed that with a nightshirt to cover the scars on his body, that might not be so bad. She wouldn't have to see them. But then he would have to take off his leg. He didn't want her to have to see that. It was too grotesque. Bad enough that his new valet had seen it.

Could he ask her to come to his bed? If she blew out the candle before she joined him under the covers, she would not have to see his body.

And then what if they couldn't manage? No, what if *he* couldn't manage? He had been a whole man the last time he had . . .

Could he ask her to be on top? Her first time—it might be difficult. If she knew anything, she would know that was not the usual way. And if she didn't know, he didn't want to have to explain . . . not their first time.

Perhaps he should have gone to a whore while he was in London to practice. He had never gone to one—he hated the idea of using someone that way—but perhaps he should have . . . No. He might have picked up some disease, and that would be even worse.

Damnation, how was this going to work?

Maria came back and must have seen something in his face. "What is wrong, Will? Are you all right?"

"No, no. I'm fine." His voice sounded like a croak. He cleared his throat and tried again. "It will be dark soon. The days are still long, but it's getting late."

She looked at him uncertainly. "Yes, it is."

"I mean . . ." He took a deep breath. "Tonight . . . If you come to me, in the dark you won't have to see me take off my leg."

She didn't say anything at first, but she looked confused. "In the dark?"

"Yes." He didn't want to face her, so he spoke to the wall. "I am . . . it is not a pretty sight. It will be easier for you if you do not have to see me."

He continued to stare at the wall, waiting for her to answer. It seemed an age before she did. What he heard was a sigh.

She put her hand on his shoulder and turned him toward her. "Will, you married me for practical reasons, and I am a practical woman who is not going to swoon at the sight of your scars. They are honorable injuries, suffered in honorable action. How dare you speak of them as something to be ashamed of? And how dare you think that I would be offended by them?"

He kept his eyes turned to the side, still unable to face her. "It's not a matter of scars. You don't know. My leg—it is one thing when

I am dressed and it is covered with clothing. But at night, when I take it off—it's this wooden thing, as if I am a marionette, being taken to pieces like a . . . like a toy."

"Oh, my dear." She put her hands on his face and turned it so that she could kiss him; it was not a passionate kiss, but a . . . he did not know what to call it. A reassuring kiss? A possessive kiss? Somehow an everyday kiss, intimate in its ordinariness.

She cupped his face in her hands so that he could not turn away. "I hope to be living with you and your leg for a good many years. We had best grow accustomed to each other." She took his arm and led him down the corridor. "Now, you may be able to undress yourself, but now that I am the picture of fashion, I need assistance. I will need your help to get out of my dress and my fashionable stays."

They reached a door, and she opened it as she continued to speak. "And, as you can see, this cottage has only one bedroom."

Indeed. He stood in the doorway. One bedroom with one bed. There it was. A large bed, with a virginal white coverlet, but still only one bed.

He turned to look at Maria, who lifted her shoulders and offered a shy smile. "I'll need your help," she said, "and not only with my stays. I don't really know what to do. Aunt Sophia's explanations were not terribly precise."

That nervous little smile of hers was probably the most seductive smile he had ever seen—probably because it was not intended to be erotic, just honest. Suddenly, his fears began to fade.

"Well then," he said, "I expect that between us, we should be able to manage to figure it all out."

He led her into the bedroom and closed the door.

CHAPTER 15

THEY STAYED AT ASHGROVE THROUGH the Christmas season, so it was already several weeks into the new year when they set out for Belford Park. Will leaned back in the carriage, still basking in the glow of the pleasures of the previous night. He couldn't help but feel a bit smug, even proud of himself, knowing that the pleasure had not all been his. Perhaps it was only because she was inexperienced, but his clumsiness and awkwardness had not disgusted his bride, not even that first time. And by last night, he had been able to bring her to paroxysms of passion more than once. Her shivers had been those of pleasure, not disgust, as he had once feared.

His contentment had even spilled over into his feelings about travel. Travel on land, that is. He had always hated carriage rides. Traveling on board ship, you had a purpose, with work to be done, but not in a carriage. In a carriage you were closed up, with nothing to do, complete control handed over to the coachman.

Now he was discovering that even a carriage ride ceased to be an irritation when it was shared with a wife. Even when that wife was drowsing on his shoulder, she provided something pleasant to look at. And since she was his wife, it did not matter that he had removed his gloves, the better to explore the softness of her. Most of her was covered up against the dust of the road, but he could trail his fingers along the lovely little curve of her neck as it rose from the collar of her pelisse, and up to the incredible softness of that little spot behind her ear. The memory of her tremor when he touched his lips to that spot brought a smile to his face.

He sighed contentedly. These past days—and nights, even nights spent in an inn—had brought him more pleasure than he had expected. He could not remember when he had last felt such peace, such . . . he was not certain what to call this feeling. He was more familiar with the feelings it was not. Anger, determination, pride, vindication—he was intimately acquainted with all of these, and pleasantly aware of their absence. But the emotion that filled him now as he held Maria curled up against him was something he could not name.

A glance out the window changed all that. His gut tightened and bile rose in his throat. They were passing through a village that he recognized. Belford Park was not far now—Belford Park and all its duties, Belford Park and all those who lived there.

Maria must have felt the sudden tension in his muscles, for she stirred and looked about her. "Are we nearing your home?" she asked.

"Nearing Belford," he said. He found it difficult to think of it as home, but then, was there any place that he called home? "This village, South Petherton, is less than a mile from the gates."

She promptly sat up, looking panicked, and began to straighten her clothes. "Goodness, that's no distance at all. Am I hopelessly mussed?"

He smiled. Not nearly so mussed as he would like her to be, but that would have to wait for greater privacy. "You look charming. There's no need for you to impress anyone. After all, you will be the mistress of the house."

She gave him a scathing look. "Oh yes, because you, of course, always arrived to take command of your ship unshaven, disheveled, with your uniform stained and wrinkled."

He blinked in surprise. She was perfectly correct. Just as the men wanted to impress the new captain, so the new captain wanted to impress the men. He needed to present himself as one worthy of authority, deserving of respect. If he did not, he would be undermining his own position.

Why would he expect it to be any different for a woman arriving to take charge of a household? She needed to establish her position from the beginning, especially at Belford Park, where she would be surrounded by people seeking to undermine her.

He couldn't admit to stupidity, however, so he harrumphed and turned to the window as she tied the ribbons of her bonnet. But he couldn't help sneaking a glance at her. It was a pleasure to watch. Whether the bonnet was anything special or even if it became her, he could not say. The pleasure was in watching her movements, so neat and economical, as if the merest touch of her fingers was enough to bring the bow into existence. His tension eased as he watched her. How did she manage to do that to him, to soothe him just by existing?

The carriage swung into the drive, past the gatehouse, a turreted building in honey-colored stone to match all the other buildings on the estate. Ahead of them was the drive, almost a mile of straight smooth road lined with leafless trees, leading to Belford. Maria leaned over to peer at the house and gave a small gasp. Most people did when they first laid eyes on it. More than two hundred years old, it sat in splendid isolation amidst its lawns. Even the trees did not dare approach too closely.

It was built in an E-shape, honoring Queen Elizabeth as did so many of the great houses built at that time. Its numerous diamond-paned windows, however, served as testimony to the wealth of the Claremont who built it. Now all those the leaded panes glittered in the afternoon sun.

A peculiar sound came from his wife. He looked over at her, and found that she was bent over, covering her face. He frowned in consternation. Surely she couldn't be weeping already? She hadn't even met Isabella and Lady Blackwell, to say nothing of Frederick.

No, he saw with relief when she lifted her head, she was not crying. She was laughing.

Laughing?

"Oh, Will, I am totally unfit to be the mistress of such a house," she said, bits of laughter interrupting her words. "Do you know what my first thought was when I saw it? Not 'How beautiful,' or even 'How impressive.' All I could think was that it was going to be a dreadful job to keep all those windows clean."

He roared with laughter, as he had not laughed in ages, and her laughter rose up again to mingle with his. They were still laughing as the carriage drew onto the graveled court at the entrance.

A footman hurried out as the coach pulled to a halt. Will accepted his help to descend, but then held out a hand himself to help his wife descend. They went up the steps, a bit slowly perhaps, but he tried to think of it as a stately pace.

Gibbs waited to greet them at the top of the steps, a beaming smile on his face. "Welcome, my lord, my lady." He bowed politely. "I trust you had a pleasant journey."

The two people standing beside him could not keep the surprise from their faces. Will decided to be amused rather than annoyed.

"Very pleasant, Mr. Gibbs," he said and turned to Maria. "My dear, you know Mr. Gibbs, but let me present Gregson, our butler, and Mrs. Bates, our housekeeper."

They looked not just surprised, but worried. He wondered why. Maria was hardly intimidating. Then he looked at his new wife more closely. She was smiling, but distantly.

"Gregson, Mrs. Bates," she said, nodding in response to their bow and curtsey. "I'm sure you will be a great help to me as I learn about this household."

"Yes, my lady." Gregson looked even more nervous. "Mr. Gibbs wa . . . told us that there would likely be some changes."

"But you needn't worry about your rooms," Mrs. Bates broke in, her hands twisting nervously. "Your maid and his lordship's valet arrived yesterday, and all has been put in order."

Maria smiled, a bit more friendly. "I'm sure they will do. But just now, I would like to have a bit of a rest if you could show me the way to my room."

"Of course, my lady." Mrs. Bates led the way eagerly.

Following, and glancing around as she did so, Maria asked, "And will there be time for me to have a bath before dinner? I feel quite dusty, I'm afraid."

Mrs. Bates' assurances faded in the distance as the women disappeared up the stairs. Will dismissed Gregson with a nod and turned to Gibbs. "Any problems?"

"None so far. I'm not certain anyone aside from the staff realizes I'm here and have taken over." He cast an eye over the two footmen carrying the luggage in from the coach and nodded to send them on their way upstairs.

Will smiled at this show of authority, glad to see that Gibbs had indeed taken charge. "Are my relatives expecting me?"

"No. As you requested, I haven't said anything to them." Gibbs smiled. "I ought to warn you that the servants are all curious about what will happen next. I believe some of them are even wagering on possible reactions."

"Let them. I'm a bit curious myself."

CHAPTER 16

Maria arrived at her room—or rather rooms—to discover a tub had already been set up in the dressing room. "Chapman, you must have read my mind."

The maid smiled. "It's a dusty trip, my lady, and I thought you'd wish to look your best when you meet the family, such as it is."

Maria nodded in agreement. From what Will had told her, she would definitely want to be armored for that first meeting.

Laying aside her bonnet, gloves, and spencer, she opened her reticule to take out the velvet bag that held one of Will's gifts—an ancient Roman onyx cameo carved with the head of Minerva, goddess of wisdom and warfare. She had not been willing to part with it even to let Chapman carry it with her other jewels.

She smiled. Yes, when she wore it on a ribbon around her neck, it would be an impressive piece of armor. From what Will had said of his relatives, they might not understand just how magnificent it was, but with Minerva to guard her, she would be invincible.

While she waited for the footmen to arrive with the water, Maria took a good look about her bedchamber.

It could be worse.

At least it was not paneled with dark wood from floor to ceiling the way the corridor outside was.

The rooms were clean enough, and there was a fireplace in the dressing room as well as in the bed chamber, but everything was a bit shabby—rather like the hall down below where they had arrived: shabby and gloomy.

The shabbiness was understandable, since as far as Maria knew there had not been a viscountess in residence since Will's mother had died twenty years ago. And that was not even considering the fact that Will's parents had always been at odds, so it was unlikely that even before that, the old viscount had been willing to indulge his wife in decorating her rooms.

Maria was not sure what the style of the dark, heavy furniture in this room was called, but she knew it had not been fashionable in her lifetime. Those heavy legs on the chairs always made her suspect that they had been intended for an obese sitter—someone perhaps like the current Prince of Wales. The thought amused her momentarily, but the atmosphere of the room remained oppressive.

Going over to the bed, she fingered the hangings. No dust went flying, but they had been hanging in place so long that the inner folds were much darker than the outer, and the linen fabric was almost brittle. A pair of candlesticks stood on the small writing table, far too few to illumine a room this size.

There probably weren't enough candles in the hall downstairs either. Gloom was everywhere.

There was plenty of work to be done here, enough to keep her busy for a good long while. She would have to talk to Will about what sort of allowance she could have for decorating. She did hope he wasn't going to be foolish and tell her to spend whatever she liked, the way her father did before the money was all lost. That sort of assurance sounded generous but was actually quite useless. If he said that, how could she know if she should be covering the walls with hand-painted silk or with whitewash?

He might be rich, as the Fortescues kept assuring her, but there was no such thing as a fortune too large to be frittered away.

She looked down at the carpet, then sat down on one of the squat chairs to take off her shoes and remove her stockings. When she stood up again, she wiggled her toes in the carpet. It was usable, reasonably soft and thick, but ugly, with those muddy greens and browns. Could they afford to replace it?

Well, if what the Fortescues had told her was accurate, they could with no difficulty. But it was not easy to adjust from watching every penny to being able to replace something just because she didn't like it!

Eventually, the footmen arrived with the hot water. It had taken them more than thirty minutes, she noted, and the water was not what she would call hot. Either the kitchen did not keep a boiler of hot water at hand, or the servants were a bit too lackadaisical about their duties.

Chapman came back after closing the door on the footmen and began to help Maria out of her traveling dress. It was odd. After all these years of getting herself in and out of her clothes, Maria surprised herself by having no difficulty getting used to the assistance of a maid. Of course, her clothes were now a good deal more complicated than they used to be and made Chapman's help necessary.

The maid must have noticed the frown on Maria's face when she looked at the carpet, because she said, "It's a decent enough carpet, my lady, but worn and ugly like so much in this house. It might do for the servants' hall, but not for the mistress's chamber. You'll have your work cut out for you, getting everything right and proper."

That sounded ominous. "With the house, or with the staff as well?"

Chapman paused to consider. "Well, I don't know that they're unwilling, but they don't go out of their way to find things to do. I get the impression that as long as he had his own comforts, the old viscount didn't care about anything else. When the master doesn't care, the staff isn't going to spend hours polishing the furniture, especially in rooms that aren't used. Then of course, for the last few years Lady Blackwell has fancied herself in charge."

"Was she or wasn't she?"

"She thought so, but the servants didn't seem to agree. My impression is that they'd say, 'Yes, my lady,' and then continue to do whatever they chose." Chapman untied the last of the laces, lifted the dress over Maria's head, and shook it out before laying it over the back of a chair.

It was Maria's turn to consider. "Will they do a good job once that's what is expected?"

Chapman shrugged as she untied the petticoat. "They may be a good, honest staff, just a bit dispirited. But it's too small a staff for a house this size."

"Too small?" The petticoat fell to the floor and Maria stepped out of it.

"Only four maids, and work enough for a dozen or more if it's to be done right." Chapman laid the petticoat aside with the dress.

Maria took a deep breath. She seemed to be doing that far too frequently these days, but it helped. At least it calmed her a bit when she ran into another gap in her knowledge. Recognizing that a bed hanging was frayed was something she could do, and she knew several ways to refurbish it if it couldn't be replaced. But how on earth was she supposed to know how many housemaids a house this size needed?

"The housekeeper seems a bit set in her ways, but it may just be that there hasn't been a mistress here—a real one—in years," Chapman continued, loosening the laces of the stays. "Once she sees that you really are the mistress here and understands that you expect things to be put right, she'll likely tell you what kind of staff she needs to get it done."

Of course, the housekeeper should know. She was the one who would be hiring the maids as well. Maria felt liberated, and not just because the stays were gone. After dismissing Chapman—help with her clothes she could accept, but she could not accustom herself to being bathed by someone—she stepped behind the screen, removed her shift, and sank into the warm water. A packet of dried lavender scented the water. She breathed in the soothing perfume and allowed herself to simply relax.

All too soon, the water began to cool, and it was time to face the world.

Chapman had laid out her costume for the evening, and Maria was glad to let the maid make the decisions. She loved the fine ivory muslin covered in delicate embroidery and with its modest train, but she shuddered at the impracticality of the costume—especially the train in this house where she doubted the floors had been swept properly.

After Chapman put the final touches on her Grecian coiffure, held in place with a green bandeau and feather, and tied the cameo on a green ribbon around her neck, she looked at herself in the mirror. It was a full-length cheval mirror on a dark mahogany stand and would have been useful had the glass not been so cloudy. Unfortunately, as it was, she appeared rather like a ghost coming out of the mist.

A knock on the door heralded Will's appearance, and the look of admiration on his face put an end to any worries about her appearance.

"I would rather like to be in the drawing room before the others," he said, sounding slightly hesitant.

Of course he would. That way the others would not notice his slow descent down the staircase.

"That sounds like an excellent plan," she said, allowing him to drape the silk shawl over her shoulders.

She wanted to laugh as they walked together down the corridor. Here she was wearing white kid slippers, silk stockings, a silk shawl, even a train—such utterly luxurious finery. Whatever had happened to the practical, sensible woman she used to be?

CHAPTER 17

SHARING A RUEFUL LOOK OF SELF-MOCKERY, Will and Maria positioned themselves carefully to face the entrance of the drawing room with the late afternoon sun streaming in through the window behind them. Will was seated in a sturdy armchair, from which he could push himself up easily. Maria sat slightly turned, having arranged her train and her shawl in graceful folds. Each held a glass of sherry.

"Now I know how actors must feel just before the curtain goes up—afraid the audience will mock them as foolish shams," Maria said.

Her husband grinned. "It's the way the captain feels when he addresses the crew before a battle—afraid they will realize he has no idea whether his orders are sensible or idiotic." He lifted his glass of sherry to her.

She could hear voices approaching and took a quick swallow of her sherry, but put her glass on the table, afraid her hand might tremble, and turned to the doorway with her best Lady Fortescue gracious smile.

The two women who came into the room stopped so abruptly that the man behind them stumbled into them, pushing the entire group forward in an awkward tangle.

The first to recover was the man, who stepped out, straightening his waistcoat, and demanded, "Who the devil are you?"

Will was by now on his feet, standing erect with one hand resting lightly on his walking stick. "Really, Frederick, is that any way to welcome me home?"

Maria stood as well. The man, who she assumed must be Frederick Dormer, Will's cousin, stood speechless, with his mouth hanging open. The two women looked equally dumbfounded, although the older one, presumably Lady Blackwell, looked more annoyed than surprised. The younger one simply looked lovely. Maria suspected she would look lovely no matter what her expression.

"Why Lord Claremont, I wouldn't have recognized you," Isabella said, sounding quite pleased. "Did your leg grow back?"

Maria blinked. She was lovely, but perhaps…a bit simpleminded?

Will managed a slight smile and looked at Maria. "My dear, may I present my brother's widow, Isabella Dormer, her mother, Lady Blackwell, and my cousin, Frederick Dormer." He took Maria by the hand and turned to the others. "And this is Maria, Lady Claremont. My wife." He lifted her hand and kissed it.

"Your wife!" Frederick's mouth snapped shut, as if to hold in his fury. His nostrils were pinched and white, and his whole body was tensed as if to pounce.

"Your wife?" Isabella simply sounded curious. "Well, you do look much better with your hair cut. Did you get a new coat? I expect that explains it."

"Why did you not inform us of this?" Lady Blackwell could not hide her anger. "How could you do such a thing without letting us know?"

Will's smile did not look friendly. "I was not aware that your permission was required."

"No, no, of course not." Frederick made no effort to smile. "It's just unexpected. I wish you happy, of course. We all do."

"And I, of course, am delighted to meet you all," Maria said, maintaining the gracious smile she had learned from Lady Fortescue. "Lord Claremont has told me so much about you."

There was a pause while she let them think about that.

Frederick headed for the sherry decanter, filled a glass to the brim, and swallowed it in one gulp. He grimaced and looked around the room. Spotting the brandy decanter, he headed in that direction and filled another glass.

Lady Blackwell took a deep breath and managed to twist her mouth into a smile of sorts. "I do hope you are not offended, Lady Claremont," she said. "It is simply that you took us by surprise."

"Indeed you did," Isabella said. "Will—Lord Claremont has been gone so long without any word that we were beginning to grow quite worried."

"Were you really?" Will said. It was more of a comment than a question.

"Oh, yes." Isabella turned to him with a smile. "In fact, Frederick was going to write to the attorneys to find out if you were alive or not."

They all turned to look at Frederick, who tossed back his brandy and refilled the glass.

"So sorry to disappoint you," Will said.

"An estate doesn't run itself, you know," Frederick snarled.

To Maria's relief, Gregson appeared at the door. "Ah, dinner is ready. Shall we?" She took Will's arm, and they led the group slowly into the dining room.

It was not the most comfortable of meals, nor was it the most delicious. Frederick took no part in any conversation and addressed himself solely to the wine, keeping the footman busy refilling his glass.

"And where are you from, Lady Claremont? Would we be likely to know your people?" Lady Blackwell peered across the soup.

"I don't know. Where are your people from?" Maria asked, deflecting the thrust. "My father was Robert Garland, a captain in the Navy."

"And my first captain when I was sent to sea," Will put in. "More recently, one of Nelson's band of brothers, and a hero in the battle of the Nile."

"A naval gentleman. How admirable." Lady Blackwell didn't quite sneer. "Is he away at sea these days?"

That question did hurt. The pain of her father's death was still too fresh. It took Maria a moment before she could reply calmly. "My father has recently passed away."

"How sad for you. And your mother?"

"She also has passed away."

"Then you are an orphan and all alone?" Isabella entered the conversation. "How dreadful. I know how lonely I felt when my dear George died, but at least I had the support of my mother and Mr. Dormer here."

Her smile of gratitude faded when she turned to Frederick. He caught himself to keep from sliding off his chair. Maria found it doubtful that he would be able to support anyone.

"So you have no family at all? How unfortunate." Lady Blackwell waved for a footman to remove the soup.

Maria smiled. "But now I have my husband and his family." Her smile faded as she looked at the dish placed before her.

"Fricandeaux de veau," Lady Blackwell said, in a vague approximation of a French accent. "Unfortunately, I fear the cook has still not mastered the recipes I gave her."

"So I see." Maria looked across at Will, who had scraped the congealed sauce off the piece of veal on his plate and was now attempting to cut the rubbery meat.

Just then Frederick slid completely off his chair, clutching the tablecloth to slow his descent, and bringing the bowls and platters of food crashing down with him.

Lady Blackwell sprang up with a shriek, but Isabella, looking at the mess that had landed in her lap, said only, "Oh, dear, my dress is ruined. At least it's one of the old black ones."

After instructing the footmen to carry Frederick to his room,

Will turned to Maria with a sigh. "And this is your new home."

"It has certainly been a memorable welcome," she laughed, "but it has been a long day. I think perhaps it would be best to retire now and allow the servants to clean up this mess."

CHAPTER 18

AT SEVEN THE NEXT MORNING, Lord and Lady Claremont came downstairs. Lady Claremont went to the small room that had, twenty years ago, been the office of the lady of the house. Lord Claremont went to the library, which had served as his father's office.

Fifteen minutes later, the cook joined Lady Claremont. The appropriately named Mrs. Potts was a stout woman of some fifty years. She had been designed by nature to be a cheerful, smiling sort. At the moment, however, she trembled on the verge of tears as she stood in front of the new chatelaine.

"I thought we might go over the menus for the coming days." Maria smiled in an effort to put the cook at ease. She was unsuccessful.

"I can't do it, my lady," Mrs. Potts managed to say, twisted her hands in her apron. "I can't cook those foreign dishes."

"That's quite all right." Maria continued to smile. "Let us begin with the dishes you do cook well."

The older woman stared for a moment, as if unable to believe her ears. "Roasts," she said finally. "I can do you a lovely roast of mutton or beef. Or steaks. I can grill you a steak just as you like it. And I've a fine hand with puddings. Pastry too. Light as air, my pastries be."

"Excellent. That will do very well to start with. Now suppose we go over the menu for the coming days."

Mrs. Potts' face fell. "Lady Blackwell gave me some more receipts she wants me to do."

"You needn't worry about that. Now that I am here, there is no need to trouble Lady Blackwell any further with household matters." Maria's smile turned steely as she drew out a piece of paper. "Since Lord Claremont and I are both content with simple meals, I think that when there are no guests, we can manage with a soup, some sort of fish, a roast, and a few side dishes. If in future we have need of more elaborate menus, I can help you to master the recipes, or we can bring in someone to assist you."

The cook straightened and stood a bit taller. "Don't you worry, my lady."

After a discussion of the foodstuffs currently on hand and those that might be needed, a determined Mrs. Potts bobbed a curtsy and left, the week's new menus in hand.

By the time Will and Maria sat down to breakfast two hours later, she had discovered a rather slovenly book of household accounts that included only sporadic entries and a household book that must have belonged to Will's mother. It was a collection of stillroom recipes, buried under a collection of Minerva Press horrid novels.

Her talk with Mrs. Potts had obviously been fruitful. The sideboard groaned under steaming oatmeal, thick cream, cold beef, grilled trout, sausages, bacon, hot rolls, fresh butter, honey, and jam. The tea was hot and fragrant.

Maria cradled her cup in her hands and enjoyed the steamy perfume. She looked around the breakfast room with an appraising eye. It was nicely proportioned, and positioned to take advantage of the morning sun. Or at least, it would enjoy the sun once the windows were well-cleaned and the faded linen drapes were replaced with something more cheerful: Toile de jouy, perhaps.

Yes, her new home seemed quite promising. She was about to say something cheerful about it when she realized that Will was not looking nearly so optimistic. In fact, he looked definitely gloomy.

So she asked. "What is wrong?"

"Frederick was right. An estate doesn't run itself." He poked at a sausage.

"Surely it cannot require your constant attendance. Lords and gentlemen are always going to London or traveling about the country."

"No doubt, but unless they are thoroughly irresponsible, they leave someone in charge who knows what to do. Or at the very least they leave an address where they can be reached." He stabbed the sausage viciously.

She bit her lip uncertainly. "Did something dreadful happen?"

"How would I know?" He shook his head abruptly. "There are bills that may or may not have been paid. There are letters that have been opened, but whether or not they have received a reply, I have no way of knowing. One of them seems to be from a neighbor about a drainage problem. Has it been dealt with? Should it be?"

He cut into the sausage angrily. "Then there is a book of accounts that I cannot make heads or tails of. A champion seems to have made my father money, though what he was a champion of, I have no idea. Then there is some woman named Eleanor who cost him money, and I hate to think what that might mean."

Before she could say anything, he swallowed the sausage and continued, "There's no help for it. I'll have to ask Frederick."

"Will he know?"

"Oh yes." He laughed bitterly. "He'll know because he thinks this should be his, and he's been waiting for me to die. Couldn't you tell? He had been hoping I wouldn't return."

"Well, yes, I admit I did get that impression as he sought to drown his sorrows yesterday evening." They both grinned at the memory. "But I don't really understand why he's here. Doesn't he have a home of his own?"

"He was so often here when I was a child that the oddity of it didn't strike me at first, but I talked to the lawyers when I was in London. It seems his father left Frederick a house and a farm and nothing else."

"Your uncle was a poor man?" Maria was surprised. "From the way Sir Roderick spoke, I assumed your entire family was wealthy."

"Frederick's father was wealthy, but he left that wealth to others, not to Frederick."

"How very odd."

"Yes, it was." Will stared moodily at the table. "Very odd. My father made him an allowance, but then never bothered to make a will himself, so there was no provision for Frederick. For that matter, there was no provision for Isabella either. She had brought no dowry, and her mother has nothing."

"Oh dear." Maria joined Will in staring at the table. "We can hardly just throw them out. It seems we are stuck with them."

Will nodded.

She stood up briskly and shook out her skirts. "Well, it's an enormous house. We should be able to manage without having to see too much of them. Now I must join Mrs. Bates for a tour of the house. I warn you, we may have to hire additional servants to take care of it properly."

Will grinned. "As you said, it's an enormous house."

IT WAS NOT SIMPLY AN ENORMOUS HOUSE, Maria realized as Mrs. Bates led her nervously around. It was an enormous mess. Unused rooms and their furnishings were coated in dust. No one had bothered to put the furniture under covers. In those rooms that were in use, everything was worn and shabby.

After the sixth hopeless room, Maria decided she had seen enough. She went over to a window, took out a handkerchief, and rubbed off some of the dust and grime. Below was a walled garden, and in the distance were rolling hills. It would be a lovely view, once the garden was restored and the windows were cleaned.

She turned back to Mrs. Bates. "You don't need me to tell you that this place is a disgrace."

"No, my lady." The housekeeper faced her squarely. "We did the best we could. Lord Claremont—his lordship's father, that is . . ."

Maria dismissed that with a wave of her hand. "It's dispiriting to work when no one cares. I can understand that. In addition, I can see that you do not have a large enough staff to maintain a decent state of cleanliness. You will need to hire additional maids. Can you find enough girls in the village who are willing and capable, or should I send to London?"

"I'm sure I can find local girls." The housekeeper stood straighter. "There's many who'll be glad to work close to their family."

"Very well, then. A week from now, I expect the house to be in reasonable order. Then we can see what needs to be done by way of refurbishment."

Mrs. Bates marched off, the light of battle in her eyes, and Maria returned to her new office feeling confident. Both the housekeeper and the cook had been perfectly willing to accept orders from her. They even seemed glad to do so. At least her inexperience wasn't obvious.

Seated at the desk, she began sorting out bills that had been shoved higgledy-piggledy into a drawer. There was, unfortunately, no indication of which ones had or had not been paid. How on earth was she to make sense of this? She could go to the butcher and ask what bills had been paid, but could she expect an honest answer?

A number of the bills were from dressmakers. Her recent experiences at the hands of Lady Fortescue showed her that these were not exorbitant, but not on the low side either. Definitely not low when one considered that they were ordered from a local woman, not even from Exeter or Taunton, no less London.

The bills and the gowns they represented presumably belonged to Isabella and her mother. From what Will had told her, they had no money of their own. If Will was going to take on responsibility for the two women, it might be a wise idea to arrange an allowance for them to avoid future unpleasantness.

CHAPTER 19

LADY BLACKWELL PACED BACK AND FORTH across the sitting room she had taken for her own, swinging the train of her morning gown at each turn. Really, Isabella thought, it was very like a cat swishing its tail—an angry cat, that is. Because Lady Blackwell was definitely angry.

Isabella and her mother had arrived in the breakfast room well before noon, only to discover that there was no breakfast. The cook had taken ages to appear in response to Lady Blackwell's demand, and then was not at all apologetic. Lady Claremont had said that breakfast was to be cleared at ten o'clock, she said.

"How dare that creature give such orders?" Lady Blackwell asked as she marched toward the window. "Who does she think she is?" she asked on the return trip.

Isabella, who had been examining the skirt of her gown and wondering if the black wasn't beginning to look a bit rusty, looked up. "I expect she thinks she is Lady Claremont. After all, she is."

"An upstart. A vulgar upstart. The daughter of no one more important than a naval officer."

"Like Lord Claremont." Isabella smiled.

"*Not* like Lord Claremont, you ninny. He at least is the son of a viscount." Lady Blackwell collapsed into a chair and put a hand to her forehead. "What is to become of us? She could throw us out. And now she is going over the bills. The dressmakers' bills that have yet to be paid. What will become of us?"

Isabella frowned. "This dress is really looking far too worn. It's been almost a year since dear George died. I really could wear gray, couldn't I? Or lavender. But I definitely need some new clothes."

"Haven't you heard a thing I said? Talking about new clothes when we could be out on the street at any moment! What are we going to do?"

Isabella looked in surprise at her mother, who was fluttering her hands helplessly. "Well," she said, "I suppose we must set about being nice to her."

"*Nice* to her?" Lady Blackwell stared in astonishment. "When she is disrupting all my plans?"

"I expect she would appreciate some help settling in."

That struck a chord with Lady Blackwell. She sat up abruptly, her eyes brightening. "Yes, of course!" She began to smile. "After all, she's just a little nobody. She won't have any idea how to behave or how to run a household like this. I can teach her. She will *need* me. Yes!"

"Perhaps." Isabella returned to examining her gown. "At the very least I need to replace the ribbons on this gown. Or perhaps use silver braid."

Lady Blackwell heaved an exasperated sigh. "Do pay attention. Perhaps you could give her advice on what to wear. She is unlikely to have any sense of fashion."

"Mmm. I don't know. That gown she wore last night was extremely elegant."

A commotion out in the hall interrupted just as Lady Blackwell opened her mouth for what was likely to be a new tirade. "*Now* what?" she demanded, heading for the door.

Isabella supposed she might as well follow.

More newcomers had arrived. This was interesting. There hadn't been this many people in the house since the funeral, and the only thing interesting about that had been Frederick's fury when he came back from the graveyard, ranting about Will's survival. These people looked interesting.

Isabella would have dismissed the older woman with a glance were it not for her very stylish bonnet. Her traveling costume was also attractive. Obviously she was a person of some importance.

Even more interesting was the gentleman with her. He was far younger—her son, perhaps? At any rate he was really quite hand-some, and his clothes too well tailored for him to be anything but a gentleman.

They were strangers to her, but obviously not to Will and his new wife, who was hugging the woman while Will shook the hand of the gentleman. Isabella stood to the side, waiting to be seen and introduced.

Her mother did not bother waiting.

"I see we have visitors, Maria. Will you present them?"

Lady Blackwell was employing her glacially condescend-ing manner. Isabella suspected that was not a good idea. After all, Will's wife did outrank her, and she did not recall her having invited them to use her first name.

Lady Claremont did indeed look startled at the incursion, but that turned quickly into amusement. "Aunt Sophia," she said, "may I present Mrs. Dormer, the widow of my husband's older brother, and her mother, Lady Blackwell." Smiling, she continued, "And may I make known to you my aunt, Lady Pellew, and Mr. Sinclair, a friend of ours."

Isabella smiled and curtseyed gracefully. Her mother managed a nod even stiffer than the one Maria's aunt offered.

Then Lady Blackwell noticed the trunks being carried in and stiffened even more. "I am so sorry I was not informed that you would be arriving today. I fear your rooms may not be prepared."

"You need not worry yourself about such household matters,"

Lady Claremont said. "I informed Mrs. Bates yesterday that we would be expecting visitors, so all is in hand."

Lady Blackwell's silence obviously required some effort, but Isabella thought it was probably wise. She herself continued to direct her attractive smiles to the newcomers while not saying anything.

It was Claremont's turn to speak. "If you ladies will excuse us, Sinclair and I have matters to discuss." With a bow, he led the newcomer slowly in the direction of his office.

Following his example, Lady Claremont said, "And I am sure my aunt would like to rest after her journey. If you do not mind, I will take her to her room, and we will see you at dinner."

Ignoring her mother's harrumphs, Isabella continued to admire Lady Pellew's traveling costume. It was a soft green cambric gown, full in back, with a matching spencer. The bonnet was one of those jockey hats in a darker green silk. On the whole, she decided that the style looked even better in reality than it had in the fashion periodicals.

CHAPTER 20

"**I**'M VERY GRATEFUL THAT YOU CAME," Will said, ushering Sinclair into the office. He sat down behind the desk, resting his walking stick against it.

Sinclair noticed the sigh that accompanied those actions. "Walking is still uncomfortable?"

"Less so all the time." Will quirked a smile. "And far easier than it was before this device. I owe a considerable debt to your uncle."

"He's as proud of this success as if he had invented the device himself." Sinclair laughed as he seated himself in the visitor's chair. "You'll need to be careful when you go up to town. He'll want to display you and your leg to all his acquaintance."

"Well, I'll not deny him anything he asks. You've no idea what a difference it has made." Will shook his head in bemusement. "And here I am, about to put myself in debt to you as well. I can't make head or tail of the account books I've seen. Look at this!" He shoved an account book across the desk.

After looking briefly at the book, Sinclair looked up with a smile. "I can't say your father employed a terribly sophisticated method of keeping his personal accounts. In fact, I'm not sure these could really be called accounts at all. All you have here is a collection of bills and a list of expenses—and pretty vague ones at that. Consider this one: *Household expenses, ten pounds.* But no indication if it's for food or roof repairs." He shook his head in dismay.

"So it isn't entirely my fault that I was having trouble making sense of all this." Will was scowling at the pile of books and papers. "The attorney in London seemed to think there were no debts outstanding. At least, no significant ones. On the other hand, he was not entirely clear on the income side of things. He has accounts from the outlying estates and from the coal mines, but he was still trying to get an accounting from Hopworth."

"Yes, well," Sinclair allowed himself a smile, "I don't think that will be forthcoming."

"And then there's this." Will picked up another book, opened it, and jabbed at an entry. "He seems to have paid a hundred pounds to some woman named Eleanor, but that's all there is about her. A mistress? A pensioner?"

Sinclair took the book and began paging through it. Then he burst into laughter. "Well, your father did manage to keep this account well enough—it's his betting book. You'll be pleased to know that he won a packet on Champion two years ago, more than enough to make up for his losses on Eleanor. Eleanor, you might like to know, is the filly who won the Derby last year. It made quite a splash. The first time a filly ever won."

Will snorted. "Typical. Horses are the only thing he paid attention to. Well, the rest of the books should be in Hopworth's house. He should be about someplace."

Sinclair looked amused, but made no comment.

Will, on the other hand, looked thoughtful. "Speaking of his house, I assume it goes with the steward's job. Do you want it? You're more than welcome to take up residence here in this house."

"The steward's house for me, I think." Sinclair said. "Not that I wouldn't be delighted to stay with you, but I think my investigations will bear more fruit if I'm not living in the landlord's pocket, so to speak."

"Pity."

A rap on the door drew their attention, and they grinned at each other like boys about to play a prank.

"Enter," Will called.

The door opened partially, and Hopworth slipped in, looking as unprepossessing as before. If anything, he looked even more pathetic than usual, hunched over, one hand clutched in the other.

"Welcome home, my lord." He smiled and bobbed his head a few times.

Good lord, Will despised that sort of cringing sycophancy. To say nothing of hypocrisy. Will wasn't sure enough yet to make an accusation, but he was fairly certain that Hopworth had been fattening his own purse at the expense of the estate. If Will found out that the cheating had affected the tenants and not just his father, Hopworth would soon lose that smile.

Hopworth was darting nervous glances in Sinclair's direction. Ignoring this, Will smiled himself and asked, "Hopworth, I was wondering about the estate books. All I seem to have here are the previous viscount's betting books."

Hopworth made a good show of looking surprised. "Ah, well, I didn't realize you wanted the *estate* accounts. Lord Claremont— the old one, that is—he never wanted them cluttering up his office here, so I kept them in my office."

With an understanding nod, Will said, "And that would be in your office where?"

"In my house. The steward's house. It's a fair walk from here, so if you let me know what you want to see, I'll be glad to bring it over." Hopworth was practically bending over with eagerness to please.

"No need for that. Mr. Sinclair here will be taking over as steward." Will waved a hand in a gesture of introduction.

Sinclair smiled in a fashion that might be considered friendly in a wolf.

Hopworth blinked. Then he blanched. "But, my lord, I don't understand. Have I offended in some way?"

"No, no, it isn't that." Will waved a hand casually. "However, it's time for me to take charge of the estate. New captain, new officers, you understand, I'm sure. Now, I expect it will take you a bit of time to pack up your gear, decide on your next bunk, that sort of thing, so you can put up at the inn in the village until you decide where to go." He looked away.

"But my lord . . ." The steward stood his ground, though nervously. He cleared his throat. "May I expect a character from you?"

Will turned back and stared at Hopworth. At length he lifted a corner of his mouth in a half-smile. "I think you had best ask that of Frederick Dormer. After all you have worked for him far longer than for me."

"Not *for* him, my lord!"

Will's smile broadened. "I only meant, you worked under his direction. I'm sure he can characterize your work far better than I."

Hopwood had lost anything resembling a smile, and his nervous bobs seemed mechanical. When he turned to go, Sinclair reached out a hand to catch him. "I'll accompany you. I assume there's a spare bedroom in the house?"

The steward nodded weakly.

"Then I will have my trunks sent over." He took Hopwood's arm to lead him out. "I'll need the keys so I can start on the books while you pack. That way you may be available to answer some of my questions before you leave."

Watching them depart, Will felt more cheerful already.

"WHO THE DEVIL ARE YOU?" A voice demanded. "And how dare you go prying through private papers?"

Too engrossed in his study of the intriguing documents in front of him, Sinclair had not even noticed that the office had been invaded. Slowly he lifted his head to look at the intruder. What he saw was a man dressed in the height of fashion, glossy boots, striped waistcoat, elaborate cravat, snug trousers, coat—and a top hat he had not bothered to remove. A riding crop was clenched in his still-gloved hand. Whoever he was, he obviously felt entitled to enter the steward's house and office without so much as a by-your-leave.

"James Sinclair, steward to Viscount Claremont. And you are?" Sinclair did not rise but tilted his head in inquiry.

The intruder checked abruptly and narrowed his eyes before answering slowly. "Frederick Dormer, the viscount's cousin. What do you mean, you're Claremont's steward? Hopworth is the steward here."

"Ah, Mr. Dormer. The viscount mentioned you." Sinclair rose slowly and nodded his head in greeting. "I am Mr. Hopworth's replacement."

"I do not recall Hopworth saying anything about leaving." The comment sounded rather like an accusation.

Sinclair smiled blandly in the face of Dormer's glare. "Really?"

Dormer waited for further explanation, but Sinclair said nothing more. He noted with amusement the way a muscle in Dormer's cheek seemed to twitch with irritation and the manner in which the riding crop was beating a tattoo against those very shiny boots. Really, if the fellow were a cat, he'd be lashing his tail about.

"Insolent," hissed Dormer before he spun on his heel and marched out.

Sinclair's bland smile widened into a grin. *So, Dormer feels entitled to enter the steward's house—and office—without so much as knocking. Interesting. I must remember to change the locks.*

He returned to the books. It had not surprised him to discover a duplicate set of books with certain variations in income and expenses. But the most recent volume seemed to be missing. Perhaps he should go and help Hopworth pack.

He must have walked with a lighter tread than he realized, since when he knocked on Hopworth's door, there was a clatter inside as if something had been dropped or overturned. There was a moment of silence before he heard footsteps within. Eventually the door was opened a crack, allowing Hopworth to peer out.

"A Mr. Dormer came to call. A friend of yours, I assume," Sinclair said.

"No, no, not a friend." Hopworth licked his lips.

"Really?" Sinclair raised his brows. "He entered so casually that I received the impression that he was on friendly terms with you."

Hopworth jerked back slightly. "I know him, of course. He is related to the family here and resides with them. But not a friend. I would not presume to call him a friend."

That slight jerk had left the door open far enough for Sinclair to enter the room, noting that the trunk by the bed was already nearly full of hastily folded clothing.

He was careful to keep both his movements and his tone of voice casual as he moved over to the window. "I see. Still, he must be eager to speak with you. He is conferring with the fellow driving the cart outside. You can catch him if you hurry."

Hopworth gasped, then coughed to hide it. "Ah, well than, perhaps I can catch him." He scurried out.

As soon as he was gone, Sinclair stepped over to the trunk and began rummaging through it. Under the linens, which had been pitched in indiscriminately, he found several books—account books, he saw when he withdrew them. There were also a number of letters. He gathered them all together and carried them back to the office, managing to avoid Hopworth on the way.

He doubted their absence would be discovered before Hopworth unpacked, and it was unlikely the man would make any complaint.

CHAPTER 21

THE SUN WAS LOW BY THE TIME DORMER RODE into the village the next day. He ordered a tankard of ale at the tavern and, despite the chill in the air, carried it out to a table by the stream. The water tumbling over the rocks made enough noise to prevent anything said here from being overheard. He took a meditative sip as he watched the water. An elderly trout, known locally as Old Sam, spent much of his time in a pool under the trailing branches of a willow on the far side, and watching for him was a popular pastime.

The wait was not long. In a matter of moments, Hopworth appeared, looking nervously about him, and slithered onto the bench. Ignoring the stream and willow, he kept a watch out for unexpected visitors.

With a sigh, Dormer passed the tankard to him, and Hopworth gulped down half the contents.

"I went to Yeovil. The bank wouldn't give me access to the accounts."

"Does that surprise you?" Dormer continued to watch the stream. "My cousin is obviously not the fool I thought him."

"Dammit! I need money!"

"Surely you've made enough the past few years. You should have a healthy sum set aside." Dormer tilted his head meditatively. "Last year alone your share should have come to . . . at least several hundred pounds."

"Yes, well . . ." Hopworth gnawed his lower lip.

"Don't tell me you've been gambling again." Dormer's smile was more like a sneer. "How many times have I told to that you should leave gentlemanly vices to gentlemen?"

"All very well for you to say. You're living in Claremont's house, living on Claremont's wealth, and you've been funneling the estate's income into your own pockets for years. The privileges of a gentleman, I suppose."

Dormer shrugged and returned his gaze to the stream. "If you like. I assume you at least had the sense to destroy the account books." The silence that followed was loud enough to make him turn his head. "You did destroy the books and correspondence, didn't you?"

"Not exactly." Hopworth swallowed noisily. "I didn't have a chance to destroy anything with Sinclair in the house, so I shoved it all into my trunk."

Silence resumed, so Dormer prompted, "And . . .?"

"And when I went to unpack, they weren't there. He must have taken them while I was talking to you."

A muscle twitched in Dormer's cheek. "What a pity. Though it's more a pity for you than anyone else, I think. I am reasonably certain that my name has never appeared on any documents. I may encounter suspicion, but there is not likely to be any proof. You, however, had best be on your way."

"What do you mean? Where should I go?"

Dormer resumed his relaxed position, watching the water for any sign of the old trout. "Why, anywhere you like. Your travels are no affair of mine."

"You can't just abandon me!" Hopworth stood, quivering with fury . . . or fear. "You're as guilty as I am. This was all your idea in the first place, your plan."

"Was it?" Dormer was unmoved. "Dear me. I don't see how anyone could think that. After all, I'm not the one who was dealing with the purveyors. I'm not the one who was keeping two sets of books. If you are found to have been defrauding your employer, I'm sure I shall be as shocked as anyone."

Hopworth stared at him, his mouth opening and closing but no sound came forth, until at last he uttered a strangled cry and fled.

Dormer continued to stare at the water, an occasional twitch at the corner of his mouth the only sign of his disturbance. He would need to go to London, he decided, and see what he could discover from his connections at the navy board. There was nothing to connect him with any misdealings, he was almost certain of that, but it would be well to make sure.

It was annoying to think that the London house was no longer at his disposal, but he did not want to call attention to his trip. The less his cousin knew about his activities, the better.

London

DORMER STROLLED ALONG WHITEHALL TOWARD THE Admiralty where the Victuallers Office was ensconced. It was doubtless an excess of caution that prompted him to have the hackney drop him off at Charing Cross, but he did not want anyone to know about his visit here—not that anyone would ask a hackney driver, but one never knew.

Part of his worry was due to the fact that he was not at all sure this visit was a good idea. Obviously with Hopwood dismissed and a new steward in his place the old arrangement could not continue. It was unfortunate, but that was not the only problem. In the past couple of years, the Admiralty had suddenly begun demanding innumerable documents and receipts for everything. He needed to be sure that there were no little scraps of paper in those piles bearing his name.

However, he was not at all sure he could get an honest answer from the clerk who had handled the transactions.

He stopped at the corner of the building. If he went in, someone might recognize him or notice him and recognize him at some later date. Was that more dangerous than the chance that his name might be on some piece of paper? After all, if it was, he could always deny it. He had never actually signed anything himself.

While he hesitated, a familiar figure came hurrying out of the building, almost as if he had been propelled—a young man dressed in the too fashionable fashion of the upstarts. Did these fellows never learn?

Jeremy Cuttlebush, for it was he, straightened his coat, adjusted his cravat, and set his fine beaver hat at a careful angle on his tousled curls. Although he lifted his chin and pushed back his shoulders as he walked, not too quickly, away from the Admiralty building, he could not entirely erase the look of worry from his face.

Not many would consider Cuttlebush the answer to their prayers, but for Dormer he was at least a possible shortcut. He resumed his stroll, following his quarry.

Unsurprisingly, Cuttlebush went directly to the nearest tavern. Deciding to allow his quarry time to down one or two glasses, Dormer extended his stroll. It was, after all, a pleasant day, and he had not been in this part of town very often. Judging from their attire, most of the men on the streets were clerks, all hastening about some business that they, or their employers, considered important.

He shuddered.

Having given Cuttlebush time to down at least two glasses of whatever, Dormer stepped into the tavern. It took him a moment to adjust to the darkness, but he decided it was a respectable enough place. Not, he decided, a place likely to supply a decent wine, but he could survive.

He ordered ale, then leaned on the bar to look around. Cuttlebush, hunched over at a corner table, was easy enough to spot. That yellow and pink waistcoat was definitely a mistake.

After a meditative sip of the ale, which was not bad at all, Dormer strolled over to join the younger man and sat down.

Cuttlebush started back in fright. "What do you want?" His eyes narrowed as he eased back on his seat. "Oh, it's you. Well, it's no use. They as good as threw me out at the Victualling Board. No one wants to know me. There'll be no more contracts after this one."

Dormer looked at him steadily but silently. Cuttlebush fidgeted.

"There's no point trying to bully me. It's not my fault. It's that damned St. Vincent pushing his nose into everything. All I know is that if we want to keep their investigators off our neck, Hopworth better have the wheat for me by Michaelmas, and I can't pay you more than forty-nine shillings a quarter. And that will leave me with damn-all profit."

"Ah well, it seems we have a slight problem." Dormer slid his mug of ale back and forth meditatively. "Hopworth is no longer with us."

"Dead?" Cuttlebush looked shocked.

"No. Dismissed." Dormer looked up with a slight smile. "It seems that my cousin is not dead after all and has returned to claim his inheritance. Apparently, the new Viscount Claremont had doubts about the old steward's honesty. He will doubtless make other arrangements for the sale of his wheat."

"Claremont?" Cuttlebush's screech was loud enough to attract the attention of a few nearby drinkers.

Dormer waited until their interest subsided. "Don't tell me you didn't even know with whom you were dealing."

Cuttlebush refilled his tumbler and took a long drink. "My father probably knew the name. It never came up when I was dealing with Hopworth. Never mattered." He slammed down the tumbler. "Claremont, of all people. Damn him!"

Now this was interesting. Dormer took a reflective sip of his own ale before speaking. "I have no objection to consigning my cousin to perdition, but how do you happen to know him? And what could he have done to you?"

"He stole Maria, that's what he did!"

"Lady Claremont? Well, it's hardly unusual for a woman to choose to marry a title rather than a mister."

"Not marry. Not after her father lost all his money. But I offered to make her my mistress. House in town and all that." Cuttlebush scowled. "It's not as if she'd have had much choice with her father dead. But then Claremont turned up. Claimed he was a friend of her father. And all those naval types came calling. Must have turned her head."

"I'm sure you are right."

Cuttlebush must have heard the sneer in those words because an ugly flush rose in his face. "And now there's Newbury! The Earl of Newbury's asking questions and poking around in the Admiralty. I'll wager that's Claremont's doing too."

"This doubtless all makes some sort of sense to you, and I can understand your irritation. My dear cousin has put something of a crimp in my plans as well. Such a pity that he's there in Somerset, alive and well, instead of safely in the family tomb where he should have been. And now he's put a new man in Hopworth's place— and in the steward's house as well. Lord knows what he'll make of Hopworth's accounts and papers."

Dormer could almost see an idea taking root in Cuttlebush's little brain.

CHAPTER 22

Belford

SOMETHING WAS SERIOUSLY WRONG. Sinclair had been able to tell that much from the books, though he didn't know precisely how it had been managed. It was high time he talked to the tenants. Unfortunately, this meant riding out to see the tenants.

It wasn't that Sinclair couldn't ride. He was a gentleman, after all, and even though he had spent most of his life in London, he had ridden around town and in the park. He had never, however, pretended to cut a dashing figure on horseback and would have been perfectly content with any slug in the stable.

The problem was, the Claremont stable didn't have any slugs in it. There were the matched bays that pulled the curricle, the team that pulled the carriage, and even the elderly mare that pulled the gig, but none of these were saddle horses. The saddle horses and hunters had been the old viscount's pride and joy. Aside from the dainty mare Mrs. Dormer—Isabella—rode, they were all spirited high steppers.

"I haven't ridden in a while," Sinclair confided to the head groom, hoping for a bit of sympathy. He didn't receive any.

The groom looked him over with barely concealed contempt, shook his head, and said, "Well, the chestnut gelding might suit.

He's getting on in years, so he's not too lively, but he knows the neighborhood well enough."

Knows the neighborhood sounded good to Sinclair. Pity he couldn't just tell the horse where he wanted to go the way he could tell a hackney driver. He managed to get mounted without embarrassing himself too greatly and set out at a brisk walk in what he was told was the direction of the Hembry farm.

Eventually, with less difficulty than he had feared, he arrived at a farmhouse. It was not the most prosperous he had ever seen, but it seemed to be in decent repair. The farmyard boasted a small herb garden and a bench under the shade of an ancient oak tree. Before he had fully dismounted, a woman appeared in the doorway.

He got his feet on the ground without disgracing himself and turned to the woman with what he hoped was a friendly smile. "Mrs. Hembry? I am James Sinclair, the viscount's new steward."

The smile didn't work. Her eyes widened and she stepped aside to let out a child hidden behind her skirt. She pushed him toward the field with the words, "Run and fetch your Da." She then blocked the door and stared after the child.

He wasn't sure if she was more angry or afraid, but she was most definitely not welcoming. "I'll just wait on that bench over there, if that's all right." He gestured toward the oak tree.

After a quick glance at him, the woman nodded, then resumed watching.

For lack of anything else to do, he watched as well.

Soon enough Hembry—it must be he—came hurrying across the field. He came to a sudden halt when he reached the edge of the farmyard and then approached more slowly. The farmer was a solid fellow, broad chested, with thick arms, carrying a hammer in his large hand.

The slow pace of his approach might be just native caution, but Sinclair doubted it. Not after the worried way he had been greeted by Mrs. Hembry.

"You'll be the new steward, then?" Hembry halted a bit further away than necessary.

"James Sinclair." He stood and introduced himself with a nod. "And you are Mr. Hembry?"

A nod was the only reply.

Sinclair heaved a mental sigh. Was this going to be his reception everywhere? "I don't want to disturb you unnecessarily, but I want to meet all the tenants, find out if there are any problems . . ."

"Problems." The word was spoken flatly, but it was accompanied by a sneer.

Ignoring the interruption, Sinclair continued, "And I had a few questions about the wheat harvest."

Hembry looked off at the fields, the stubble touched with frost, awaiting the end of winter. "So, you'll be wanting the same arrangement that other fellow had. I let you sell my wheat for the price you set or I'll be evicted like the others."

"No."

"No? You want more?" Hembry's face reddened and he lifted the hammer as he came closer. "Be damned to you then. We're all of us barely managing to feed our families as it is. My family has held this farm for a hundred years or more, but if yon lord wants more from us, he can pull the plow himself!"

Sinclair held up his hands and backed away. He had no desire to end up in a brawl. "I mean no, you mistake my meaning." When Hembry halted his advance, Sinclair continued. "What I was hoping to get from you was information."

"Information." Hembry did not sound friendly, but at least he was no longer advancing to battle.

Sinclair took a relieved breath. "Yes. Hopworth is gone, and the books he left behind don't seem to make sense. I was hoping some of the tenants could explain what's been going on."

Hembry looked at him silently. Sinclair couldn't remember having been examined in quite this way since he was a schoolboy standing in front the headmaster.

At length the farmer said, "His lordship—I heard that he told Hopworth not to evict Parsons." He waited until Sinclair nodded confirmation. "Mayhap things will be different. We'll see." He turned and headed for the house. When Sinclair didn't immediately follow, he said, "Well, come along then. We'll need some ale."

WILL WAS ONCE MORE SETTLED IN THE LEATHER CHAIR in the library. It really did fit him comfortably, he decided. Just the right height to leave ample leg room under the desk. The desk in turn, with its broad walnut expanse, provided ample room for books, papers, maps—whatever he was working on.

Sinclair, he noticed, was not settling quite so comfortably into the visitor's chair. In fact, he was lowering himself quite gingerly onto the cushioned seat.

"What's the matter?" Will asked, concerned. "Are you injured?"

"Only in my pride," said Sinclair with a grimace. "I have ridden very little in recent years, as my fundament is reminding me." He leaned back with a sigh. "This morning I covered I don't know how many miles visiting the farms of five of your tenants. I believe I have earned the scorn of a number of urchins who viewed my passage with amusement."

Will couldn't restrain a smile. "My father and brothers were noted for their horsemanship and for their horses, I am told. At least my leg spares me the burden of expectations in that arena. I have the perfect excuse to ride in a carriage."

"Don't be too comfortable with that idea. I can assure you that the lanes around the estate will offer you a bumpy ride however you travel. It's probably not a high priority, but one day you may want to do some improving there."

Will shrugged. "That can wait. What have you learned?"

"It actually started out as a beneficial arrangement for the tenants." Sinclair eased himself back cautiously and began to tell his tale. "It occurred to them some years ago that they could probably get a better price for their wheat if they got together and sold the entire crop from the estate to the corn merchants, instead of competing against each other in the market. They talked to the steward, who agreed to handle things for them. And indeed, they did do better, at least at first. He sold the crop to a corn merchant who had a contract with the navy victualling board, and they all managed to benefit."

"Is there some problem with this? Were they cheating the navy?"

"Probably not. Or at least those contracts are put out to bid, but there may have been some clerk who made sure Cuttlebush was awarded . . ."

That made Will sit up. "Cuttlebush? That miserable scoundrel? Are you serious?"

"Did you know him? He was a major purveyor for the navy and I'm pretty sure he was the one involved in this. With this agreement, he could give the tenants a better price than they might have gotten elsewhere and still make a profit on his navy contract."

Will snorted. "I'll wager it was a hefty profit."

"No doubt. But then a few years ago things changed. Your father's steward retired, and your cousin, who was pretty much running things for your father, hired Hopworth. At about that time, Cuttlebush died, and it looks as if his son took over."

"Ah, the son must be the scoundrel I encountered. The bastard who was sniffing around Maria's skirts. And so that was when the foxes entered the henhouse?"

"Yes, I'd say that sums it up pretty well. I don't know whose idea it was, but they fixed the price for the tenants—and your father—at forty shillings a quarter." Seeing Will's confusion, Sinclair explained, "That's eight bushels. The navy buys wheat by the quarter."

Will nodded but continued to frown. "So the navy set the price at forty shillings?"

"No, no. Hopworth and Cuttlebush fixed the price your father and the tenants received, and they never changed it. The navy buys at more or less market price. They have to, or no one would sell to them. And what with the war demanding more and more resources and the occasional bad harvest, the price was rising to fifty or sixty shillings a quarter. After the bad harvest a couple of years ago, it was over a hundred and forty shillings."

"Good God. Why did the tenants agree to such an insane arrangement?"

"They weren't given a choice. If they refused, they were told they would be evicted."

"But this can't be right. Surely there must have been something they could have done." Will had gotten to his feet and made his way to the window, where he stared out. In the distance, off to the side of the orchards, he could see a field that last summer had been covered with ripening wheat. "There must have been something."

"What?" Sinclair, who had also risen, raised a sardonic brow. "Complained to the magistrate? Even if the magistrate hadn't been a friend of your father, what charge could be laid? Holding the tenants to a bad bargain?"

Will cursed softly before turning back. "You assured them that this . . . this . . ." He hammered his walking stick against the floor. "Damnation! I don't know what to call it. Theft is what it was. Outright robbery. You assured them that it was at an end?"

"Of course, though I am not certain that they believed me. Hopworth has vanished, but your cousin is still in the neighborhood and there is a rumor that young Cuttlebush has been seen in the neighborhood." Sinclair hesitated. "I don't know what he hopes to do. Just sniffing around it seems."

Will considered, then shook his head decisively. "That miserable little worm can't be important. No, I'd wager it's Frederick who's behind this scheme. It has his greedy prints all over it."

"There's no evidence. I'll be writing up a report on the scheme for St. Vincent at the admiralty, but I don't know that there will be any way to bring charges."

"There won't be any evidence against Frederick. He's too sly to put his name on anything. But I know him. He was involved."

Sinclair studied Will's stiff posture. "Begging your pardon,

Claremont, but you have not had anything to do with your cousin since you were a child."

Will turned around with a twisted smile. "You may be right. Frederick may have changed from a sly, meeching bully to a kind, generous fellow. Or at least to a decent human being. You may be willing to believe that. But it's proof of his innocence I'd need to see before I believe it."

"No, HANNAH." MARIA WAS SPEAKING TOO SHARPLY, she knew, but the maid was exasperating. Lazy and slovenly. "You can't just wipe the oil on the furniture and leave it. You have to take a second cloth and polish it." She took a closer look at the cabinet and added, "And you need to dust it before you polish it."

Hannah glared. "Lady Blackwell never had any complaints."

"Well Lady Blackwell is not your employer," Maria snapped. "And you will not be employed much longer if you don't learn to do a proper job."

Just then Aunt Sophia came in. "Good heavens, Hannah, are you still dusting this room? You must have started two hours ago."

"Well, Lady Blackwell came in, and she wanted me to run an errand for her. Couldn't very well say no, now, could I?"

Maria and her aunt exchanged glances. "Very well, Hannah. Just get on with the task now. It would be nice to have the room finished before dinnertime."

Maria took her aunt's arm and led her to her office. There they could be reasonably sure of privacy. She closed the door before bursting out, "That woman is going to drive me mad. So help me, it seems that she manages to interfere with everything. If I assign a maid to work in the sitting room, she sends her to find a book that she left in the drawing room. Or if it isn't there, perhaps she left it somewhere else. And an hour later, once she's involved half the household in searching for it, she realizes that it had just slipped under her chair."

"I know, dear, I know." Aunt Sophia patted her arm. "It's an intolerable situation. You really shouldn't put up with it."

Maria sat down, frowning. "I need to talk to Will. He said something about providing them with an allowance. Do you suppose we could find them someplace else to live? Isabella isn't such a problem. She's rather like a cat. As long as she's warm and fed, she's content. But her mother! I do not think I can live under the same roof with her much longer."

HAVING WAVED OFF INQUIRIES ABOUT HIS ABSENCE with an airy, "Business affairs, y'know," Frederick settled himself on the settee and waited for Lady Blackwell to tell him what had happened while he was away, as she was obviously bursting to do.

"Oh, of course." She fluttered her handkerchief in the air. "You have your own estate to worry about."

The flash of fury across his face was instantly erased. He was certain she would not have noticed it. But any mention of his "estate"—a house barely large enough to qualify as a gentleman's residence, falling apart because there was no income to maintain it—had bitter bile rising in his throat.

Lady Blackwell obviously had not noticed because she continued. "It was so generous of you to devote so much time to managing this estate for your uncle. I swear, Lord Claremont seems to have no idea how much in your debt he is. I feel I must upbraid him for his ingratitude."

"Please do nothing of the sort!" He had spoken too sharply, so he managed a smile to soften his words. "He has suffered enough, poor fellow, with those dreadful injuries. I would not want him to feel under any obligation to me."

"You are so full of kindness, Mr. Dormer. Your cousin has none of the graces that should adorn a man of his station. I swear, he has no notion of the behavior appropriate to a gentleman."

"Surely he has not been rude to you or your daughter?"

"Rude?" She sniffed. "If you consider barely acknowledging our existence rude! We almost never see him, and when we do, at dinner, he shows no interest in us. He is all consideration for his wife's aunt, that Lady Pellew, but for Isabella? His own brother's widow? And for me? We might as well be invisible."

"Well, you can hardly expect much by way of conversation from an ignorant seaman."

Continuing with her grievances, she said, "Now that wife of his discarded all my menus and allows that miserable excuse for a cook to provide meals that belong in a pothouse rather than on a gentleman's table. And the servants only obey her, and if she is not about, they go to Lady Pellew. As if I had not been managing the household for all these years!"

Frederick permitted himself a cynical smile, being aware of just how badly the household had been managed.

"She wants to throw us out, that's what she wants. I just know it." Lady Blackwell looked both furious and frightened.

"Now, now, Claremont can hardly throw his brother's widow out of her home."

"Claremont!" Lady Blackwell sneered. "He has no notion of his obligations. He has not even called on the neighbors yet. He spends all his time closeted with that new steward of his or up in that long empty room on the third floor."

That caught Frederick's attention. "The long gallery? I would not have thought there was much of interest there. As I recall, there are barely any furnishings. Certainly nothing of any value."

She sniffed again. "As if he would know, any more than that creature he married. Though she goes about with the housekeeper, poking and prying, talking about refurbishing. As if she would have any notion what is fashionable."

Frederick smiled. Lady Blackwell could be trusted to pry and put the worst possible interpretation on anything she discovered. As for himself, he needed to discover what on earth Will found of interest in the long gallery. The view? Unlikely. His cousin had never struck him as a man to go into ecstasies over the landscape. Something else? But what?

CHAPTER 23

Every day, Will retreated to the long gallery. It was certainly not a cozy retreat. Situated on the third floor and running the length of the house, the gallery was a cavernous space, almost two hundred feet long and more than twenty feet wide at its narrowest. Yet it was the one part of the house that Will remembered with any fondness.

As a child he had come up here to escape.

No one else in his family ever came here, and even the servants neglected it to this day. The furnishings were sparse—a pair of chairs by a fireplace and an occasional table that had not found a place elsewhere. One side of the gallery was hung with paintings, most of them portraits, that no one cared about. His father had possessed one painting of which he was inordinately proud, a Stubbs of a horse and dog, but that was kept in the library, a room where children were not welcome. The other side of the gallery was lined with tall windows that let in plenty of light and could be opened to let in a breeze.

None of that mattered to Will now, any more than it had when he was a child. What did matter was that none of his relations came up here. In fact, no one came up here. He could practice walking back and forth completely unobserved.

Here he exercised in privacy, safe from mocking eyes, safe from pity. His footsteps beat their irregular pattern in the echoing gallery—long, short, long, short—and the leg gave an audible click with each step, but there was no one to hear. He was beginning to think that his stride was less irregular than it had been. It was certainly less painful than it had been that first week in London.

His strength was increasing too. By now he could stay on his feet for close to half an hour. But he still walked slowly, even on level ground. He checked his pocket chronometer, which had survived his dunking in the waters off Copenhagen. It still took him more than ten minutes to walk the length of the gallery seven times, and he estimated that was no more than a quarter of a mile. He was determined to improve.

Then one day he heard footsteps—not just the echo of his own—approaching. No one should be coming up here. No one ever had, and he was damned if he would allow anyone to intrude now. He came to a halt and stared at the door, prepared to repel boarders if anyone intended to invade his retreat.

The door opened, and Maria peered in. Maria. He felt all his tension dissolve. Maria was different.

She looked hesitant as she offered a smile. "Am I intruding?"

He returned her smile with no hesitation. "Never," he said, and realized that he meant it. After all, he thought wryly, there was little reason to feel self-conscious or embarrassed before a woman who has seen you naked with all your scars.

But it was something more. He did not resent her presence. Instead, to his surprise, he actually welcomed it. She was the only one he did not mind seeing him limp down the gallery. Her presence actually helped him, gave him courage. She understood what he was doing and did not despise his weakness.

"How peaceful!" She turned in a circle, taking in the entire space. "How wonderfully peaceful and quiet!"

"No one ever comes here," he growled. That didn't sound precisely welcoming. He hoped he hadn't offended her because he truly didn't want her to leave.

She didn't seem offended, because she was still smiling as she looked around. "Would you mind if I joined you here?"

Mind? He had not expected the sudden jolt of pleasure that he felt at her suggestion.

"Mind? Of course not. You are welcome anywhere in this house." Not perhaps the most gracious of invitations, but he was in danger of begging her to stay, which would not do at all.

She looked at him as if she understood what he meant, and not just what he said. "It's all rather chaotic down below," she said. "Mrs. Bates has taken on some new maids, and they are all madly cleaning—at least, they are when Lady Blackwell doesn't decide to set them to doing something else. I'm afraid it makes them nervous to have me looking on—my presence is to blame for the destruction of at least two pieces of china, and I am so ignorant that I have no idea if they were valuable pieces or not."

He grinned at her. He could not get over how pleased he was to have her company. "I'll admit to being responsible for more than a few casualties myself."

She turned one of the chairs to maximize the light, opened the basket she had brought, and sat down with a pair of cushions to mend.

He frowned at the basket. "Shouldn't the maids be doing the mending?"

"They will when we acquire a few more of them," she said. "But in the meantime, I need something to occupy my hands while I think about what needs to be done. Besides, this is somewhat creative mending. These two cushions were on a bench under a window in one of the rooms, but moths have been at them. The needlework is quite lovely, so I would like to rescue them rather than replace them if I can."

He grunted, hoping that sounded as if he understood, and went on his way. Each day he could walk a little longer and a little less awkwardly. He was perfecting the rhythm of his walking stick, and he even managed a bit of a twirl with it.

"That cane now looks like a decorative accessory, not a walking aid." Maria smiled approvingly at his latest flourish. "You will have to acquire some more impressively decorated sticks."

"Like those with a carved silver head? I would look like a dandy."

"And why shouldn't you? Or perhaps you could have one with the handle that looks like the figurehead on a ship."

He came to a stop and actually considered that before he chuckled. "No. I would feel a fool. But I did see one that a fellow was showing around at a tavern one time. There was a lid on the handle and when you opened it up there was a bawdy picture inside."

"You shock me, my lord." She shook her head in mock reproof before she turned back to her sewing.

He thought about that as he continued down the gallery. He hadn't shocked her, of course. Very little seemed to shock her. She had none of those dying-away airs that some women put on so they could lay claim to delicacy. She had something far better—strength and steadiness. She would be able to stand up to whatever the world threw at her, good or bad.

She also seemed to have something on her mind, he thought, noting the slight frown that did not seem to be caused by the cushion. He stopped in front of her. "Something is worrying you. Out with it."

Putting down her needlework, she gave him a rueful smile. "Chapman tells me there are rumors Cuttlebush is in the neighborhood. I wasn't sure if you had heard."

He scowled. "Yes, I heard."

"But you didn't tell me."

She was annoyed, he could tell. "I didn't want to worry you."

"Oh, Will! Ignorance isn't bliss. It's dangerous. I can't think of any good reason for that toad to make an appearance."

"He can't harm us."

She gave him a skeptical look. "Do you think he has turned up here because he wishes us well?"

"What can he do? But it's getting late. Let's go down."

She started for the staircase ahead of him, looking back at him with a smile when suddenly . . . she was no longer there.

He heard a shriek as he stared at the place she had been, the place she should be. The emptiness froze him to the bone. There were thumps and thuds—and then silence when the shriek was suddenly cut off—a terrifying silence.

CHAPTER 24

WHEN HE REACHED THE HEAD OF THE STAIRS, he saw her lying sprawled on the landing below, motionless. He could not shout for help. He could not even speak. He hobbled—damnation! All he could do was hobble like a wretched beggar down the innumerable steps, hopping half the time as he clutched the banister.

Useless, he was useless, a pitiful, useless excuse for a man.

It took an eternity for him to reach her, and by the time he did, he could see that she was still breathing. That prayer had been answered at least. She wasn't dead. But her eyes were closed. Somehow she had landed with one of the pillows under her so that her head hung down, barely touching the wood of the landing, while her feet were still on the steps above.

He sat—or rather, he crumpled—down beside her. Tentatively, he reached out to press two fingers on her throat. A pulse was there, strong and steady. He sucked in a deep breath and the sound of it broke the silence.

From Maria came a slight moan as she started to lift her head.

"Don't move!" He barked the command, before continuing, a bit more quietly, "I need to see how badly you are injured."

"How unutterably foolish." Her words were muttered into the cushion.

"Not foolish at all. I have had far more experience of injuries than you, and I know what I'm talking about."

That sounded reasonably calm, he thought. Now if he could just stop trembling.

"I didn't mean you. I meant how foolish of me to go tripping over my own feet like that. I feel quite ridiculous." She started to try rising again, but he put a restraining hand on her shoulder, and she subsided.

He moved his fingers carefully over her head. "Does your neck hurt? Your head?"

"My pride is severely injured, I fear, and I expect a few bruises to appear in the near future, but I do not think I have suffered any serious injury." She started to push herself up.

"I told you not to move."

If he were able to smile at the moment, he would have done so at the annoyance in her voice. Instead, he continued to probe carefully as he moved his hands carefully over her arms and legs. Nothing seemed to be broken.

Thank heaven for her thick hair . . . and for those ridiculous cushions. The one under her had kept her head from striking the floor, and the other was caught between her and the paneled wall.

"Good gracious! What has happened?" Mrs. Bates came running and stumbled to a halt at the foot of the stairs, trailed by two maids, all wrapped in aprons and all of them wide-eyed.

"Have a pair of footmen rig up a stretcher for my lady and send someone for the doctor." When they all remained frozen and staring, he barked out, "Now!" and they immediately scurried off.

"You are making a ridiculous fuss over a stupid fall." Maria actually looked apologetic.

He said nothing. He couldn't. All he could do was sit there clutching her hand tightly.

James and Harold created a stretcher by the simple expedient of taking down one of the doors. They lifted Maria onto it carefully, following Will's instructions to keep her neck and back as immobile as possible as they carried her to her room. Somewhere in the back of Will's head came the thought that they must have had experience of injuries, so efficiently did they manage the task, but he put the thought aside for the moment. For the time being he wanted only to hold her hand as he limped along beside her.

Once she had been laid down on the bed, Lady Pellew took charge. She didn't bother trying to evict Will, but worked around him, removing Maria's shoes and stockings, bathing her face with lavender water, and making soothing noises.

Will sat there, feeling guilty. He was still holding her hand half an hour later when the doctor arrived. Dr. Bright was a brisk fellow, with a youthful face but grizzled hair. Will knew he had been to the house a few times to see servants who were injured or ailing, but he had never met the man himself. He refused to leave the room and watched intently as Dr. Bright felt Maria's limbs and gently turned her head, much as Will had done.

"This is really excessive," Maria protested. "I feel like quite enough of a fool without having everyone make such a fuss over my clumsiness."

"Mmm," said Dr. Bright, turning her foot gently from side to side. "What you are is a very fortunate lady. No broken bones, not even a sprain. You'll have some colorful bruises on the morrow, and the aches and pains will remind you to watch your step, but you should be fine in a few days."

"I'm well enough right now . . ." she began.

The doctor spoke over her. "You'll stay in bed for a day or two. I'll bleed you now, and then you'll have a dose of laudanum to help you sleep. Mrs. Bates has a good salve for the bruises, I know, and you'll be needing it for the next few days."

When he had finished, Mrs. Bates took the detritus from the

bleeding away, and Chapman brought in a pitcher of warm water to clean Maria before putting her into a clean night rail.

The doctor took Will by the arm and led him into the corridor. "She should stay in bed at least through tomorrow, and she shouldn't do anything too active for a few days after that. She probably won't be able to even if she wants to." Then he gave Will a sharp look. "You're looking worse than your lady. That's often the way of it when those we care for are injured."

Care for? No, that wasn't it. He had promised to protect her, and he had failed utterly. Once he would have been able to catch her when she stumbled. But now . . . Half a man. That's all he was. A useless cripple.

When Will remained silent, Dr. Bright patted him on the shoulder. "I know you've probably had your fill of medical advice, and it looks as if you've come along remarkably, but you're going to need to get some rest yourself, and a bite to eat won't come amiss."

The words seemed to be spoken in some foreign language, and it took a while for them to penetrate the fog surrounding his mind. "Eat?" He shook his head to clear it.

Bright must have thought he was disagreeing because he said, "Yes, eat. Your lady won't need you to be passing out tomorrow. She'll be needing you to lean on."

This time Will shook his head in disgust. Lean on him? When he couldn't even stand on his own two feet because he didn't *have* two feet?

"Now Lady Claremont will be asleep in a few minutes, and she needs the rest." The doctor kept droning on. "Let her aunt and her maid take turns sitting with her tonight, and I'll be back to check on her tomorrow." He bustled away.

Will wanted to protest, but what was the use? He was of no use, in any case.

Sinclair and Gibbs had been conferring a short distance away. They turned to him.

"How is she?" Sinclair asked.

Will swallowed. "The doctor said nothing seems to be broken, though she's badly bruised."

"Tomorrow will be bad for her," Gibbs said in the voice of experience. Then he turned to Sinclair. "I'll stay here for now. You might send one of the footmen later."

"Right." Sinclair nodded and took Will's arm. "You, my lord, need to come with me."

Sinclair led him away as if he were a child, but Will couldn't find it in himself to object. They ended up in the library, where Will was surprised to see the candles lit. He had not realized that it was full night already.

Something was bothering him though. He scowled as he tried to remember. Then he realized that Gibbs had said he was staying there, outside Maria's chamber.

"Why?" he asked. "Why is Gibbs staying there?"

Sinclair pushed Will down into a chair. "That's what I need to talk to you about." He found the decanter of brandy, poured a hefty measure into a glass, and handed it to Will. "You'll be needing this."

Will took the glass and slammed it down on the table beside him. "Stop trying to manage me and tell me what the devil is going on."

Lifting his hands in surrender, Sinclair said, "It wasn't an accident."

When Will simply stared at him in silence, he continued. "I went up to see why Lady Claremont might have slipped, and I found that a thin cord had been tied across the steps. It must have broken when she tripped over it, but this piece of it was still attached to a nail driven into the skirtboard." He held out his hand with a coil of brown horsehair twist.

"Fishing line," Will said, staring at it in horror. "But why . . .? Who could wish Maria harm?"

Sinclair shrugged. "She is expecting more of the servants than they are accustomed to doing. It is possible that one of them may have resented it."

Will shook his head. "That would be out of all proportion to the offense. In any case I have seen no sign of any such resentment. Have you?"

"Neither of us would be likely to see it, but there is another possibility. Lady Claremont is familiar with household accounts. She expects them to be kept more accurately than has been done in the past."

Will's head snapped up at that. "Has she accused anyone of theft?"

"No. In fact, she went out of her way to make it clear that she was not interested in anything in the past. It is only what happens in the future that concerns her."

That brought a smile to Will's face. "That's the way to get the crew on your side."

Sinclair nodded in agreement. "But there is something else. Lady Blackwell and Mrs. Dormer."

"What of them? Maria has simply lifted the burden of running the house from their shoulders. All they have to do is sit around and . . . do whatever it is ladies do when they have nothing to do."

"Apparently they do not view that as any great boon. At least Lady Blackwell doesn't." Sinclair smiled as Will's look of curiosity. "Chapman says that she tries to undermine your lady's authority every chance she gets. And those below stairs have commented that whenever your wife turns her back, Lady Blackwell glares at her with murder in her eyes."

"Why? Maria has never done her any harm."

"She disrupted her plans. According to the gossip, Lady Blackwell was just waiting for the year of mourning to end. Then she planned to have her daughter marry your cousin, who was expected to be Lord Claremont until you appeared."

"Marry Frederick? Oh, that would be something!" Will guffawed. "Much though I would like to see him with Lady Blackwell for a mother-in-law, I somehow can't see it happening unless poor Isabella suddenly acquires an enormous dowry. Lady Blackwell is a fool."

"There is another possibility." Sinclair stepped back to lean against the desk, half sitting on it. "Tell me, does Lady Claremont often join you in the gallery?"

"No." Will was startled by the question. "No, today was the first time."

"Then the trap may not have been intended for her. Does anyone wish you harm?"

The fear and worry and uncertainty that had been swirling around in Will's mind concentrated into a dagger of fury. "Frederick." He spat out the name. "Of course. Who else could it be?"

"Possibly. He is heir to your title so long as you have no son. But he is not the only possibility."

Will snorted. "Who else?"

"Hopworth, for one. I've seen enough creative accounting in the estate books to suggest that he may well be guilty of a number of transgressions that could have him hanged or transported if you decide to prosecute. And he may have had collaborators."

"No, it was Frederick. I'm sure of it. The sneaking, cowardly villain. I'll tear him to pieces." Will was on his feet now, pacing back and forth, slamming his cane down with each step.

"Don't be too hasty. You may have another enemy in the neighborhood."

Will halted to stare blankly at Sinclair. "Who?"

"I'm not sure, but one of the grooms was in the tavern a few days ago, and there was a stranger asking about Belford and about you. A young man, very fashionably dressed, but not really a gentleman according to the groom. He said his name was Smith, but I'm fairly certain he is Cuttlebush, the partner in the wheat scheme."

"He isn't just the thieving purveyor. He's the nasty little fellow who was hanging about making scurrilous advances to Maria. I threw him out." A look of satisfaction crossed Will's face. "But I don't see how Cuttlebush could manage to set a tripwire on the staircase. How could he have gotten in? How could he even know I'd be up there? No. It has to be Frederick."

"He may well be guilty," said Sinclair, "but keep an open mind. We don't even know if he was in the house this afternoon when the cord was tied."

"Even if he was absent, he could have had an accomplice."

Sinclair nodded. "But don't forget that the same is true of Cuttlebush. It would be well to learn the names of any accomplices. Preferably without creating a scandal that will send them running for cover."

Will set his jaw. "I'll not have Frederick in my house any longer. Not where he can harm Maria."

CHAPTER 25

JUST AS THE DOCTOR PREDICTED, Maria slept through the night. Will knew this because he had spent the night sitting by Maria's bedside himself. It had been a bit of a struggle to achieve that position. Chapman had protested vigorously, but Lady Pellew had taken one look at him and decided it was pointless to argue.

In the morning, his wife was still sunk in that drugged stupor when the maid returned, still looking miffed at having her place usurped. Unapologetically, Will took himself off to his own chamber to be washed, shaved, brushed, and dressed in pristine linen, immaculate coat and vest, and beautifully polished boots.

Thus armored, he was prepared for the confrontation to come.

He descended the main staircase easily enough and raised a hand to summon the footman standing by the front door. "Tell Mr. Dormer to attend me in the library as soon as possible."

The footman looked uncertain. "Yes, my lord, but . . . Mr. Dormer may still be abed."

Will smiled. It was a satisfied smile. "You have my leave to wake him."

In the library, Will settled himself behind the desk to wait. He realized that he had begun to feel as if he belonged here. This had become his desk, covered with his papers, quite as much as the desk in the captain's cabin on the *Hector* had been his, with his charts and papers.

The draperies had been drawn back, and through the windows he could see the orchard, the trees with buds beginning to swell. That reminded him that he still had not investigated the situation of the tenant Hopworth had wanted to evict. What was his name? Priest? Proctor? No, Parsons. That was it. He took a piece of paper out of the drawer and made a note of the name.

Will leaned back in his chair. That was the day that had sent him off to see Garland, to meet Maria. He ought, he supposed, to feel a certain gratitude to Hopworth. The anger he had felt that day, not just at Hopworth but at Isabella and Franklin, had sent him down the path that had led him to Maria.

Maria.

The thought that someone had dared endanger her roused such a murderous fury in him that he . . .

He took a deep breath. No, he could not actually prove that Frederick was guilty of this attack. He could not prove it, though it was just the kind of sneaky villainy one could expect of him. But he was damned if he would allow the viper to remain in this house where Maria was vulnerable to his attacks.

So he waited.

Eventually, and without bothering to knock or to cover his yawn, a disgruntled Frederick strolled in and flopped into a chair. "What is it you want to see me about so urgently at this ghastly hour of the morning, Cousin?"

Will looked at him in silence for a long minute. "You will be pleased to know that Lady Claremont was not too seriously injured yesterday and passed the night in reasonable comfort."

Frederick put on a brief look of confusion, and then said, "Oh, right. I heard she took a tumble. She's all right, then? Good to hear, I'm sure, but is that what you dragged me out of bed to tell me?"

"No, I just thought you might be interested." Will settled himself comfortably in his chair and rested his hands on the arm rests, rather like a king settling himself on a throne. "What I wanted to speak to you about was your position in this household. I am, of course, grateful for your oversight of things after my father and brothers died and while I was recovering from my injuries. However, I cannot impose on you any longer."

The sulky irritation drained from Frederick's face to be replaced by wariness. "I don't think I understand your meaning."

"As I understand it, you have an estate of your own, the one you inherited from your father. Surely that property could benefit from the same careful attention that you have given to Belford."

"That estate, as you call it, is a house that has been uninhabited for twenty years, surrounded by a farm producing barely enough income to cover the rates. My *father*"—Frederick imbued the word with scorn—"succeeded only in laying waste to the place. He sold off most of the land and what's left isn't enough to support a gentleman in decent style."

"Dear me. I had no idea." Will made a slight effort to look sympathetic but was not particularly bothered by his lack of success. "In that case, the place is most certainly in need of your attention. You must remove there at once."

"What do you mean?"

"I mean that it is high time you took up residence in your own house on your own estate."

"You can't be serious."

"But of course I am."

Frederick leaped to his feet, wariness replaced by outrage. "You can't do that. This is my home. It has always been my home. The viscount brought me here to live when I was still a child. He always told me that this would always be my home."

Will nodded. "True. I remember that throughout my childhood you were always here. Quite his favorite, you were." But when Frederick began to relax slightly, Will continued, "However, he made no provision for you in his will. You are not mentioned at all. Of course, there was no will for you to be mentioned in. Doubtless an oversight, but there you have it."

Frederick stared in amazement. "This can't be. You're throwing me out? You're throwing me out of my own home?"

"You are mistaken," Will said coldly. "This is not your home. This is *my* home, and I see no need for your presence in it."

Expressions of shock, outrage, and fury chased each other across Frederick's face. Fury was the final victor. "You'll not do this to me, you crippled bastard. You don't know . . . *I'm* the one who belongs here, not you. You a viscount? You grotesque excuse for a man, a monster to frighten children! You're not fit to even set foot in this house. Why do you suppose the viscount shipped you off to sea? You and that doxy you married are the ones who should be driven away."

Will stood up and leaned forward with his fists on the desk. He kept his voice low. "Enough. You will depart immediately. I will have the servants pack your things and send them after you. Now get out."

There was a moment when it seemed that Frederick might throw himself across the desk at his cousin—Will half-hoped that he would try it—but the moment passed. Instead, Frederick pulled himself together. "You bastard. You really are a bastard, you know. Did you never guess?"

With that, Frederick spun about and stormed out of the room. Will heard the footsteps growing faint as he travelled down the hall. Then the slam of the front door reverberated through the house. Will stared at the door, unseeing, thinking about the past.

A moment later Gibbs came in, looking dubious.

"Tossed him out, have you?" Gibbs sounded disapproving.

Returning to the present, Will said, "Did you expect me to keep him around, endangering my wife?"

Gibbs shrugged a shoulder. "I'd not have been surprised if you sent him packing the day we arrived. Never could see that he had any business being here in the first place. But now, well, it would have been easier to keep an eye on him if he were still hanging around the place."

"It will be a good deal easier to keep an eye on the place to make sure he keeps away." Will heaved himself up and headed for the window, his cane muffled by the thick carpet. He stared out at the vista of bare trees and hills under heavy gray clouds, the estate Frederick coveted. It would have been simpler if his father could have left the blasted place to Frederick in the first place, the laws of entail be damned. God knows he would never have begrudged it to him.

But now? Now Maria had been attacked. That was intolerable. Frederick had sealed his own fate.

Will turned back to Gibbs. "Lady Claremont is to be guarded at all times. She is not to go anywhere alone."

"She may not care for that."

"She may not care for it, but she is not a fool. She'll see the need once I explain it to her. I'll not have her falling into another trap intended for me." He began pacing again.

"And will you be guarded as well?" Gibbs looked phlegmatic but sounded sarcastic.

Will snapped around to glare at Gibbs, but then looked down at his cane and smiled. "It would only be sensible, I think, to protect myself. Tell me, Gibbs, do you know where you could procure a swordstick for me? And I will need a sheath and knife that I can keep in my boot. At least with a wooden leg I need not worry about stabbing myself."

Will thought for a moment, then added, "And it would be as well if Maria were armed too. She'll need a knife she can strap to her leg. I'll start teaching her how to throw it."

MARIA WAS THOROUGHLY CRABBED. She hurt all over. She was humiliated by the fact that she had been so stupid as to not watch where she was going and fall downstairs. She was annoyed with herself for snapping at Chapman when the maid had only been helping her. She had absolutely refused to get back in the bed, so now she was sitting by the window wrapped in an utterly unnecessary wool shawl with a blanket over her legs.

She could now see more than the walls and bed hangings, though whether this was an improvement was not clear. The view was lovely, and it was a gloriously sunny day making her incarceration in the bed chamber all the more frustrating.

To make matters worse, soon after dismissing her maid, she had realized that she actually would be more comfortable lying down, but she didn't think she would be able to get back to the bed without help. The fact that this situation was entirely her own fault did not improve her disposition.

When Will opened the door, she was torn between being delighted to see him and annoyed that she must appear so useless. Then she was simply worried. He looked so thunderous that she feared he was seriously angered by her fall. It made her just another burden for him.

"How are you feeling?" His angry look eased slightly.

"Battered and bruised and exceedingly stupid for having neglected to watch where I was going. I am so sorry for causing all this trouble. You are not to waste any more time taking care of me."

He pulled up a chair so he could sit beside her, still looking upset.

"Really," she said, feeling a bit defensive, "there is nothing wrong with me that a day or so of rest won't cure. I'm sure that between them, Aunt Sophia and Mrs. Bates will keep things under control. You needn't worry that Lady Blackwell will try to take over again."

"What are you talking about?" He looked a trifle confused as well as worried.

"There's no need for you to be so annoyed." She was feeling a bit annoyed herself. "I hardly took that tumble on purpose, and it is unlikely to seriously discommode you."

"You think I'm annoyed at *you*?" He sat back and stared at her. "Good God, it's myself I'm angry with. I should have realized that my bedamned cousin was dangerous. My heedlessness put you in danger."

It was her turn to feel confused, and she returned his question. "What are you talking about?"

"Your fall—you didn't stumble. You were tripped. There was a cord tied across the stairs."

"What? But that's ridiculous!" She couldn't take it in. "Why would there be a cord across the stairs? What purpose could it serve?"

"Precisely the purpose it accomplished—to send someone tumbling headlong down the stairs."

"You mean it was deliberate? It wasn't an accident of some sort?"

"Precisely." His mouth flattened.

"I don't understand. It makes no sense. Who would want to trip me? Lady Blackwell? I know she dislikes me, but . . ." She shook her head. "One of the maids? I know one or two of them resent being told to work more diligently, and there's one, Hannah, who manages to stop just short of disrespect, but . . ."

"You may not have been the intended victim. I doubt anyone even knew you were up in the long gallery with me. But anyone might have known I was there."

"You mean it was a trap set for you? That's—that's *wicked*!" She started to get up but winced as her body objected to the movement. "I won't have it!"

He seemed to find that amusing, because he stopped looking so distressed and actually smiled at her. "And I won't have anyone endangering my wife, so I've sent Frederick packing."

"Your cousin? It was him? Are you sure?"

"Can I prove it? No. But he's done that sort of thing before." His angry look was back.

She stared at her husband with horror. "But you never said anything. What did he do?"

"Not recently, nothing recent. But when we were boys . . ." His voice trailed off and his jaw tightened.

"Will Dormer, you tell me exactly what sort of things he has done."

"Looking back, it seems foolish. I could never have proven any of it. I didn't even dare accuse him. But things happened. I got locked in the icehouse, and it was only by accident that the cook needed some ice and sent a servant who found me. When we were all climbing on a cliff, a boulder came tumbling down and barely missed me. One day I was sent back to the house on an errand, and a mantrap had been left in the path." He shook his head. "Things that were easily explained as accidents, mistakes, but I knew. I was only a child, and I can't explain how I knew, but I did."

Maria looked thoughtful. "He must have thought he had inherited when your father and brothers were all killed in that accident last fall. Didn't you tell me that they all thought you had died?"

"So the lawyer told me. Apparently the first reports after the North Sea battle had me listed as dead. It was only at the funeral for my father and brothers that he found out I was still alive." He gave a surprised laugh. "Poor Frederick. How disappointed he must have been. One could almost feel sorry for him."

LADY BLACKWELL'S FACE WAS FLUSHED more by anger than by haste as she rounded the yew hedge in the garden. "This is preposterous. If you wished to speak to me there is no reason why you could not call at the house."

Frederick rose slowly from the stone bench on which he had been sitting. "Unfortunately," he drawled, "my cousin seems to feel that I am no longer welcome at Belford. Hence my invitation to you."

Lady Blackwell sniffed. "Hannah slipped me your note and seemed to feel I must pay her for the privilege of receiving it."

"She is a trifle mercenary, one must admit, but she has her uses."

"No doubt. Especially for gentlemen."

"True. Quite true." Frederick smiled a bit complacently. "But she can be trusted to see to her own advantage, so a shilling now and then is only sensible to ensure a . . . a line of communication, shall we call it?"

Another sniff. "Well, what is it that you needed to *communicate* in this hugger-mugger fashion?"

Frederick's face tightened. "I need to know what my cousin and his wife are about. I need to keep informed of their comings and goings."

"Hah!" She barked an unpleasant laugh. "You wish a sort of court calendar? One would think they were the royal family."

"That amuses you? Just remember that you have no real claim on him. He could throw you out at any time."

"As he did you."

"Yes. As he did me."

They glared at each other, with no friendly feeling softening their exchange.

It was Frederick who chose to soften first. He managed a twisted, almost apologetic smile. "There is no need for us to argue. We have both been displaced by my cousin and his wife."

"I, at least, still reside under his roof," she said stiffly.

"But not with any guarantee of security."

When she tightened her lips and looked away, he pressed his advantage. "You need to find a husband for your daughter," he said. "One who can provide for both of you."

She looked at him for a long minute before she spoke. "Are you proposing to marry Isabella, *Mr.* Dormer?"

"I am not precisely in a position to do so at the moment. However, who knows what the future holds?" He lifted his hands and shrugged. "Life is ever uncertain."

"Uncertain. Yes, it is that." She continued to look at him, waiting.

He was the one who finally surrendered. "But perhaps two people who are willing to cooperate, let us say, might find that cooperation makes life just a little less uncertain."

"Possibly," she said.

"So you will keep me informed of my cousin's plans?"

Although he was trying to maintain an unworried air, she could hear the urgency in his voice. "Perhaps," she said.

"You can use Hannah. She is willing to carry messages."

"For a price."

"My dear Lady Blackwell, everything comes at a price."

CHAPTER 26

CUTTLEBUSH WAS FEELING FRUSTRATED. IT WAS a familiar sensation. Since he was not a man of great self-knowledge, or any other kind of knowledge, he could not understand his failure to make headway among the shoals of bumpkins washing up on the shores of the tavern. He was calling himself Smith, just in case Hopworth might have mentioned him by name.

The dolts were more than willing to allow him to buy them a mug of ale—or cider, which seemed to be the preferred beverage here—but received his hints about Claremont's probable iniquity with blank stares.

The only one who had much to say to him was an ancient who seemed permanently ensconced in the settle by the fireplace. He was more than willing to talk. Unfortunately, he spoke in a dialect made even more incomprehensible by his lack of teeth.

At least there didn't seem to be any rumors about the arrangement he had entered into with Hopworth and Dormer, so it was possible that Hopworth had gotten rid of any incriminating correspondence. Dormer had doubtless been clever enough to avoid having his name anywhere. Unfortunately, he and Hopworth had been unable to conduct their business in person. Letters had been necessary, and those letters were, perhaps, overly specific about their plans—and he had written and signed those letters.

If Hopworth was possessed of an adequate sense of caution, he had burned those letters. Unfortunately, Cuttlebush had some doubts about Hopworth. Had the letters been destroyed? He couldn't count on it.

If only he could ask Hopworth.

But the steward had vanished. Nobody seemed to know where he had gone. That did not seem to bother anyone. He could hardly blame them. Hopworth was not a man to make friends of those beneath him, and Dormer was not a man to worry about anyone but himself.

It sounded as if Hopworth had departed in haste after he lost his post. It could be that his departure had been too hasty for him to be able to take care of any incriminating paperwork. If he was planning to disappear, he probably thought it didn't matter. He could take his profits and start a new life elsewhere.

But Cuttlebush couldn't do that. He had a business, he had a wife, he had a position in the community. He did not intend to lose any of that. This particular arrangement might be at an end, but that didn't mean he was finished. Just as long as there was nothing to incriminate him.

Now that St. Vincent was First Lord of the Admiralty, he was snooping into everything and trying to impose discipline. If he could, he'd be flogging the purveyors as if they were his blasted sailors.

If he could only be sure there was no evidence left behind. No one had come along to clap him in irons yet. That could mean Hopworth had been kind enough to burn all those incriminating letters . . . or it could mean they hadn't been found yet.

Cuttlebush stood in the lane, staring at the steward's house, the house where Hopworth had once lived, and worked—the house where any letters Cuttlebush had written might have been left behind.

It looked empty. Well, at this time of day, it ought to be empty. Any steward worth his salt would be out and about. He could just go up and knock on the door. If anyone was there, he could make some excuse about admiring the place. It was quite a decent house, after all.

He steeled himself and knocked.

Silence.

He knocked again.

When there was still no answer, he tried the door. *Locked.*

He looked around for likely place to hide a key, but the place was bare of ornaments, and when he felt the lintel over the door there was nothing. So he made a circuit of the house, checking the windows. Not a one of them was conveniently open, and all of them seemed to be locked.

Hmm. This new steward was not a very trusting sort, unfriendly of him.

He considered breaking a window to get in but decided against it. If someone came by and noticed, he'd be trapped with no plausible excuse for being here. No, nighttime would be safer. With a frustrated backward glance at the locked door, he headed back for the inn.

Ten-year-old Johnny Hembry, who had been watching the stranger, thought his behavior strange enough to mention when he got home for dinner. His father thought it strange as well, strange enough for him to take young Johnny to tell Sinclair about it.

"Sounds like the fellow staying at the inn, calling himself Smith," Hembry added when Johnny had finished his tale.

To their surprise, the information brought a smile to Sinclair's face. "Splendid!" he said. Then he noticed the startled looks on the Hembrys' faces. "Smith's name is really Cuttlebush, and he's one of the fellows who have been cheating you and your fellow tenants in recent years," he explained. "Now, if you, Mr. Hembry, would be good enough to drop by the tavern before you go home for the evening, you might mention that I have gone to Yeovil and plan to be away overnight."

Hembry thought about it, and then asked, "Why? Seems to me I could just tell the others who he is and what he's been doing. We could take care of him ourselves."

"Doubtless you could, but there's no need for you all to find yourselves on the wrong side of the law. I think there's a fair chance he'll try to break into my house if he thinks it's empty, and then we will catch *him* on the wrong side of the law. And then I can take him to London and turn him over to Lord St. Vincent."

"Lords!" Hembry snorted. "Not like lords are going to take an interest."

"Ah, but you don't know St. Vincent. He's recently been appointed First Lord of the Admiralty and he's furious about all the corruption that's been going on. He's spent most of his life at sea, and that corruption is the cause of all the bad food and lack of supplies that he and his men have had to suffer. He would be delighted to make an example of Mr. Cuttlebush and his colleagues."

When Hembry still appeared unconvinced, Sinclair added, "Perhaps you know some men who would be willing to help me keep watch tonight?"

Smiling slowly, Hembry thought he might.

IT HAD BEEN DIFFICULT TO CONVINCE CLAREMONT that he should not take part. No one wanted to point out that no matter how well he could walk with his artificial leg, he was still not likely to be of much use in a fight. It was his wife who found the argument that would save his pride.

"If you take part in this," she said, "Cuttlebush could argue that you are persecuting him because of a private quarrel. It will be best if you do not appear."

Claremont sulked, but submitted.

When the others moved into position, it was already dark even though the church clock had only just chimed eight. It was decided that Sinclair would remain in the house, since breaking into an occupied dwelling was the more serious offense. Since there could be no fire on the hearth and no lamp could be lit, it was a dark and chilly wait. He had considered setting himself up on the sofa with a blanket to keep warm but decided that he might fall asleep if he were too comfortable. It seemed unfair, since the others were all outside at the mercy of the wind. He set a hard chair next to a window that looked out on the road to the village and prepared to wait.

At first the men outside stood in the shelter of the trees near the road, but eventually decided that one or two watchers would suffice while the rest sheltered in the comfort of the barn safely out of the wind. A half hour turn as watchers seemed fair enough.

Even so, it was a long, cold wait, and the clouds rarely let the moon appear. Still, when Cuttlebush put in an appearance not long after midnight, there was no difficulty in following his progress. With a bundle over his shoulder and a lantern in his hand, he stumbled and crashed about, winning the scorn of the countrymen, even those with no knack for poaching.

The original plan had been to allow him to break into the house, but to the surprise of the watchers, he made no attempt to open a door or window. Instead, he began fussing about in front of the front door and seemed to be blocking it.

It was Hembry who first realized what was in order. He lifted his head to sniff, and then swore. Lamp oil!

"He's out to burn the place down," Hembry shouted.

Indeed, Cuttlebush had lit his pile of kindling and lifted the lantern, preparing to throw it through a window, but he froze at Hembry's shout. He dropped the lantern and started to run but got no farther than a few feet before he was seized by some very angry farmers.

Sinclair had been able to see Cuttlebush's approach from his window and shook his head at the man's pitiful attempt at stealth. Had the idiot no idea how much noise he was making? He didn't quite know what to make of the sounds at the door—it didn't appear to be an assault on the lock—but his amusement faded when he smelled the oil.

He flung open the door and hurried out, kicking the flaming kindling away from the house and using his coat to beat out the flames. Two of the farmers who had been guarding the place came to his aid, since they couldn't get close enough to Cuttlebush to join in the pummeling.

It was over almost too quickly. A stray piece of kindling flared up on the gravel of the pathway and just as quickly winked out. When Sinclair turned to see what had become of Cuttlebush, he saw the fellow curled up on the ground making sniveling noises while Hembry and his friends looked on in disgust.

Sinclair walked over and nudged Cuttlebush with his foot. Cuttlebush twitched and whimpered a bit louder.

"Pathetic creature, isn't he?" Sinclair turned to Hembry. "It's hard to believe he had the courage to engage in theft the way he did."

"Well, he'll not be thieving again," Hembry said with satisfaction. "They hang you for arson, don't they?"

"That they do," Sinclair said. Any further response was drowned out by Cuttlebush's cry of protest.

"No, they can't hang me!" He struggled first to his knees and then to his feet. "I never meant to hurt anyone." He clutched Sinclair's arm. "They told me you were away, that the house was empty. No one was hurt. And besides, the house wasn't even damaged!"

With a look of fastidious distaste, Sinclair removed himself from Cuttlebush's grasp. "Whether the building was occupied or not, damaged or not, is irrelevant. The punishment is the same." He turned away.

"Nooo!" Cuttlebush scurried after him, snatching at his coat-tails. "You have to listen to me. It wasn't even my idea. It was all Dormer's doing, him and Hopwood. They were the ones who worked it out."

Sinclair smiled.

Cuttlebush continued to babble feverishy. Sinclair continued to smile. The farmers continued to glower.

At length, Sinclair turned to Hembry. "I hope you will not mind, but rather than hang him, I would like to take him to London in the morning. I believe Lord St. Vincent would like a word with him."

Hembry and his friends looked uncertain.

"Lord St. Vincent is the First Lord of the Admiralty," Sinclair told them, and relayed what he had told Hembry earlier.

Hembry, who seemed to have become the spokesman for the farmers, still looked dubious. "He'll not get off scot-free, will he?"

"Oh, I doubt that," Sinclair said softly. "I seriously doubt that."

Hembry looked around at his fellows for agreement, and then nodded. "I reckon we can trust you then. I doubt we'll get the money we were cheated of, but at least he'll get his dues."

"That he will." Sinclair smiled. "I can promise you that."

CHAPTER 27

WHEN WILL AND MARIA CAME DOWN to breakfast the next day, they found a cheerful Sinclair waiting for them with Aunt Sophia at his side. "I assume that smug look on your face means your trap was successful," Will said.

"It was." Sinclair continued to smile. "Mr. Cuttlebush did not, however, attempt to burglarize my house. Apparently he was not sure he would be able to discover all the possibly incriminating paperwork. So he tried to burn the place down instead."

"Good heavens!" Maria gasped. "Was anyone injured?"

"Well, Cuttlebush is a trifle battered, and a few of your tenants have bruised knuckles, but on the whole, we came away in decent shape. And once he was informed that the punishment for arson is hanging, Cuttlebush was more than eager to confess all in hopes of a reprieve."

Will grunted. "I suppose that means you feel entitled to a bit of smugness."

Maria looked dubious. "Will he deny that confession once he isn't surrounded by men who want to hang him?"

"He would probably like to do so," Sinclair acknowledged. "That is why I had him write out a confession, with three copies, signed and witnessed. One has been delivered to the magistrate, one I have right here for you, and one I will take with me to the Admiralty, along with Cuttlebush himself. I believe St. Vincent will probably wish to question Cuttlebush himself."

With Maria hanging over his shoulder, Will snatched up the document and read it quickly. "Frederick was behind it! I told you so, didn't I? He'll not get away this time."

"Well, as to that . . ." Sinclair shook his head. "He may not end up actually convicted in a court of law. Unless some physical evidence can be uncovered, documents or letters, it may be difficult to build a case against the cousin of a peer based on nothing but the word of an admitted criminal."

"He may not end up in prison, but that is not the worst that can happen to him." Aunt Sophia smiled cheerfully. "The magistrate will have read this confession, we have read it, and all the men who were present last night know about it. By this evening, everyone in the district will know about it. He will be completely disgraced."

"As if he'll care," Will muttered.

"Oh, he will care," Maria said softly. "He is a very vain fellow. According to Chapman, the servants believe that he is furious not because you accused him of causing my accident but because he no longer lives here, in this house. His own house is not adequate for his sense of consequence."

"Never forget that he thought you were dead and that he had inherited your title and estate," Aunt Sophia reminded Will. "He has been talking as if you are a usurper."

Will did not appear convinced.

"And on Sunday, we will go to church," Maria said. "It's high time we showed ourselves."

Will looked at her in horror. "Are you out of your mind? You must be daft to think I'm going to put myself on display that way."

"We will both be on display. Yes, people will stare, but they will stare because you are the new Viscount Claremont and I am your new wife. They will stare because they will have heard about

Frederick's misdoings, his shameful abuse of your father's trust. They will want to know if your uncovering of his misdeeds means that you will now be a good landlord for your tenants and a good neighbor for them all."

Will snorted. "They will take one look at my scars, at my patch, and run, terrified that I am a pirate who will spit their babies on a sword."

Maria sat back and frowned at him in exasperation. "Honestly, Will, your vanity grows tiresome."

"Vanity?" he snarled.

"Yes, vanity. Because you are not as perfectly handsome as you once were, you have decided that you are now monstrous. Ridiculous. I doubt you have even looked in a glass in all the time you have been here."

"I don't have to look in a glass to see how people react to my appearance." He slashed his hand angrily through the air. "It took the servants here months to be able to look me in the face."

She shook her head. "That is because you always scowled so ferociously at them. You terrified them. Tell me, did Lord Newbury shrink in horror at the sight of you? Did any of the people you encountered in London do so?"

"You think they weren't startled?"

"Startled, perhaps, but I expect they got over it quickly enough. Now, the longer you keep yourself immured in this house, the more people will build you up into some sort of monster in truth. Attendance at church tomorrow is the perfect way to show them that you are a handsome and elegant gentleman who happens to have a limp, an eyepatch, and a few scars as a result of his heroic service in the navy."

"You have no idea what you are talking about." He leaned back and shut his eyes. "No idea."

"Yes, I do. So long as I have known you—now I mean, not when I was a child—I have not seen a single person shrink from you in horror. Not when we were at Ashgrove, not when we were traveling. But I have seen the servants look lively when you scowl at them. I would wager the men on your ship did as well."

He didn't open his eyes, but she could almost feel him retreating. Then he did open his eyes and sit up. "You should not attempt it. You have been injured and you still need to rest. You cannot go traipsing off to the village."

She wanted to laugh at the way he seized on this as a possible escape, but she only smiled and shook her head. "We will take the carriage. I need only walk from the carriage to the church and back again. That is no farther than the distance from the drawing room to the dining room." When he simply gave her a disgruntled look, she continued, "I will order the carriage for nine thirty Sunday morning."

LADY BLACKWELL HAD SENT A MESSAGE declaring that she did not choose to attend church with yokels and tradesmen, so the carriage was not as crowded as it might have been. Lady Pellew and Maria were accustomed to attending services every week, and Isabella considered it a grand outing, so the three ladies were smiling as they set out on their short journey to the church.

William sat stiffly in his place, looking grimly determined.

Peering out the window, Maria could see the bell tower of the church well before they arrived. It was an unusual shape, octagonal, and made of a yellowish stone that looked almost golden in the morning sun. As they drew near, she could see that the church was much larger than the one she had been accustomed to attending. Though it looked very old with its long windows in their pointed arches and with actual gargoyles at the corners of the roof, it seemed to be in good repair.

Impressive . . . uncomfortably impressive, rather like Belford Park. She had been hoping for something a bit cozier. Something familiar. Instead, she was going to have to make an effort to live up to the church she attended as well as the house she lived in.

Her shoulders began to sag under the weight of it all. She was supposed to be a viscountess. No, she actually was a viscountess.

But why would anyone believe that? She was still the same Maria Garland who wore dresses that had been turned and remade more than once. The fact that her pelisse was now lined with fur didn't change who she was. Would people take one look at her and shout, "Imposter"?

She wanted to shrink into the corner of the coach, but then she looked at Will, sitting there as grim as if he were on the way to his execution. No shrinking allowed, she told herself. She lifted her head and put on a serene expression.

When the carriage pulled up before the church, the people who had been standing around, chatting in the weak sunlight of the late November morning, all fell silent and turned to look.

"See?" Will said through gritted teeth.

Maria kept calm as she spoke. "They aren't staring at you, Will. They can't even see you. They're staring at the carriage because they haven't seen it here before. They're curious, that's all."

The groom opened the door and let down the steps. Will allowed him to help in his descent from the carriage and turned to help Maria.

She smiled and muttered, "You need to smile too, Will."

He managed to force the corners of his mouth up and said, "Certainly, my dear," before turning to help the other two ladies descend.

They walked slowly along the path to the church, Isabella beaming, Maria and Lady Pellew smiling as they walked the gauntlet of curious stares. Will managed to not glower.

Maria suddenly bethought herself of something. "Will, is there a family pew?"

"How the devil would I know?" His jaw was still clenched.

"Will," she protested. "We're at church!"

"How the *deuce* would I know? As far as I can remember, I've never been here before."

"Never . . ." But before she could say any more, they were inside. An elderly man stared at them and then at the carriage. He bobbed his head in a jerky bow and ushered them to a box pew at the front. Apparently there was a family pew . . . but they had never attended?

Really, she thought, her husband's family was most peculiar.

Will had not been lying when he said he could not remember being here before, but when the usher opened the door of the pew, it was suddenly familiar. He could almost see his mother entering the pew first, followed by him and his brothers, with his father bringing up the rear. Frederick had been with them too, sitting next to his father just as Will himself sat next to his mother.

He sat down with a thump in the place that had been his father's. Maria looked at him with concern, but he shook his head. It was not his leg that had caused his ungainly descent but the attack of memory. Curious that memory should revive here, in a church he may have attended but in which he paid little attention.

When he first returned to Belford Park, he did not even recall the location of many of the rooms. He had to be directed to the drawing room and had followed the others in order to reach the dining room.

Perhaps that was not so very strange. Children were not welcome in formal rooms, and at ten years of age, he had been only a child when he left. Children might not have been particularly welcome in the church either, but at least their attendance was expected. Proper behavior was also expected. He remembered his mother's hand coming down on his leg when he was swinging it, trying to see how close he could come to the front wall of the pew without actually kicking it while the vicar roared from the pulpit.

Amazing, how vivid that unimportant memory was. For it was, he thought, unimportant. He could remember nothing significant about the day or the service, just his mother's thin hand in its pale kid glove coming to rest on his leg.

Thinking back on the thinness of her hand, he realized that she must have already been ill with whatever disease it was that carried her off. And that was another oddity—he had no idea what illness it was that had killed his mother. He had not even known she was ill. There had been no time for questions because it was only a day or two after her death that he was sent off to sea.

The oddness of it had never struck him as a child because children never think there is anything odd about the things that happen to them. They know of nothing outside their own experience. But now, looking back, he could not help but think it odd.

He was recalled to the present when everyone stood for the entrance of the vicar. He was not the roaring vicar Will now remembered from childhood. This was a scholarly-looking gentleman of perhaps forty years of age who peered out at the congregation with an expression of solemnity on a round face that looked as if it smiled more often than not.

The vicar almost stumbled over the opening prayer when he caught sight of Will and the ladies in the family pew. Recovering quickly, he continued in a clear, pleasant baritone that could doubtless be heard in the back of the church as well as in the front pew. There was no roaring, Will was relieved to note. Nor was the sermon, when it came time for that, a ranting tirade.

The vicar spoke about the need for hope. Well, that was a sentiment Will could share. He glanced at Maria, sitting at his side and listening attentively to the service. The realization struck him that he had been feeling more hopeful ever since he met her.

A less comforting thought struck him when they stood to leave the church at the end of the service. He turned to Maria with a panicked whisper. "I don't know the vicar's name." It was, of course, something he would be expected to know.

But Maria just smiled and whispered, "He is Mr. Gilbert. Octavius Gilbert."

Why was he surprised? He should have realized that she would know, just as she already knew the names of all the servants at Belford. He started to smile back at her but then he looked past the vicar—Mr. Gilbert—standing by the door of the church. Small knots of people were scattered around the churchyard, chatting with each other—and waiting, no doubt, to get a good look at the scarred cripple who was now the viscount.

He gritted his teeth and tried not to scowl as he made his way down the aisle, Maria on his arm, his walking stick beating its slow tattoo.

Nonetheless, when they greeted the vicar, he seemed quite pleased to see them. "We were delighted to learn that you had survived the engagement up in Denmark," he said, beaming cheerfully. "The original news was that you had died, you see. And then it was actually at the funeral of your father and brothers that we learned you were still alive. It turned a sad occasion into one of rejoicing."

"I suspect not everyone rejoiced," Will said dryly.

Mr. Gilbert's beaming smile faded a bit. "Well, I'm sure that once Mr. Dormer recovered from his surprise, he too was pleased."

"Oh no," said Isabella innocently. "He was quite furious for ages."

The embarrassed silence that followed her remark was mercifully cut short when some of the people who had been gathered about came up to be introduced.

The first were Sir Thomas and Lady Fanshaw, an older couple, rather stiffly proper. Will knew Sir Thomas to be the local magistrate with whom Sinclair had arranged the disposition of Cuttlebush. He did not know if the formality of his greeting was habitual—Sir Thomas wore a wig and breeches and Lady Fanshaw still powdered her hair—or if it indicated some disapproval about the way the situation had been handled. But Maria's smile had a softening effect on them.

Mr. and Mrs. Upstone were younger, close to his own age, and lived in the village. He was a solicitor, he announced, a trifle defiantly, and relaxed only after Will did not seem to be put off by this. He had an intelligent, observant look about him that Will appreciated.

The Maltbys had a property just beyond the village. A middle-aged pair, they appeared contented with their lot in life without looking smug. Their daughter, Alice, was not more than a year or two younger than Maria, and smiled at as if she would like to be friends. The Maltbys' son, Matthew, was a young pup still growing into his hands and feet. Far from being put off by Will's injuries, he appeared almost worshipful, and had to be pulled away by his father to stop him from peppering Will with questions.

An older gentleman, Mr. Horatio Aberdare, lived at Musgrave House. His was the largest property in the neighborhood other than Belford Park, and the others spoke of it in voices tinged with awe.

Will began to suspect he had been foolish to learn so little about his neighbors. They seemed pleasant enough, even likeable.

Maria had been smiling and chatting with them all, but he could feel her beginning to sag beside him. Mrs. Gilbert, the vicar's wife, noticed even before Will did.

"Now we've all heard about your dreadful accident," she said, "and happy though we are to see you so well recovered, you mustn't over-try your strength." She turned to Will. "You really must take her home and see that she rests."

He grinned at the authoritative tone telling him to do just what he intended to do. "Aye, aye, Mrs. Gilbert," he said, saluting her with his stick.

"That went well, I think," said Lady Pellew once the carriage was underway.

"Hmm?" Will was looking at Maria to make sure she really was all of a piece.

"I am fine, my lord," Maria said to him, "and I also think it went well."

"I suppose it did," he said, thinking about it. People had seemed a bit nervous at the start, but he'd been nervous himself. At least no one had recoiled at the sight of him.

Perhaps, just perhaps, he had been making too much of his scars.

CHAPTER 28

MARIA HAD INVITED THOSE SHE MET AT CHURCH to call, assuring them that they would be welcome at any time, but she would certainly be at home on Wednesday. She had worried that such an informal invitation might not be acceptable.

Fortunately, Lady Pellew knew better. She could hardly believe that Maria did not realize that no one would ignore an invitation from Viscountess Claremont and an opportunity to visit Belford Park. She rolled her eyes when her niece wondered if anyone would visit and warned the staff to expect callers.

Consequently, Mrs. Potts had freshly baked cakes, both plain and iced, prepared. Mr. Gregson saw to the polishing of the silver tea service and filled decanters with sherry and madeira. Mrs. Bates had the parlor maids dusting and polishing every inch of the drawing room and filled bowls with fresh potpourri.

There was an orangery attached to the house, but it had fallen into disrepair after years of disuse. Mrs. Bates and Mrs. Potts discussed the possibility that if the master and his wife planned to entertain, it might be restored and put to use once more. Their eyes gleamed, the one thinking of enough hothouse flowers to fill a dozen vases no matter what the season, the other of bunches of grapes and even a pineapple to grace the table.

When the clock struck two on Wednesday afternoon, Maria was thinking no more than a few hours ahead. Just in case someone did call, she had dressed in a white muslin afternoon dress topped with a high-necked yellow overdress and her Kashmir stole. The stole wouldn't be needed if she sat by the fire, but when she entered the drawing room, she saw that Lady Blackwell had taken that seat and was rather ostentatiously reading a book of sermons.

Lady Pellew, walking in with Maria, was amused. "I had not realized that you were so fond of devotional literature, Lady Blackwell. I am almost embarrassed to reveal that my own taste in literature runs to horrid novels."

Just then, Mrs. Gilbert was introduced. After greeting everyone and being seated, she turned to Lady Pellew to ask, "Did I hear you mention horrid novels? I declare, they are a great weakness of mine."

"Really?" Lady Blackwell asked with raised brows. "Surely as a vicar's wife you should have a mind above sensational literature. I myself am drawn to works like Law's *Serious Call*."

"Are you?" Mrs. Gilbert smiled politely.

Isabella looked up from her needlework. "Oh yes. Mama has been reading that book forever. In fact, I don't know that I have ever seen her read any other." She smiled a smile of innocent ignorance.

Mrs. Gilbert's polite smile turned into a choked cough. "I'm afraid I found Law rather tedious. When I have time to read, I greatly prefer works like *The Castle of Wolfenbach*."

"One of my favorites!" declared Lady Pellew. "I do like a story with truly villainous villains, and that one has two. I have just finished another book by Mrs. Parsons, *The Mysterious Warning*. It has more dark family secrets and ghostly apparitions. Absolutely delicious! Have you read it?"

When Mrs. Gilbert said she had not yet had that pleasure, Lady Pellew immediately sent a servant to retrieve the book from her bed chamber so she could lend it to her new friend.

Before Lady Blackwell could do more than simmer in silence, tea arrived, and with it additional visitors—Sir Thomas and Lady Fanshaw, followed by Mr. Aberdare and the Maltby family without the son. Maria poured tea, nervously but gracefully, and sent a servant to ask Will to join them since Sir Thomas and Mr. Maltby seemed to be looking around in search of him.

Mr. Aberdare, however, seemed quite content to sit by Isabella, admiring her needlework and offering gently amusing observations that had her looking happily content. Maria could not fail to notice that although Isabella was smiling, Lady Blackwell was not. Since there was nothing Maria could do about this, and since she cared very little whether Lady Blackwell was happy or not, she turned to the other ladies.

All of them proved to be devoted readers of novels, and so were discussing their favorites. Lady Fanshaw favored the tender sentiments of *Evelina*, Miss Maltby had been thrilled by *The Mysteries of Udolpho*, and her mother championed the realism of *Castle Rackrent*.

"It cannot be denied," Mrs. Maltby said, "that far too many landowners neglect their duties, and it is their tenants who suffer for it. It may be that novels like Miss Edgeworth's will do more to bring the problem to people's awareness than any number of speeches in parliament."

Miss Maltby rolled her eyes at her mother's speech, but only briefly, and Maria thought she was the only one to notice.

Lady Blackwell, still smarting from the general disdain for volumes of sermons, flattened her lips. "Surely," she said, "it is the laziness and intemperance of the lower orders, especially among the Irish, that are responsible for their woes."

Mrs. Maltby drew herself up, but before she could speak, her husband put a hand on her arm. "My dear, perhaps these discussions could wait for a later date, when we are all better acquainted."

Taking a deep breath, Mrs. Maltby released it in a resigned sigh. "No doubt you have the right of it, Mr. Maltby. I beg your pardon, all of you, for allowing myself to be carried away."

"Not at all, Mrs. Maltby. Not at all." Will was standing in the doorway, apparently having overheard the last part of the book discussion. "The duties and responsibilities of landowners are something that should concern us all, and I am feeling sorely my lack of knowledge. I am hoping you gentlemen will be able to help me."

Sir Thomas narrowed his eyes at Will. "Dormer, your cousin, isn't here?"

Lady Blackwell sniffed loudly, but Will ignored her and said, "No, he has returned to his own estate, which is doubtless in need of his care."

Mr. Maltby sat back and exchanged a smile with Sir Thomas. "Well, then . . ."

Now it was Will who narrowed his eyes. "Perhaps you gentlemen would care to join me in my library while we leave the ladies to their literary discussions?"

Sir Thomas and Mr. Maltby accepted the invitation with alacrity. Mr. Aberdare stayed behind at Isabella's side. Lady Blackwell still did not look pleased, but Isabella appeared quite content.

Mrs. Maltby looked regretfully after the gentleman, then glanced over at Lady Blackwell, whose lips were tightly pressed together. She sighed and said, "The weather has been quite mild for this time of year, has it not?"

Maria gave her a sympathetic look. "Since I have never before lived in this part of England, I am actually curious about the weather. There has been no lady of the house in more than twenty years, and the gardens have been sorely neglected." Catching a look of outrage on Lady Blackwell's face, she added, "Of course Isabella and her mother did their best, I am sure, but it is difficult when one has the responsibility without the authority."

"Indeed," Mrs. Gilbert put in, "and I fear that the late Lord Claremont had very little interest in the gentler pursuits. It must have been very difficult for you." She patted Lady Blackwell's hand, and Maria choked down a laugh when the look of outrage increased.

Just then, Mr. Aberdare and Isabella rose. Turning to her mother, Isabella said, "Mr. Aberdare is going to take me for a ride in his carriage."

"But . . ." Lady Blackwell was finding it difficult to find words for this new outrage.

"No need to worry, my lady." Mr. Aberdare bowed slightly. "I will take care your daughter is not chilled."

They departed before any more could be said.

"There is no need to worry, you know," said Lady Fanshaw. "Mr. Aberdare has a most comfortable landau and an excellent coachman."

"But I know nothing about him," protested Lady Blackwell.

"Oh, he is a highly respectable gentleman with a most attractive property," said Mrs. Maltby. "Indeed, I believe he is one of the wealthiest men in the county."

Lady Blackwell's mouth slowly closed.

WILL WAVED HIS GUESTS INTO HIS LIBRARY, where they settled comfortably in the chairs by the fireplace. When he joined them there, he realized with a start that he had not automatically slipped behind the desk, using it to hide his leg, and positioning himself to keep his scars in shadow. These men had seen him in the bright light of day in the churchyard. They had not shrunk from the sight then and did not appear to do so now.

Could it be that Maria was right, and that his appearance was not as terrifying as he thought?

Putting that thought aside, he said, "I'm afraid we've left the tea behind, but may I offer you a glass of claret?"

"You certainly may," said Sir Thomas.

Mr. Maltby grinned his agreement and looked around appreciatively. "I've not been in this room in a good many years," he said. "I must say it looks a good deal more welcoming."

"That would be my lady wife's doing," Will said, looking around as well. "We're a bit short on books, however."

"Well, I don't recall your father and brothers being great readers," Maltby said.

When they had all been served, Sir Thomas took his first sip of wine, looked at Will in surprise, and said, "Remarkable!"

"Yes. It seems my father was very attentive to questions of vintage. Unfortunately, the rest of the estate does not seem to be in as good condition as the cellars. We've been uncovering a number of problems."

"Well, at least you've replaced that idiot Hopworth. Never could understand why your father hired him." Sir Thomas grimaced. "Didn't seem to have the least notion what he was doing. Good to see the back of him."

"I gather it was actually my cousin who hired him. My father seems to have turned over management of the estate to Frederick." Will was careful to keep his tone neutral.

Maltby smiled and shook his head. "No need to be diplomatic about it. We've all heard what Dormer did, even if Sir Thomas here is the only one who's actually read that scoundrel's confession."

"Now, now," Sir Thomas growled, "can't convict a man on the word of a villain like that."

"Well, you have to admit, no one would think that fool Hopworth would dare set up an arrangement like that on his own," Maltby replied. "And anyone would agree that it's exactly the sort of nasty scheme Dormer would think of. Cheating tenants who have no defense against him."

"Damn fortunate that this is cider country," Sir Thomas said. "Most of the farmers hereabouts depend on their apple crops to see them through the year."

"Dormer couldn't do anything about that. There's the estate mill, and the tenants use it because it's convenient and cheap," Maltby said with satisfaction. "But if he tried to raise the price, there are other mills nearby the tenants could use."

"It will take me a while to sort out who was cheated and of how much," Will said. "But eventually Sinclair and I should be able to get it sorted out. I assure you that the tenants will all get what's owed to them."

Both Maltby and Sir Thomas blinked at that. "Good God, man, no one thinks you're to blame," Sir Thomas said. "Dormer is the one who should be paying them back."

Maltby raised a brow. "Not that he's likely to be able to do so even if he's willing. Going about as a tulip of fashion, as he does, to say nothing of driving those showy high steppers, costs a pretty penny. Never gave the impression of being provident with his money."

Will shook his head decisively. "Even if it is proven that my cousin is to blame—and I'm not sure that is likely—I am the one who is responsible for the tenants on the estate. When I inherited the title and the estate, I also inherited the obligations that come with it."

The corner of his mouth lifted in a crooked smile. "After all, when the captain takes over a ship, he can't ignore damage to the hull just because it didn't happen on his watch. And it's not as if the estate can't afford it."

Sir Thomas harumphed to cover a smile of approval.

Maltby leaned back and eyed Will consideringly. "I do believe my wife and I will appreciate having you and your wife for neighbors. You must come to dinner one day this week."

THAT EVENING, AS WILL AND MARIA RETIRED to their chamber well content with their encounter with the neighbors. While brushing out her hair, Maria could not help but think how lovely it would be if Mr. Aberdare married Isabella and removed her and her mother from Belford. She sighed with pleasure.

"Is something the matter?" Will looked worried.

"On the contrary. Isabella returned from a ride with Mr. Aberdare filled with enthusiasm for his luxurious carriage, his beautiful house, and his kind care for her comfort. It sounds to me as if she has a serious suitor."

"Aberdare?" Will frowned. "What would he want with a ninny like Isabella?"

With a laugh, Maria took his arm. "She may be a bit of a ninny, but she is extremely pretty. I know you married me for my fitness to run your household and so on, but many men prefer a pretty ninny."

"No, you're wrong." Will's frown deepened.

"You think not?"

"I don't mean that she isn't a ninny. I mean you're wrong about why I wanted to marry you." He lifted his hand to her face and traced a finger along her lips. "I wanted to marry you the minute I saw your glorious smile. It lights up my world."

"Oh!" She had to hold tightly to his arm for a moment because the ground had shifted beneath her feet.

"I think I fell in love with you right there on your doorstep when you smiled at me." He was looking at her with bemusement as he caressed her cheek.

"Oh, Will!" She flung her arms around him. "I love you so very much. I didn't dare tell you because I thought you might feel even more obligated." She pulled her head back to look up at him. "Are you sure? It's not just because you promised my father?"

"Your father . . .?" He looked stunned. "That's ridiculous. But what you said . . . You mean it? You really love me?"

"Of course I do. How could I not?" She smiled up at him.

Wrapped around each other, they tumbled down on the bed, and no further conversation was needed.

CHAPTER 29

Hannah strolled into the sitting room, looking not at all as respectful as a housemaid should look. From her seat by the fireside, Lady Blackwell glared at her.

Not at all cowed, Hannah said, "He's waiting for you out in the shrubbery."

Lady Blackwell added raised eyebrows to her glare, but that had no noticeable effect on Hannah. At length she gave up and asked, "Who is waiting?"

"Mr. High and Mighty Dormer," Hannah said. "Only not so high and mighty now, is he?"

"How dare you speak so disrespectfully of your betters?" Lady Blackwell quivered with outrage.

Hannah shrugged. "My betters? I'm not the thief, hiding in the shrubbery. If you want to see him, he's there."

"Insolent," Lady Blackwell hissed as the watched the maid saunter out of the room, hips swaying like the doxy she was. She remained seated, indecisive, drumming her fingers on the arm of the chair. One of her fingers snagged, and she looked down.

The chair was covered in brocade, in a color that had once been vivid but was now faded to a muddy green. Enough of the threads were broken to easily snag a fingernail. The chair should have been recovered—or replaced—years ago.

That woman was refurbishing the house. She and her aunt were always putting their heads together over samples of fabric—as if they knew anything of true elegance. But they had as yet done nothing about this room, the one she had chosen as her own sitting room.

Why would they, she thought bitterly. It's only the sitting room provided for a poor relation. That's all she was now, a poor relation—not even a relation—just a dependent, hoping that she would not be turned out.

She had had such plans for the house when Isabella became the viscountess! She could have made it into a showpiece, the glory of the county. Such entertainments they could have had, such glorious balls and festivities. She would have been the envy of society.

Then those drunken fools drove themselves over a cliff and ruined everything. Now she was reduced to worrying about survival, frightened by the intrusion of Dormer.

What was he doing here? He must be out of his mind. He had to know that his perfidy had been discovered. He couldn't possibly be expecting her to help him, could he?

Why hadn't he fled by now? Surely he didn't think she could help him leave England. He knew she had no money of her own—he was the one who had been enriching himself at his uncle's expense. All she had ever gotten from George and his father were complaints about her extravagance.

They spent what they wanted on horses and brandy, she thought bitterly, while she and Isabella were berated if they bought so much as a ribbon to trim an old bonnet.

If what the servants were saying was anywhere near the truth, Dormer had siphoned off thousands of pounds. He couldn't have spent all of it on his clothes. He probably didn't pay his tailor anyway. And he had been living here, at Belford, with no cares.

What could he want from her?

She wanted to ignore him. She wanted that very much. Was there any reason why she couldn't stay right here in the sitting room, as if Hannah had never entered with that presumptuous summons? Her hands clenched as she remembered the girl's effrontery. How she had wanted to slap the insolent smile from her face.

The chit had never dared behave that way when she had been in charge of the household. Now that little nobody Claremont had married was lording it over all of them. As if she had any notion how a nobleman's house should be run. As if . . .

This was not the time for that. First, she had to consider how Dormer might affect her position. Could he do her any harm? She suspected that he was aware of certain discrepancies in the household accounts. One day when she had been making entries in the account book he had appeared in his silent way, looking over her shoulder. He had not said anything, not really. He simply laughed that superior laugh of his and commented that she had a curious grasp of arithmetic.

But it had been no more than a few shillings that had gone into her purse. Well, a pound or two now and then. But no more than that, and only because George and his father were so mean.

Dormer himself had stolen hundreds, maybe thousands of pounds. Who knew how much? He was in no position to cast stones in her direction. He would not be able to distract attention from his crimes by pointing at her peccadillos.

No, she was surely safe from him. She sat back with a contented smile.

But then she had another thought: Isabella. Could he know something to her daughter's detriment? That could not be allowed. Not now, when the very wealthy Mr. Aberdare was showing interest. He would be the perfect husband for Isabella. And Claremont could certainly be trusted to see to it that the trusts and settlements would be all that they should be, if only because he would be glad to see the last of her and Isabella.

Was it possible that Dormer could threaten that future? Perhaps she did need to see him. She stood and looked out the window. The sun was shining, but weakly, and a blustery wind shivered the shrubs. She would need her warm cloak, but there was no need to bother a servant to fetch it. She took a quick look about her on leaving the room. There was no need for anyone to know she was stepping outside.

IT WAS BLOODY COLD. AT LEAST THE YEW HEDGE was thick enough to block some of the wind—but not all of it. Dormer cursed silently as he moved back and forth along the path. His fashionable coat was not thick enough to keep out the icy chill, and he had to stomp his feet to keep them from freezing.

The curses were mainly directed at his misbegotten cousin, sitting warm and smug in the house that should be his. He, Frederick Dormer, was the one who should be Viscount Claremont. It was his! He had the title and the estate in his grasp and then it had been snatched away by that smirking Sir Roderick.

And hadn't he enjoyed himself. "Oh, but didn't you know? Surely your uncle must have told you that Will survived," Sir Roderick had said, laughing up his sleeve all the while.

No, my *uncle* didn't tell me. He didn't tell any of us. Why would he? It wasn't as if any of us cared, one way or the other. Not until my *uncle* and my two *cousins* drove over a cliff.

I'd wish you were burning in Hell for that little joke, *Uncle,* but you're already there, aren't you? Even standing in that pit of fire, you're probably laughing at the result. You think it's a fine joke, don't you?

Bedamned to the lot of you. I'll win yet, just wait and see.

He continued stomping up and down the path. At last, Lady Blackwell came into view, looking as pinched and bitter as ever. He shook his head. It was one of the mysteries of life that such a scrawny crow could produce a luscious morsel like Isabella.

He pulled himself together and by the time she was close enough to speak, he was leaning casually on his walking stick, looking utterly impervious to the cold. "So good of you to join me," he said.

She sniffed, her mouth pinched as if life were naught but bitter lemons. And perhaps hers was. The thought made him smile.

"I don't know what you find so amusing," she snapped. "Not with everyone in the neighborhood declaring you a thief. I'm surprised they aren't out hunting for you already."

"Really? Whatever makes them think I'm a thief?" With effort he kept his voice smooth and maintained his smile.

"Don't pretend you don't know. That fool Cuttlefish or whatever his name is tried to burn down Sinclair's house with Sinclair inside it. When they caught him, he poured out the whole story, how you cozened your uncle and his tenants, letting everyone know that you were behind it all."

"Dear me. He said all that, did he? And people believed him?" It was requiring an effort to sound casual, but he believed he accomplished it. At any rate, Lady Blackwell began to look uncertain.

"Well, of course they believed it. Why wouldn't they?"

An uncertain, defensive tone was creeping into her voice. Good. Really, it was almost too easy to undermine her certainty.

He put a purr into his own voice. "Perhaps, my dear lady, because it isn't true. I deny his accusations absolutely. The cur is obviously lying in an attempt to minimize his own guilt by implicating his betters. Surely you were not taken in by such an obvious fabrication."

She looked shaken by his certainty, definitely shaken. But then she recovered, at least slightly. Her mouth returned to its tight little smile. "Taken in? Well, if I was taken in by what you term a fabrication, so was everyone else. Not just Claremont, but the Maltbys, the vicar and his wife, and even Sir Thomas, who is, you may remember, our local magistrate. They all seem to find no difficulty in believing you to be a villain."

Rage blinded him momentarily. He clenched his hand on the

walking stick to keep it from trembling . . . also to keep from slashing it across her smug, stupid face.

Pulling himself together, he said, "Fools are easily duped. They will soon find that there is nothing but the word of a frightened miscreant to implicate me. They will then be scrambling to offer me their apologies."

Although he believed he had spoken with admirable composure, she remained dubious enough to shake her head. "If that is true," she said, "I wonder that you are skulking about here in the shrubbery rather than calling at the front door."

"You may recall that my cousin is less than fond of me. I have no desire to exacerbate his temper merely to enquire after you and your daughter." He was determined to maintain a pleasant smile on his face.

She sniffed. "Well, since you are so concerned for our welfare, you may be pleased to know that Isabella has a new admirer, Mr. Aberdare."

"Aberdare? Why, he's an old man."

It was Lady Blackwell's turn to smile. "He's also a rich man. Very rich. Therefore you have no need to worry about us any further, and there is no need for any more of these shrubbery encounters. It is far too cold."

With that, she turned and hurried back to the house. Not quite fleeing, but not with great assurance either. However, her uncertainty was not enough for him. He needed someone to tell him what was going on inside the house. Hannah? He thought about it. She might be of some help, but not enough. She would not be close enough to either Will or that wife of his to know what they were planning, what they were thinking.

He needed someone else.

CHAPTER 30

GIBBS TOLD HIM IT WAS NECESSARY.
Sinclair told him it was necessary.

Maria told him it was necessary.

Will was gradually coming to realize that he was going to have to visit his tenants. There was really no other way to learn what they were like, what they could do, what they needed. It didn't matter if they flinched at the sight of him. They were going to have to become accustomed to it.

He refused to take the carriage, however, complete with driver and grooms. He was not trying to overawe the tenants, after all. Instead, he was trying to get to know them, to win their trust. After his father's neglect and his cousin's exploitation, they would be foolish to trust him at the start. They didn't know him. That was why he agreed to this in the first place.

He was going to take the gig. It was a solid, unpretentious vehicle, built to travel over rough country roads, with no effort at elegance or even comfort. What's more, he was going to drive it himself.

Driving was not an accomplishment that filled him with pride. There had been little need for it in the navy, and even though he had been practicing, he was not at all confident of his skill with the reins. Nor was he pleased by the effort required to get himself on and off the driver's seat. It was high off the ground and involved pulling himself up with the strength of his arms as much as pushing himself up with his good leg. *Ungainly* and *awkward* were the adjectives most likely to be applied to him.

Unfortunately, the alternative was to be always dependent on others. He would rather look like a clumsy oaf than be dependent. It was slightly less humiliating.

Maria was going with him. She had insisted, and although he had demurred, he had to admit that he was grateful. It wasn't just that he always enjoyed her company, but he had to acknowledge that she would ease the way, put people at their ease. If they found it too distressing to look at him, they could look at her instead.

He had pretty well mastered getting onto the seat in the gig. He knew exactly where to place his hands and where to place his foot to enable him to swing himself up with a minimum of fuss.

Helping Maria into her seat was a different question. He simply couldn't do it. Fortunately, she was not a fragile little flower and considered herself perfectly capable of getting into the gig by herself. She didn't even wait for the footmen, who were placing baskets under the seat.

He grinned at her as she settled herself, wrapping her cloak around her. She glanced back and frowned.

"Oh dear," she said. "I was supposed to let one of the footmen help me up here, wasn't I? I keep forgetting. It seems so silly to wait for help to do something I've done by myself all my life."

"What would Lady Blackwell say!" Will laughed as he lifted the reins and told the horse, an elderly mare named Blossom, to start. To his relief, she did. Totally unperturbable, she ambled down the drive, taking the turning to the right at his direction. Will continued to be surprised at this.

"It's not just Lady Blackwell," Maria said. "Your aunt was quite emphatic on the point, and Aunt Sophia agreed. It's apparently part of the behavior expected of the nobility. And your uncle pointed out that paying someone to do something we could do perfectly well ourselves provides employment to those who need it."

"A roundabout way of doing that, it seems to me." He frowned as the gig bounced. The road was in poor condition, just as Sinclair had said, and the cold weather had frozen the mud into ruts and ridges that were impossible to avoid. At least, he could not manage to avoid them. Blossom was more concerned with her footing than the comfort of her passengers.

"Sorry," he muttered as Maria bounced off his side.

"Not your fault," she said cheerily as she straightened her bonnet. "But I do think some attention to the roads will need to go on the list of things to do. How does one go about repairing a road?"

"Absolutely no idea."

"I have no idea either, but I'm sure someone must know." She pulled out the sheet of paper that had been folded in her muff. "Now, according to Gibbs' directions, we should be coming to the Wheelers' farm soon."

And indeed, as soon as they topped the brief rise in the road, there was a farmhouse off to the side. It was a substantial house, built of stone as were all the buildings he had seen. There were a number of other buildings around, built of the same stone. A barn, he supposed, and buildings for various animals.

This was insane. He had no idea what he was doing. He was an actor in a play, stepping on stage with no idea what the play was about and no idea what his lines were. He should just turn around and . . . too late. There was a small boy standing in the doorway staring at them. He pulled Blossom to a halt.

"Good morning, young man," Maria said in a cheerful voice. "Are your parents about?"

The boy stared a moment longer and then disappeared through the door.

"Not a delighted greeting," Will said, settling the reins in place and preparing to get himself safely on the ground. Maria had mastered the art of getting down while keeping an eye on him without making it obvious that she was doing so. He appreciated that.

By the time he was prepared, hat on his head and walking stick grasped firmly, she had removed one of the baskets from the gig and walked by his side to the door, where she knocked firmly but politely. After a longish minute, the door opened slightly, and a woman peered around it.

Will doffed his hat. "Mrs. Wheeler? I am Lord Claremont, and this is my wife. We've come to pay a call on you and your husband."

Her eyes widened, she gave a short gasp, and she gave the boy a shove out the door, saying softly, "Go fetch your Da." Then she straightened up, wiped her hands on her apron, and bobbed a curtsey. "You'd best come in then." She opened the door wide, looking none too happy about it.

Nonetheless, Maria entered with a smile on her face and placed the basket on the table that occupied the middle of the room. "We weren't here at Christmastide, so we are bringing somewhat belated gifts. It's nothing much—some tea, preserves, a cheese, and sweetmeats for the children."

Mrs. Wheeler seemed more frightened than anything else as her eyes darted back and forth between her visitors. "There's naught wrong, is there?"

"Of course not." Maria kept smiling cheerfully.

Footsteps outside—hurrying steps—came to a halt when a man burst through the door. Mr. Wheeler, presumably, held out a hand to his wife and drew her to his side. "We're paid up through the quarter, m'lord. There's naught owing," he said truculently.

"Good heavens, man, I never meant to suggest such a thing." Will smiled in what he hoped was a benevolent way. "I merely wanted to make the acquaintance of my tenants, a bit belatedly, I fear. I have been remiss in taking on my obligations. You must ascribe this at least in part to my ignorance. My experience at sea is not of much use on land, and I'm hoping you and your fellows will be able to tell me what needs to be done."

The distrust did not vanish. "Beggin' your pardon, sir, but your father never had naught to do with us. He left all that to Mr. Hopworth."

"Yes, well . . ." Will cleared his throat. "Hopworth is gone, and I find that some things have been badly managed and others neglected. For example, there seems to have been nothing spent on the repairs and improvements that are my responsibility, and I find it difficult to believe that in the past five years, no repairs have been needed."

Wheeler snorted. "'Make do,' he'd say. 'Make do.' So if I didn't want to drown in my bed, I'd have to find a way to repair the roof myself." He frowned suspiciously at Will. "Be you serious?"

"Indeed I am."

They looked over at the women. Maria was sitting on the floor, making the acquaintance of the Wheelers' son and a toddler of indeterminate sex. Mrs. Wheeler was standing over them, looking shyly proud of her offspring.

"You go along," Maria called to Will. "We're fine here."

They went out to the farmyard, and Will was pleased that Wheeler made no effort to accommodate his limp. The farmer paid no attention to it whatever, just as he paid no attention to the scar and eyepatch. Of course, by now everyone in the vicinity must have heard what he looked like, even if they hadn't seen him. Still, no one flinched.

Maria seemed to be right. He did make too much of his injuries. Doubtless their own concerns were of more importance to the tenants . . . a humbling thought.

The Wheelers' farmyard did not greatly impress Will, being both muddy and odiferous, as were the pigs, cattle, and poultry. He did not make any comment, however, since he had no idea if this was the common state of farms and livestock.

He could, however, see that the barn needed a new roof. The patches were obvious even without Wheeler pointing them out.

He took out a notebook and pencil to write this down. He also wrote down Wheeler's forceful suggestion that a strong, healthy bull was needed if the dairy herds were to flourish. Several breeds were mentioned, and Will dutifully wrote down the names.

When they returned to the house, Wheeler and Will were in charity with each other and discovered that their wives had also achieved an amicable accord. They shared a pitcher of cider before travelling on the next farm.

By the end of the week, Will and Maria had visited almost a dozen farms, with about twice as many still to come. By the third day, their arrival was no longer viewed with alarm, and by the end of the week Will thought he might need another notebook.

He had tramped through each farmyard and discovered that the Wheelers' yard was one of the better-kept ones. Maria had sat in numerous kitchens, admiring offspring and acquiring receipts for various ailments. Together they had drunk mugs of cider and eaten oatcakes with appropriate relish.

Each farm had its specific needs—repairs and even replacement of some of the farm buildings, new varieties of seed, clogged irrigation channels. Several streams were themselves clogged, and a couple of bridges were in danger of collapse. There was some argument over who was responsible for repairing a fence that had allowed a goat to feast on Mrs. Durbin's kitchen garden. Mrs. Durbin was inclined to think that the appropriate recompense was roast goat, and Mr. Durbin had a hard time keeping his wife from taking an axe to the creature.

Will began to think that maybe he could manage this viscount business.

ALTHOUGH IT WAS NOT LONG AFTER FOUR in the afternoon, the sun was setting, and the curtains in the drawing room were drawn against the chill of the evening. Candles were lit, providing plenty of light for needlework or reading, and a brisk fire danced on the hearth. Even so, the ladies all had warm shawls wrapped around their shoulders.

Will had pulled a chair up to a table and spread his notes out in front of him. He frowned and moved some papers from one pile to another, then he scowled and shifted even more papers.

Finally, he heaved a sigh. "I'll be glad when Sinclair returns. I have no idea which of these complaints are justified and no idea what should be done about them. Am I really expected to provide a bull to service my tenants' cows?"

"He will probably be a very happy bull if that is to be the extent of his duties." Maria said with a grin.

Lady Blackwell looked up from the pages of Law's *Serious Call* and sniffed. "That, Lord Dormer, is hardly a subject that should be raised in the presence of ladies. And you, Lady Dormer, should not understand such a reference."

Aunt Sophia rolled her eyes, and Isabella turned a page of a recent issue of *The Gallery of Fashion*.

Maria sent a scornful look in Lady Blackwell's direction. "I cannot believe that ignorance is ever a desirable accomplishment. But that reminds me . . ."

She turned back to her husband. "There's something else I'd like you to consider. There are quite a few children on the estate and in the village. Some of the mothers are able to teach their children their letters, but there doesn't seem to be any other opportunity for learning. Do you think it would be possible to establish a school?"

"Oh, now that's an excellent idea," Aunt Sophia said, perking up. "It's always so awkward when servants are unable to read. You can't leave them notes. And if they don't know their numbers, they come back from the shop with the wrong change."

"More seriously, they don't know when they've been cheated," Maria said.

Aunt Sophia nodded and then frowned thoughtfully. "Are there any buildings in the village that could serve as a schoolhouse, or would one have to be built?"

"Whoa!" Will said with a laugh. "Before you begin building, there are a number of other things to consider."

Lady Blackwell nodded, tight-lipped, but Aunt Sophia asked, "Are there? What things might they be?"

Will smiled at her patiently. "For example, you would need a teacher, and he would have to be paid. I don't know if the parents would be willing to take on the expense."

"But surely they would see that schooling would open up so many more opportunities for their children," Maria said.

"What nonsense." Lady Blackwell slammed her book closed. "You are talking foolishly. There is absolutely no need to school such children. It can only give them ideas above their station and lead to unrest. Look at what happened in France once the proper people were no longer in charge. If you ask me, it is utter folly to coddle your tenants."

Angry red patches flared on Maria's cheeks. "In that case, it is probably just as well that no one is asking for your views," she snapped.

"Well, I never . . ." Lady Blackwell stood up. "The late viscount never considered such nonsense, and neither did Mr. Dormer. They knew how to demand respect and run an estate properly."

Will looked at her coldly and did not bother to get to his feet. "Did they? It seems to me that their only concerns were for their own comfort and convenience. That hardly makes them exemplars of responsible management."

There was a brief silence, finally broken by Isabella. "A ruff around the neck seems to be quite fashionable at the moment, but I do not think it particularly attractive. What do you think?" She held up the fashion plate for the others to see.

Will and Maria looked at each in disbelief. "I'll send a note to Maltby, asking if we may call one day," he said. "He may have some sensible advice for us."

CHAPTER 31

For a change, the day was bright and sunny. Not precisely warm—it was only February, after all. Still, the biting wind had subsided, and it was possible to believe that spring might soon come.

Maria stood on the steps and looked around approvingly. The drive had been raked smooth. The steps were swept clean even if there were still some repairs to be done. Behind her, the windows were sparkling clean and the brasses on the door were polished. Fresh paint was still on the list of things to be done, but the list no longer overwhelmed her.

She would take the sun as a hopeful sign. Things really were going well. Perhaps she was not ready to stride into London and take society by storm, but she saw her way clear to managing her household, and she might be finding a place for herself in the local community.

Already, she and Will had gone to church and spoken to people. Neighbors had come to call. They had driven out to call on tenants. And no one had made her feel that she was inadequate, that she could not possibly be a real viscountess. In fact, in the months since her marriage, the only person who had ever tried to diminish her was Lady Blackwell. She was not someone she would ever need to take seriously.

More important was the change in Will. He had gone into those encounters with trepidation, saying it was only because she insisted. Well, she had insisted, and she might have been wrong. People might have been repulsed by his scars. They seemed unimportant to her because she knew him—loved him. If she had been wrong . . .

But as it turned out, she hadn't been wrong. People were eager to meet him. Even the tenants, once they realized he wasn't there to gouge more money out of them were happy to meet him. Some of them had helped trap Cuttlebush and expose Frederick for the worm he was. If anything, they saw Will as a naval hero, someone they were proud of.

Now he was standing beside her, waiting for a groom to bring around the gig so they could call on the Maltbys. As if it were a perfectly ordinary occurrence.

His jaw was not clenched. He did not grip his walking stick so tightly that his knuckles were white. Her hand rested on his arm, and she could feel that the muscles were not tense.

A groom brought the gig around, its green paint sparkling clean. That probably wouldn't last too long since the warmer days meant the frozen roads were turning muddy. It was just as well that placid Blossom was in the traces, since she would not be inclined to splash through puddles.

Feeling perfectly ladylike, Maria went down the steps on her husband's arm and allowed the groom to help her into the gig while Will swung himself up on the other side. Then she let Will tuck the carriage robe over her legs without taking care of it herself. If she could keep this up, she might eventually be able to turn herself into one of those helpless creatures always suffering from the vapors.

Will grinned as if he could read her thoughts and started Blossom on her steady way. They rolled smoothly down the drive, and the road was not too bad to the church and through the village. Maria found she was actually enjoying the trip. She had not seen much of the surrounding area since her arrival, having first been occupied with household matters and then recuperating from her fall.

Will's walking stick was propped between them on the seat, and she was absent-mindedly fingering the knob as she admired the hilly landscape. Suddenly something snapped, and the knob detached itself from the cane.

Will turned at her gasp and smiled before returning his attention to the reins. "Yes, that's a swordstick. I asked Gibbs to get me one before I realized it's of no use to me."

When she withdrew the blade, with its wicked point, she asked, "Why is it of no use? It looks quite frighteningly lethal to me."

"Lethal enough. The problem is that for me a walking stick is not just a decorative accessory. If I were to withdraw the sword, I could no longer use the stick for balance. If I tried to fence with it, I would fall flat on my face." He grinned. "I would just have to hope my opponent falls down laughing."

She pushed the blade back into the stick, then practiced releasing it and closing it a few times. "Perhaps women should take to carrying such sticks. The surprise of such a lethal weapon in the hands of such a frail creature might be very effective."

"An excellent idea. I'll tell Gibbs to get one for you."

"Yes, but I shall want it in a paler wood, I think. This dark finish looks much too serious. And perhaps with a pretty gilt handle."

He chuckled. "Perhaps a few gemstones as well to embellish it."

"Ah yes. Then it shall look utterly frivolous, and no villains would ever suspect." She sat back contentedly to enjoy the trip.

The road's condition was not good, but neither was it hopeless. Blossom was content to move at a placid pace that did not endanger her passengers. She did not carry them along at a rapid pace either, but that was the price they paid. The fields they passed were still covered with the stubble of last year's crops, and the trees of the orchards stretched out their bare branches. But every now and then, a tree or shrub displayed the pale color and swollen tips that foretold spring.

Soon they were traveling uphill, a steeper rise than Maria had expected, on a road worse than the ones they had been traversing. "I'm told this is a much shorter route," Will said, "though not one to take in bad weather. Or on a dark night. It takes us along one of the few cliffs in this area."

"Is this where your father and brothers came to grief?" Maria looked about nervously.

"Yes, but they were driving at night and driving much too fast, and they were all drunk. A recipe for disaster on any road. I think you can feel safe with Blossom."

He smiled, and she returned his smile, but still felt a few qualms.

They came around a bend, and although one side of the road was heavily wooded, the view off to the other was quite impressive, more impressive than Maria would have liked. The distant hills could be seen so clearly because there was very little between the road and empty space.

Blossom seemed to find that empty space intimidating. She slowed her dignified pace even further, picking her way carefully through the bumps and furrows of the road. That deliberation made it even more shocking when she suddenly reared up, neighing wildly, in response to the sound of a shot.

The horse's cries were echoed by Maria's. Will's shouts were louder still. But none of these quite drowned out the sound of a wheel cracking.

As Blossom swerved and kicked, the gig swerved and tilted until, accompanied by the passengers' cries, it went over with a terrific crash.

Fortunately for the passengers, it fell away from the cliff, flinging Will and Maria onto the road. Mercifully for both of them, Blossom's thrashing smashed the gig just far enough away to miss the fallen passengers. It missed only by inches, but it missed.

The noise faded away. Blossom ceased to carry on once there were no more loud noises to distress her, and the smashed gig kept her in place. She looked around briefly, but saw nothing to unnerve her further, so she huffed a sigh, put down her head, and waited.

Maria slowly opened her eyes. For some reason—she had no idea what it might be—she had shut them tightly when the world fell into chaos. She opened them slowly because she was more than a bit worried about what she might see.

The first thing she saw was Will's arm, lying still on the road. "Will," she whispered, fearing the worst. Then she realized that she was lying atop her husband, her head resting on his chest, and she could feel his heart beating steadily. Slightly relieved to know he had not been killed, she lifted her head to look around.

Though he was certainly alive, Will's eyes were still closed. Not an encouraging sight.

She rolled off him, trying to do as little damage as possible in case there were broken bones, and then knelt at his side. She could not see any blood. His hat was knocked askew, partly crushed under his head. Had it cushioned him when he fell? Gingerly, she touched his skull, watching to see if he winced in pain.

He remained immobile.

Wishing for some water, a stream, anything with which to wet her handkerchief so she could wipe his face, she rummaged in her reticule for something useful. She should be the sort of aristocratic lady who carried a vinaigrette. Unfortunately, she was not given to fits of the vapors, so she had nothing of any use. She could spit on it, she supposed.

Before she was driven to such lengths, Will groaned and opened his eyes. He groaned again and shut them. Then with a sigh he opened his eyes once more and blinked.

"What the hell happened?"

To Maria's relief, he sounded more annoyed than anything else. "I don't really know," she said. "All of a sudden Blossom reared up, the carriage sort of flipped in the air, and the next thing I knew, I was lying on top of you on the ground."

He pushed himself up with a grunt and sat there, looking around and scowling. "Are you all right?" he growled.

"Yes. You cushioned me nicely."

"Glad to be of service," he said absently, wincing as he tried to heave himself up. Giving up, he turned to scan the area. "Do you see my cane anyplace about? Damned if I can manage without it."

She looked around as well and saw it tangled in some of the wreckage of the gig at the side of the road. "I'll get it."

"Be careful! We don't want you pulling that mess down upon yourself," he called out as she knelt down to reach for it.

"It's perfectly safe," she said, flattening herself on the road and stretching her arm carefully under the splintered boards to catch hold of the cane.

"You are ridiculously difficult to dispatch." Frederick sounded disgusted as he stepped from the trees.

Startled, Maria scratched her wrist and caught her breath as she withdrew the cane. More forcefully, Will uttered an oath, and demanded an explanation for his cousin's appearance.

Ignoring that, Frederick stood casually at case, a pistol dangling from his hand. "Only you would drive out with a horse too slug-gish to bolt even when shot. I cannot imagine how anyone man-ages to think of you as a gentleman."

"You shot Blossom?" Maria sat down and turned to face him in outrage. "You took out your temper on a poor dumb animal?"

"It was only a slight graze," Frederick said, giving her a slight bow before turning back to Will. "The team the viscount was driv-ing responded in much more expected fashion, but then he was a capable enough whip."

"Are you accustomed to using horses for target practice?" Will sounded perfectly cool as he seated himself more comfortably, his arms around the knee of his good leg. "It seems a peculiar pastime."

Ignoring him, Frederick continued. "The viscount, being a true gentleman, naturally drove a spirited pair, and had them racing along at a far better pace than the plod you prefer. When they bolted, horses, carriage, and passengers all went over the cliff in most impressive fashion."

Will and Maria froze as they stared at him, not wanting to believe what they had just heard. Speaking very carefully, Will said, "Are you saying that you killed my father and brothers?"

"*Your* father?" Frederick laughed, but not with amusement. "Didn't you realize? Why do you suppose he shipped you off to the navy as soon as your mother died? He wasn't your father, you fool. He was *mine*."

"That's preposterous," Will said. "Your father was his brother."

"Ah yes, his brother." Frederick shook his head as if in disbelief. "Were you truly so blind? Did you not see that they hated each other, those brothers? The older one with the title and estate and the younger brother with a miserable inheritance that was barely more than a farm. Each trying to do the other a bad turn, each one marrying the bride his brother wanted, and finally each one seducing his brother's wife and leaving a cuckoo in the nest."

Maria listened to this with growing horror. "How fortunate you were, Will, to have been sent to the navy. If Frederick is telling the truth, you must be grateful to have escaped this positively Gothic family."

"It's true enough. Whether you believe me or not hardly matters at this point." Frederick shrugged, but the casual gesture was belied by the way he kept his gaze intently on William.

While Frederick was so occupied, Maria seized the opportunity to slip the swordstick under a fold of her skirt where she could try to release the catch without detection.

Will looked as if he thought Frederick's claim possible. "It would explain . . . It would explain why he seemed to dislike me."

"And why he favored me." Frederick smiled unpleasantly. "I was the one he treated as a favored son. You were a nothing. You were always a nothing."

Will shook his head sadly. "Better a nothing than a thief and a murderer. Are you boasting of what you have done? That seems foolish, even for you."

"Are you under the impression that you are going to walk away—I beg your pardon. I mean *limp* away—from this little accident?" Frederick inquired, assuming an exquisitely courteous manner. "Because I assure you, you will not. You will soon be tumbling over the cliff despite the delay caused by your lumpish excuse for a horse. Therefore I feel perfectly safe in disclosing past secrets."

"But as you can see, we didn't tumble over the cliff, and it seems to me you might have some difficulty in persuading us to do so."

Frederick smiled and held up his pistol.

"Yes, but you already fired it at poor Blossom," Will pointed out.

"And I had the foresight to reload it."

Maria found the catch on the swordstick and slipped it out of its case. Will, she could see, was fiddling with his boot. She could not tell why but supposed it might be well to distract Frederick.

"But Frederick," she called out, "don't pistols have only one shot? And there are two of us you will need to dispatch."

Another figure emerged from the trees. "How good it is then that he has me to assist him," said Isabella. "And I have a pistol as well." She smiled as she held it up.

"Why would you want to do that?" Maria was genuinely curious.

"Spare me the condescension." Isabella dropped the smile. "I will finally be Lady Claremont. That fool George said his father was on his deathbed when we married. But it turned out I was the fool for believing him."

"It seems you're not such a witless noodle as we thought," Maria said thoughtfully.

"Or perhaps you are," said Will, drawing attention back to himself. "Do you truly expect Frederick to marry you? He'll inherit nothing but the entailed bits of the estate, which won't add up to much. And as a viscount he will surely rank high enough to command a bride with a decent dowry."

"Oh, he will marry me," Isabella said, aiming a smug smile at Frederick. "After all, I know what he has done."

Frederick glared at her.

Maria now had the sword part of the swordstick safely in her hand, but she didn't think she could stand up to use it before Frederick or Isabella, pistols in hand, noticed. "I don't see how knowing what Frederick is doing can help you. You will be as guilty as he."

Will was sitting up now. "If I were you, Isabella, I'd be a bit worried. Frederick seems to be making a habit of eliminating people who get in his way."

"Shut up!" snapped Frederick, turning to Will and cocking his pistol.

That turn placed Frederick quite close to Maria, but with his back now to her. Using all her strength, she stabbed the sword into the back of his Frederick's knee. At the same time, Will threw the knife he had taken from his boot. It embedded itself in Frederick's shoulder.

Frederick shrieked. His hands flew up as his leg collapsed beneath him, and the pistol went off.

Isabella shrieked as the ball from Frederick's pistol struck her. Her own pistol fell from her hand harmlessly as she collapsed.

With an equine shriek, a horse burst from the trees, dragging a curricle, and galloped down the road.

Blossom lifted her head, saw nothing of interest to her, and returned to her own equine meditation.

The echoes from the gunshots faded, the hoofbeats of the frightened horse vanished into the distance, and the shrieks turned into sobs and moans. Maria stood up, returned the sword to its case, and stepped around Frederick to help Will to his feet. She handed him his swordstick, and he walked over to remove his knife from Frederick's shoulder.

Frederick gave another shriek of pain as Will did so.

"Not a mortal wound, I think," Will said, looking down at his cousin. "I suggest you use your cravat to staunch the bleeding.

Maria, meanwhile, had gone over to Isabella, who was sobbing for help. Ignoring the sobs but picking up the pistol, Maria bent over to examine the wound. "I don't think it's a terribly serious injury. You seem to have escaped with little more than a scratch. I suggest you use your petticoat to bind it up."

Isabella stopped sobbing long enough to gasp, "You're a cold, cruel woman!"

Maria gave her a disbelieving look and turned away to join Will. He had gone over to Blossom and was surveying the wreckage of the gig. It was obvious that it would not be of any use in getting them home.

"We had best start walking," he said. "It can't be more than a mile or two to the village."

That sounded perfectly sensible, but Maria knew how hard it would be for Will. His walking had improved wonderfully, but walking that far down a steep road would have to be painful.

She looked at the horse. Blossom seemed to sigh.

"What about Blossom?" she asked. "We can't just leave her here."

He looked at the horse too. "I suppose we should bring her with us. We'll need to get all those straps off her."

They set to work, undoing buckles, lifting off straps, and cutting the reins where they had become entangled with the wreckage. The horse stood there, waiting stoically.

When they had finished, Blossom actually perked up, as if relieved to be set free. Maria looked at her. "Do you suppose she'd be willing to let us ride her?"

Blossom turned to them with what Maria could swear was a look of disbelief.

Will snorted. "I'm not a horseman. I've not even been on a horse in years. And without even a saddle?" He shook his head. "Have you ever been on a horse yourself?"

Maria rubbed the horse between her eyes and Blossom snuffled as if pleased. "Well, no. But she doesn't seem as if she'd mind."

"Trust me. She would mind. She would most certainly mind. And if you've never been on a horse, you'll be far safer on foot."

"Are you sure? Nothing seems to bother her. She didn't even mind gunshots."

"Maria, I know you are trying to make things easier on my leg, but believe me. I would rather cover a few miles limping on my leg than try to ride a horse that may never have had a rider on her back before." He smiled and rubbed his knuckles against her cheek. "But thank you for the thought."

CHAPTER 32

THEY SET OUT DOWN THE ROAD, followed by Isabella's wail and Frederick's curses. With no one attempting to ride her, Blossom was a comfortable companion, perfectly willing to keep pace with Will's halting progress.

After the short stretch where the road neared the cliff—the stretch where Frederick had intended them to plunge to their doom—woodlands edged the road on either side. Despite the sun's best efforts, the bare trees did not look cheerful. They just looked dead. An occasional path could be seen through the undergrowth, but whether it was for rabbits or for poachers, Will had no idea.

Dead trees did have one advantage, he decided when he spotted some branches on the ground. He found first one and then another that would serve as a sturdy walking stick once he trimmed off the twigs. The sword stick was elegant, but was better suited to a stroll down a smooth garden path than to a trek down a rutted dirt road.

One of the sticks he gave to Maria. He could see that she was limping even more than he was. For a moment he feared that she was doing so in an effort to assuage his pride. But that thought lasted only for a moment. He knew perfectly well that she was not an idiot. She must be in pain.

So he asked. "What's wrong?"

She made a face. "These lovely, elegant shoes I wore to impress the Maltbys? The soles are so thin they might as well be made of paper. I am making the acquaintance of every pebble along the way."

He looked down. They were quite pretty shoes. Green leather and very dainty. But as much as he appreciated them, he could recognize that they were not at all what one would choose for a trek over rough country. In addition, it was easy to see her shoes, because she was holding up her skirts to keep them from dragging through the dirt.

"Chapman is going to be very distressed over the state of your attire. We shall have to replace that gown as well as the shoes, I fear."

She looked at him. "Your boots are scuffed, your breeches are torn, your coat is muddied, your cravat is missing . . ." She frowned. "What happened to your cravat?"

Somewhat sheepishly, he confessed, "I gave it to Isabella to bind her wound."

That earned him a sniff before she continued, "I at least have my bonnet, battered though it is. Your hat has completely vanished. And you are criticizing *my* attire?"

He grinned, and they continued down the road, bickering cheerfully to distract themselves from the walk and all that had happened.

As it turned out, their march did not last too much longer. Once they reached level ground, a farmer driving a wagon came out of a field onto the road. He stopped abruptly when he saw them. "M'lord, m'lady, what's amiss?"

Fishing quickly through his memory for a name, Will said, "Mr. Durbin, isn't it? Well met. As you can see, we've had a bit of an accident."

Durbin frowned. "Aye, that I can see. And with Blossom? I wouldn't have thought she'd enough spirit for that."

Will turned a laugh into a cough. "I'll not have Blossom maligned. It was through no fault of hers that we came to grief, and it was her own good temperament that kept it from being worse."

"Well, you'd best climb aboard. The wagon's not fancy, but it can get you to the Park well enough." He frowned. "Unless you be needing the doctor? M'lady isn't looking any too spry, no more are you."

"No, no need to bother the doctor. But . . ." Will looked at Maria, who was indeed looking a bit green. Still, she managed a smile. "But I would appreciate it if you could take us to Sir Thomas, the magistrate."

Durbin's eyes widened. Will hesitated to explain, but Maria said, "All the county will know soon enough, Will. There's no point in trying to avoid a scandal."

"True enough." He nodded and turned to the farmer. "It's a sorry tale. My cousin, Mr. Frederick Dormer, tried to kill us. He's back on the road, along with Mrs. George Dormer. They are both more in need of the doctor than we are, but I would like to report the matter to the magistrate as soon as possible."

"Dormer." The farmer spat the name out as if it were a curse. "And I'll wager he tried it from hiding, not being one to show his face."

"Well, yes, he did." Will couldn't restrain a smile. "But thanks to Blossom's refusal to panic, to say nothing of my lady's courage and quick thinking, he failed."

"It's right glad I am that ye came through safe and sound, m'lord, and I'm thinking the rest of us hereabouts'll say the same. Now if you and your lady'll get up here on the back of the wagon"—he shook out a couple of sacks to cover the wagon floor—"I'll have you to Fanshaw in no time."

Leaving Blossom behind to be returned to Belford Park later, Will and Maria settled themselves on the back of the wagon and Durbin turned his horse toward the Fanshaw residence.

"Will . . ." Maria shivered slightly.

"Don't worry. You'll be safe and warm in no time," Will said, putting an arm around her shoulders and dropping a kiss on her head. "You were magnificent. Calm and courageous. You are a wonder."

"Will . . ." She grabbed a fistful of his coat and leaned her head against his chest. "Do you remember my saying that I was not susceptible to vapors? I believe I may have been mistaken. I think I am about to succumb."

He held her close as she shivered and murmured consoling endearments until the tremors ceased. It took a while.

She slowly withdrew from his arms, her face turned away in embarrassment. "Please excuse me, I don't know how I came to behave is such a silly, cowardly fashion."

"Cowardly!" He laughed softly. "I have rarely seen trained warriors face danger with such aplomb as you did. Keeping your head and making use of the swordstick—it was amazing. And completely unexpected by those two idiots."

After thinking about it for a moment, she managed a tremulous smile. "I was so angry with them that I didn't even stop to think. But we did do well, didn't we?"

"We make an unbeatable combination." He pulled her to his side again.

"Mmm." She settled comfortably against him. "I didn't mean to go all to pieces now that it's over. I feel quite foolish."

"You should have seen me after my first battle. I'm told I managed well enough while it was going on, but when the cannons stopped roaring and we were called to order, I was hanging over the side, casting up my accounts."

She looked up at him doubtfully.

"I swear it." He held up his hand. "And then I was reassured by the bosun that most midshipmen do the same after their first brush with combat. You, my dear, are managing far better than most."

"Well, in that case, I'll not resign my commission."

"Resign? As if I would ever accept your resignation! I'm afraid, my love, that you are commissioned for life."

And if it was a slightly improper display of affection for a gentleman to keep his arm around his wife and for her to keep her head on his shoulder for all to see, they cared not a whit.

That peaceful interlude was ended far too quickly. Durbin took them over the farm roads between the fields, and they arrived at Fanshaw's door in no time at all.

Needless to say, their arrival in such a disheveled and bedraggled state caused considerable consternation. Once the Fanshaws were assured that neither Will nor Maria was seriously injured, they settled into practical hospitality.

Lady Fanshaw whisked Maria upstairs to a bedchamber where a good fire was blazing on the hearth. There she was firmly cosseted; one maid helped Maria out of her stained and wrinkled gown, another brought pitchers of hot water so she could wash herself, a third brought a wrapper that she slipped into once she was washed, and a footman brought a glass and a decanter of brandy.

Lady Fanshaw poured a healthy measure into the glass and handed it to Maria. "Drink this while Nancy brushes out your hair. And then you must lie down and rest. I am dying to hear all the details of your ordeal, but you look much too done up to provide a coherent account." She smiled. "Don't worry. This is only a delay. I shall insist on a full accounting later."

Maria sipped the brandy and felt the warmth of it spread through her limbs. She lay down on the soft feather bed and let the maids pull a comforter over her. She closed her eyes until they left the room, but once she heard the door close, they sprang open again.

Her feet were weary enough. Indeed, her whole body was weary, and grateful to be embraced by the soft feather bed. Her mind, however, refused to rest.

The coming scandal was not her fault. In no way could it possibly be considered her fault. Could it?

Should she have realized how dangerous Frederick was? She had thought of him as, really, nothing more than an annoyance.

A foppish drunk. Tiresome, but hardly lethal. She knew Will disliked him—loathed him, more precisely. But she had thought that was just the result of childhood quarrels. She had clearly underestimated the jealousy, the hatred on Frederick's part.

As for Isabella, well, that angered her. She had completely misread the girl. She had thought her naught but a pretty nitwit and had actually been considering that some sort of income should be provided for her as George's widow.

Hah! Talk about nurturing a viper! Well, she was welcome to try her wiles in Botany Bay!

But none of that was going to do anything to mitigate the scandal they were facing.

If she hadn't pushed Will to involve himself with the community and neighbors, they wouldn't have been on that road to be ambushed by Frederick. Would that have made a difference?

Probably it would not. Frederick would have found some other way to attack Will, and it might have been more successful.

No, it was better this way. Frederick would not be able to attack Will again. At least not physically. But . . .

But there was that venom he was spewing about Will's father being his own father and not really being Will's father at all. It would not matter in one way. There would be no way to prove it, after all. But it would be a lurid tale for the broadsheets, and the scandal would be whispered all over—not just in the neighborhood, but across the whole country.

Will would hate that. It would drive him right back into his shell.

If only she had stabbed higher and killed Frederick!

DOWNSTAIRS, WILL WAS ALSO GIVEN BRANDY, but not until after he had given Sir Thomas a concise account of what had occurred, and Sir Thomas had dispatched men to retrieve Frederick and Isabella. The magistrate also sent a man to fetch the doctor and warn him that a couple of patients were on their way.

Once that had been accomplished, the two men settled down in front of the fire in Sir Thomas's library. Will did his best to stifle his groan as he sank into a chair and stretched out his leg.

Politely ignoring the stifled groan, Sir Thomas sat down in the other chair. "Bad business, this." He shook his head. "A bad business indeed."

Judging that this needed nothing but a sign of agreement, Will nodded and took a swallow of the brandy.

"Knew your father and his brother both when we were young, but we were never close. They were always a bit wild, mad for horses, you know, and up for any kind of dare. I was a cautious type, never ready to run with that crowd. A bit envious, I admit. They were the ones everybody watched, the ones all the girls admired."

The slight, reminiscent smile on his face faded to a frown. "When they were boys, they were as close as could be, those two. Nobody could ever figure out what drove them apart, but they came home one day at daggers drawn. From that time on, if one of them could do the other an ill turn, he would. Did you ever know what it was that caused the trouble?"

Will shook his head. "I was never in my father's confidence. He rarely even spoke to me if he could avoid it."

"A strange man. He and his brother both." Sir Thomas shook his head. "And now the son of one is trying to kill the son of the other. A strange family."

Will rolled the glass in his hands. He had not mentioned Frederick's claim that he had also killed Will's father and brothers—if his father actually was his father. One way or the other, they were all dead. It was bad enough, more like a stage tragedy than real life. He did not want to make it any murkier than necessary.

However, he did want to know what would happen next, so he asked, "What happens next?"

Sir Thomas sighed and shook his head yet again. "A bad business. I'm afraid there will be no way for you to avoid the scandal. But at least there's no need for you to face it today. My carriage can take you and your lady home. When they bring Mr. Dormer and Mrs. George in, the doctor will take care of them here. I won't hold court until the morning—you'll have to appear to give witness against them, but I don't think your lady need be present. They'll have to be tried at the assizes, so once they are well enough to travel, I'll send them to Taunton, and they can be held there until it's time for the sessions."

Will sat there silently, thinking. Finally he said, "I meant to kill him, you know. It was only an accident that I missed."

Sir Thomas sat up straight at that, and emitted a few interrogatory sounds.

"I'm quite good with a knife." Will smiled gently. "There are all those long stretches at sea when nothing much is happening. I honed my skill at throwing a knife."

"Yes, but . . ." Sir Thomas stuttered a bit.

"He intended to kill Maria as well as me. It was only Blossom's placid nature that frustrated his attempt."

"Ah. Fortunate, that."

"Yes. And it is only because he jumped when Maria stabbed him that my knife landed in his shoulder, and not his heart. She saved me from murder."

Sir Thomas smiled as if all was suddenly clear. "But you did not kill him. We have no need to worry about what might have been. What actually happened is clear enough."

A commotion outside drew their attention, and the door was flung open. One of the grooms stood there, twisting his hat in his hands. "Beggin' yer pardon, sir, but Mr. Dormer, him we was supposed to collect . . ." He gulped.

"What about him?" Sir Thomas demanded.

"Well, sir, we brought back the lady. Doctor Bright's with her now. But she said Mr. Dormer went over the cliff."

"What?" Will roared, and Sir Thomas echoed him.

"That's what she said," the groom repeated. "We'll be taking the wagon around down there to . . . to . . ."

"To see what's there," Sir Thomas said. "Yes, that will have to be done. Go ahead." He waved the man out.

Will stood dumbstruck.

CHAPTER 33

Frederick Dormer was not dead when the party from Fanshaw arrived at the base of the cliff, but he was not far from it. He clung to the arm of the first man to reach him—Gregson, the head groom—and held on until he had gasped out what he was determined to relate. He demanded that Gregson repeat the message before he finally let go.

He was only semi-conscious by the time they reached the doctor but managed to gasp out enough of his story to surprise the man. Doctor Bright, in turn, told Gregson that he had best tell Sir Thomas right away.

"What!" Sir Thomas exclaimed. Then he stood, thoughtfully gnawing his lower lip. "It's been warm enough these past days that the ground's not hard frozen. There may be footprints, marks, that will show who's lying. We'd best get Mattick to come with us. A gamekeeper may be better at reading the ground."

The gamekeeper was located soon enough, so it was still light by the time Sir Thomas and his men reached the site of the accident. Mattick signaled them to stand back while he studied the ground.

"Nasty spot, this," Sir Thomas said. "This would be where old Claremont and his sons came to grief, no?"

Gregson nodded. "As well his lordship was driving Blossom this time. Anything livelier and they would have been smashed up like his father."

Mattick looked up from where he was crouched on the ground. "Come this way, Sir Thomas, and take a look."

Sir Thomas duly came. "What am I looking at?"

"This is where Mr. Dormer fell. You can see the bloodstains."

Sir Thomas nodded.

"But he didn't walk away. Those footsteps coming near him, but not too near—that would be Lord Claremont. You can see the way he limps and uses his stick." Mattick then pointed out smaller footprints. "Those would be a woman's. And you can see where someone was dragged along. Those scrapes there would be the backs of his feet."

"Go on!" Gregson said. "You can't tell me that a little woman could drag a man along that way."

"He's not such a big fellow." Sir Thomas thought. "Could Claremont have done it himself?"

Mattick shook his head. "Look, you can see where he and his lady unhitched Blossom and started walking down the road. The drag marks go right over their tracks, wiping out a path. It had to be done after they left."

Gregson walked carefully over to the section Mattick pointed out and crouched down. He shook his head. "I see what you mean, clear enough, but I can't rightly believe it. That little woman? He wouldn't just lie there and let her pull him along and roll him over."

Mattick returned to the spot where Dormer had first been wounded and looked around. There were a number of rocks littering the area. He picked up a few to examine and then discarded them. Eventually he found one that prompted him to grunt in satisfaction.

He carried it over to Sir Thomas, who had a notebook out and was making a sketch of the scene.

"I'd wager she used this to stun him, enough so he wouldn't fight as she dragged him along," Mattick said. "But he probably came to just before she rolled him over the side. That's how he knew she was the one that tried to kill him."

"Ah." Sir Thomas shook his head sadly. "I couldn't believe she had tried to kill him. Didn't think it was possible, but I'm afraid you may have the right of it. That rock—we'll need to take that with us. Now, both of you, look at this map I've made of the scene. Is it accurate?"

When they had looked it over and nodded their approval, he closed the notebook and said, "You'll both be needed in magistrate's court tomorrow and, I fear, at the assizes." He looked apologetic. "It can't be helped."

WHEN LORD AND LADY CLAREMONT GOT INTO Sir Thomas's carriage to be taken home, they looked considerably improved over their arrival. They had washed and rested, and their clothes had been sponged, brushed, and pressed. Her bonnet had not survived, and his hat had been lost, but other than that, Maria thought they looked quite respectable.

Even so, it did not take her long to notice that something new was bothering her husband. "What is it, Will? You look even more upset than you did before."

"It's nothing . . ." he began, trying to look reassuring. Under her disbelieving look, he reconsidered. "No, you're right. You might as well know. When the men went to retrieve them, Frederick wasn't there. Isabella said he had thrown himself off the cliff. Apparently he said he didn't want to give me the satisfaction of seeing him hang."

"That's horrible!"

Will shook his head. "I'm having trouble believing it."

"Well, I suppose I can understand his not wanting to go through that humiliation," she said slowly.

"I'm having trouble with the notion that he actually believed he might hang. He was far more likely to believe he could wriggle his way out of it, convince everyone to . . . well, not forgive him, but at least keep it quiet to avoid the scandal. Send him off to live abroad or some such."

"I don't wish to sound bloodthirsty, but personally I would be quite willing to see them both hang. When I think how sympathetic I felt about Isabella despite her harridan of a mother! I was even ready to encourage a match between her and Mr. Aberdare." Maria tightened her mouth and frowned.

Will wasn't quite listening to her. He was still frowning over his own thoughts. "He probably thought I'd be willing to let him go to keep him from telling everyone that I'm a bastard, not my father's son."

She looked at him carefully. "Does it bother you?"

He tilted his head as he considered. "Not really. It's not as if my father—if he was my father—ever played a part in my life, other than sending me off to sea. And I can't really complain about that. I was happy to be in the navy." He turned to her with a smile. "And, of course, that is how I came to find you."

She smiled back.

"No," he said, "what bothers me is that I feel like an impostor. I'm not prepared to be a viscount, a landowner, all the things people around here seem to expect me to be."

"Now you are being foolish. As everyone will tell you, you are doing a far better job of it than your father ever did, or than Frederick ever did."

"Perhaps I am. But, you know, I still might have let him go except that he was going to kill you as well as me." He pulled her close and rested his head on hers. "I was terrified that I might not be able to stop him."

"But you did."

"With your help."

"Isn't that the way it's supposed to be?"

"It is in this best of all possible marriages."

She smiled. "May you continue to think of it that way.

Nonetheless, I would prefer to avoid such dramatic episodes in the future."

The rest of the brief journey passed in mutual expressions of connubial happiness, so that when they arrived at Belford, they were still presentable though not quite so pristine.

Once inside, footmen relieved them of coat and cloak with only a momentary hesitation as they reached for nonexistent hats. Gregson hovered politely in the background.

Will turned to him. "Ask Gibbs to join us in the drawing room. Also, Lady Pellew and Lady Blackwell." He turned to Maria. "Tea?"

"Not just now."

"Very good, sir." Gregson started to back out.

"And I think it would be best if you and Mrs. Bates were to join us as well."

Gregson managed not to stumble as he withdrew.

Maria sank into the chair by the fire. "It's such a pleasure to have a lovely fire burning away when we come home."

"Are you cold? Would you like a shawl?" He looked around as if he expected one to appear.

"No, no. It's just . . . it's the whole day, I suppose. It's left an icy knot in me. I try to ignore it. I tell myself that it's over. We're safe. No harm really came to us. Then all at once I'm shivering again. Not because I'm cold, but . . ." She shook her head. "I don't think anyone ever hated me before. No one ever wanted to kill me. It's as if my world has tilted. I'm not sure I am seeing things properly."

Half-standing, half-sitting on the arm of the chair, he took her hand, caressing it carefully. "I know what you mean. In battle, the men on the enemy ship were trying to kill me, I suppose, just as I was trying to kill them. But it wasn't personal. There it's the enemy you're fighting, not an individual, not a real person.

"This was different. Frederick and Isabella were trying to kill us. They hated us. And that hatred turned us into something less. It filled me with such rage, such hatred, that I wanted to kill them. And that's not an emotion I ever want to feel again."

"Yes," she said. "That's it exactly." She looked at him with a crooked smile. "But that doesn't mean I'm ready to forgive them."

Lady Blackwell arrived, looking pinched and resentful, as usual. Aunt Sophia looked slightly surprised by the solemnity, but made no comment when Will invited them all to be seated. Gibbs, Gregson, and Mrs. Bates stood near the door.

"My daughter is not here yet," Lady Blackwell said when Will was about to begin.

"No, she is not," he agreed. "Nor will she be. That is part of what I need to tell you all."

Lady Blackwell paled and clutched her throat. "You've driven her away! You're sending us away! But where shall we go? What shall we do?"

"Please, Lady Blackwell, calm yourself," Maria said. "Let Lord Claremont explain what has happened." Somehow, she felt that using Will's title made the occasion more formal, less personal. Though nothing could actually prepare Lady Blackwell for the blow that was about to fall. She could pity the woman, though she could not like her.

Looking around, Maria could see that they were all looking apprehensive. Gibbs started to say something, but Will shook his head.

"There is no easy way to say this," he said. "While my wife and I were on our way to pay a call on the Maltbys today, my cousin, Frederick Dormer, tried to kill us."

That produced an uproar. Will waited quietly until it subsided, and continued. "He was assisted by Isabella, my brother's widow."

Lady Blackwell's first gasp was followed immediately by a shriek. "No, no! You're lying! That can't be true!"

"I'm afraid it is," Will said, and continued quietly recounting what had happened.

Lady Blackwell grew increasingly strident in her cries of protest. Maria started to get up to go to her, but Will's hand on her shoulder kept her in her seat. Instead, Aunt Sophia and Mrs. Bates went to her aid and half-led, half-carried her from the room.

In the silence that followed their departure, Maria looked up at Will. She saw a familiar face but an unfamiliar, stony expression. This was the captain directing his ship in battle. It was both frightening and comforting. No matter what the danger, he would know what to do.

"Captain?" Gibbs asked tentatively.

Will relaxed his grip on her shoulder and finished his account, including what Isabella said had happened after he and Maria left.

Gibbs looked grim. "I'm not surprised that your cousin would try an ambush—skulking in the shadows sounds all too like him. But Isabella? I wouldn't have thought she could lift a pistol, no less use one."

"Trust me," Maria said. "She wielded it with no hesitation."

"She said he threw himself over the edge? So you'd not be able to see him swing?" Gibbs shook his head in disbelief. "Death before dishonor? I'd not have thought him the type."

"No more do I." Will shrugged. "But that's what Isabella said."

CHAPTER 34

SIR THOMAS ARRIVED ON THE CLAREMONT'S doorstep bright and early the next morning. He was ushered into the breakfast room where Will and Maria were still eating. Although Will seconded his wife's invitation to join them, he did not like the solemn expression on the magistrate's face.

His misgivings were soon justified. Over a cup of coffee, Sir Thomas told them what Frederick had said.

Will sat back in his chair. "That sounds more like Frederick," he said slowly. "I found it difficult to believe he would kill himself. But Isabella? Could she possibly have done such a thing?"

"I don't doubt her willingness to do it," Maria said acerbically. "After yesterday, there is nothing I would put past her. But would she have the physical strength to do it? Of that I am not so certain."

"That was my thought too," Sir Thomas said. "But I went up to the site of the attack with Mattick, my gamekeeper." The magistrate smiled slightly. "It seems he is as good at tracing human tracks as he is at tracking game. He walked us through the marks that showed where you had fallen—everything that had happened."

The magistrate shook his head. "It was remarkable. But then he showed how Dormer had been pulled along after you had left, and found a rock that she could have used to stun him so that he wouldn't struggle."

Maria lost all color from her face and started to sway.

Will, who had been watching her during Sir Thomas's exposition, was at her side instantly. "My dear, there is no need for you to hear this."

Sir Thomas also came to his feet. "Bless my soul, my lady, I did not think. I should never have spoken of such things before you."

"I do beg your pardon," she said. "I don't know what came over me. It just seemed so, so cold-blooded. I always thought of her as rather simple-minded and naive in the way she would blurt things out. But not malicious."

"I know what you mean," Sir Thomas said, patting her hand. "She always struck me as almost childlike."

"Childlike?" Will shook his head. "Only if by childlike you mean utterly selfish, completely uninterested in anything except as it affected her. She has always seemed to me to be the most utterly self-centered person I have ever known."

"But she is so pretty," Maria protested.

Her husband laughed. "And that is how she gets away with it so easily."

Sir Thomas looked startled at the notion, and began to protest. But then he frowned, pensively. "Do you know, I think you may be right. I was going to say that she was always very pleasant, but then, come to think of it, she never went out of her way, if you know what I mean. Even when we visited, back when your father was alive, it was her mother, Lady Blackwell, who acted as hostess, doing all that fussing about that ladies do."

"I always though Lady Blackwell was a bit, well, pushy, always wanting to take charge. But perhaps it was simply that someone had to run the household if Isabella couldn't be bothered to do so. Now I feel a bit guilty." Maria smiled a bit. "But not too guilty. I was also rather annoyed at Isabella for not doing anything to help when we were trying to get the house in order."

Will did not feel particularly amused. "It seems her idea of getting the house in order involved removing us." He turned to Sir Thomas. "What happens now?"

"Well, that's not too certain. Mr. Dormer is in no condition to make a statement. Dr. Bright is doing his best, and I know how he hates to lose a patient, but he's not holding out any great hope. If Mr. Dormer doesn't recover enough to at least make a sworn statement—"

"But you said he told your groom what happened," Maria put in.

"Yes, but what a man says when he's half out of his mind with pain . . ." Sir Thomas shook his head. "No jury would want to hang a woman on that."

"And what does she say to the accusation?" Will was feeling a bit cynical.

"She says he asked her to help him to the edge, but then he tried to throw her over. She struggled and he fell." Sir Thomas shrugged.

"Do you believe her?" Maria asked.

"No, but without Dormer to testify, I'd wager any jury would."

"I'd wager you're right," Will said. "Damnation! I don't know if I hope he survives so that he and that nasty little cat can get what they deserve, or hope he dies so that we can escape without a scandal. And isn't that a shameful way of thinking in either case."

"Where are they now?" Maria asked with sudden sharpness.

"Dormer is in Dr. Bright's care. There's no worry about his escaping, not in his condition. As for Mrs. Dormer, well . . ." Sir Thomas hesitated. "I don't suppose you'd care to take charge of her yourselves?"

The look of horror on Maria's face answered that question.

"I think not," Will said. "But I can see the difficulty. There is a strong possibility that should he live, Frederick will charge her with attempted murder, so letting her go would be foolish."

"On the other hand," Sir Thomas said, "there is a strong possibility that Frederick will die before he can make such a charge, and what evidence is there against her? Some marks in the dirt that will be gone the first time it rains."

"The gatekeeper's cottage," Maria said. "No one is living in it, but it's in fairly decent condition. She can stay there while she recovers from her wound with Lady Blackwell to take care of her."

"But what's to stop her from running away?" Sir Thomas protested.

"Running away? Isabella?" Maria looked incredulous. "She considers a stroll in the garden to be vigorous exercise. She requires a servant to fetch her shawl from the next room. All we need do is tell the grooms she is not permitted to order a carriage and she will be imprisoned as thoroughly as though she were in Newgate."

Will gave a sharp laugh. "Very good, my lady. In your charity you allow her the tender care of her mother. I think that provides at least a temporary solution. Don't you agree Sir Thomas?"

"Bless me," said that worthy. "I believe you have it. That will work very well. I'll have one of my men transport her from the doctor's house."

With that Sir Thomas departed, a smile on his face.

An hour later, Will was not smiling. He was tempted to do so, but he feared Maria would take that amiss. He had taken refuge in the library and left her to tell Lady Blackwell about the arrangement, judging that she would no doubt take it better if it were explained to her by another woman.

It was useless to pretend Lady Blackwell had taken it well. Even with two closed doors between him and the hysterics—and he felt guilty about the closed doors—he could not completely mute that lady's objections. He and Maria, Lady Blackwell cried, were cold and unfeeling, and had been determined to persecute Isabella from the moment they arrived. They were jealous of her beauty, that's what it was.

Eventually the shrieks subsided. From where he remained, secluded in the library, Will could hear the sounds of Lady Blackwell's descent. He did not breathe easily until he heard the door close behind her.

Maria entered looking indescribably weary. Will opened his arms and she walked into them. Fortunately, he had the desk at his back and had no difficulty supporting her as she leaned on him.

Eventually she lifted her head. "I was sorely tempted to hit her over the head with a candlestick and have her dragged from the house, but Aunt Sophia dissuaded me."

"I could hear her shrieks," Will admitted.

"I finally convinced her that the gatehouse would be preferable to the village jail, which is one end of the cellar in the constable's house where he locks up drunks to sober up."

Will made sympathetic sounds.

"It's entirely our fault, you see. You were supposed to be dead, and then Frederick would have married Isabella, and everything would have been fine."

Still murmuring consoling sounds, he led her to a well-cushioned settee, tucked a throw over her legs, went over to the decanter, and poured a hefty dose of brandy. "Drink this," he said. "You've earned it."

She took a sip and blinked. "Brandy?"

At his nod she took another small sip, and then another. "Oh my, I could grow fond of this. It makes me feel as if, as if a heavy weight has just been lifted from my shoulders." She smiled blissfully. "No wonder gentlemen are so fond of it."

"It has its uses," Will said, sitting beside her and tucking his arm around her.

A few hours of peace descended on them and on the house. Aunt Sophia popped her head in to assure them that she would take care of having everything packed and transported to the gatehouse.

Gibbs stuck his head in to assure them that everyone in the stables knew the gatehouse residents were not to order any sort of transportation.

After a while Gregson brought in a tray with hot tea, roast beef sandwiches, lemon biscuits, and a warm bread and butter pudding with a meringue on top. Maria had been half dozing, but the pudding roused her at once.

She swallowed a spoonful with a look of bliss. "Everyone's coddling us, aren't they."

Will agreed. "Do you mind?"

"Not at all. Mind, I wouldn't care to be coddled all the time, but today, today I truly appreciate it."

Their quiet content lasted until late in the afternoon, when Sinclair returned from London, bounding with excitement and flourishing a warrant for Frederick's arrest. He was full of enthusiasm as he spoke of the corruption Cuttlebush had described to Lord St. Vincent. The First Lord of the Admiralty was outraged, quite properly outraged, in Sinclair's view.

Sinclair himself was properly outraged when he heard of the attempt on the lives of Lord and Lady Claremont, but he exploded when he was told of Frederick's own injuries.

"It can't be!" he said. "I won't allow it."

"I'm afraid it isn't up to you," Will said mildly. "The fair Isabella made a determined effort to end his life, and she may have succeeded."

"You don't understand. Cuttlebush told us enough about corruption in the Navy Board to thoroughly whet St. Vincent's appetite. But Dormer is the one who knows the names, who knows who the higher ups are. I must speak to him at once!"

"That may be impossible."

"It must be possible!"

"Sinclair, be reasonable. The man was thrown from a cliff—the same cliff that proved fatal to my father and brothers. Dr. Bright is doing his best, but he is not optimistic about Frederick's chances of survival."

"Then I must speak to him while he still lives!" Sinclair rushed from the house to catch the groom who has leading his horse to the stable.

Maria came to stand by Will as they watched out the window. "Mr. Sinclair is a bit of a mystery," she said.

"Yes. I suspect that his presence here was not simply the result of a desire on the part of Lord Newbury to do me a good turn."

She stared at her husband. "You think he had a reason for wanting to come here?"

"Let us say, I believe he has more connection to Lord St. Vincent than he let on." He smiled at her uncertain look. "There is no need to worry. I have no doubt that he is on the side of the angels, and people have given shelter to angels unaware before this."

THE NEXT MORNING, THERE WAS AGAIN A VISITOR in the breakfast room—a gloomy, frustrated Sinclair. He looked exhausted and disheveled. The clothes he wore were the same ones had traveled in the day before, and the shadows under his eyes blended into his unshaven cheeks. A footman held a chair for him, which caught him before he collapsed.

Maria poured him a cup of coffee and set it before him. Will buttered a piece of bread and put it on his plate. Sinclair grunted an acknowledgement.

After he had inhaled the coffee, he grimaced. "Sorry. I shouldn't have inflicted myself on you in this state."

"Never mind that," Will said. "I gather you do not bring good news."

"Now that," Sinclair said, "is a matter of debate. Your cousin, Dormer, died last night."

There was a brief pause.

"You will understand if we do not burst into tears," Maria said.

"But you regret his death?" Will asked.

"Not the fact of it, but the timing." Sinclair massaged the back of his neck wearily. "I wish he had restrained his murderous impulses for another day or two to give me an opportunity to question him."

"About his cheating the tenants on the estate?" Maria asked. "But surely that's all taken care of now that it's been exposed."

Sinclair waved that away. "No, it's about his dealings with the Navy Board that I wanted to question him. St. Vincent has been going after the corruption there—it's truly incredible. And on top of that, the waste in the shipyards is unbelievable. A workman needs a four-foot board, so he takes the topmost piece, cuts off his four feet, and tosses the rest on the scrap heap, no matter that it was a twenty-foot plank to start with."

Will smiled. "You're making my frugal wife shudder."

Sinclair smiled ruefully. "Sorry, my lady. It's just that such careless stupidity makes my blood boil."

"Mine too," she said. "But stupidity isn't corruption."

"No," he agreed. "The corruption comes with the purchasing. The Navy Board purchases vast quantities of supplies. There are more than 100,000 men to be fed and clothed quite apart from building and maintaining the ships. Vast quantities of everything from grain to canvas to barrels to cannon balls must be ordered. And some people are getting rich in the process."

Sinclair began to pace around the room. "And in the shipyards themselves? Men are paid for being on duty twenty-four hours a day for months on end even though they barely put in an appearance. Instead of building ships, a crew is set to build a deck and boathouse for one of the officers. And there seems to be a cartel that controls the timber market."

He turned to face their startled looks. "Oh yes. St. Vincent is certain that the timber cartel is driving up the price, and he suspects that there is something of the same sort when it comes to wheat. Dormer seems to have been involved, and I had hopes that he could be persuaded to name names."

Will cursed softly. "You could always trust Frederick to watch out for Frederick. What will you do now?"

"Try another route." Sinclair sighed. "St. Vincent had hoped that this truce with France would give him a chance to root out the worst of it, but he's encountering opposition at every turn. There are too many office holders who consider bribes and 'gifts' to be just the ordinary perquisites of their positions. And I doubt this truce will last much longer."

The subdued silence which followed this observation was not broken until Will smiled wryly and said, "So Lord Newbury sent you down here to do more than put my house in order. I gather we shall be needing a new steward."

Sinclair nodded, embarrassed. "My uncle always has his fingers in a number of pies. But I'll find you a replacement before I leave. It shouldn't be difficult. This estate could be a real jewel, and any agent worth his salt would love to get his hands on it."

CHAPTER 35

FOR THE SECOND DAY IN A ROW, Sir Thomas arrived on the doorstep of Belford Park. With no urgency to his message, he had ridden over at a leisurely pace and arrived well past noon. Still, while his news might not be urgent, it was likely to create an awkward situation, and he was not certain how Lord Claremont and his lady would react.

So it was with hesitant steps that he followed the footman who led him to the sitting room where Claremont and his lady, along with Lady Pellew, were comfortably ensconced by the fire. He waved them back when they started to stand, shaking his head, and took the chair the footman drew up for him.

Maria took one look at him and said to the footman, "Wine and biscuits, please." Then she turned back to Sir Thomas and said, "Unless you would like me and my aunt to leave?"

"No, no," he said. "Lady Fanshaw told me to be sure you were included in this discussion." He smiled hesitantly. "She has very strong feelings about including ladies in any discussion that involves them."

"I know these ladies agree," Will said, "and so do I."

"So let us begin." Maria smiled. "We know that Frederick Dormer has died. That leaves Isabella Dormer to be dealt with. I somehow doubt that she is overcome with guilt and pleading for mercy."

Sir Thomas opened his mouth but then decided not to speak. He simply nodded.

Lady Pellew said, "I expect she completely denies Mr. Dormer's accusations, and insists that she never wished to do any harm. With trembling lips, she whispers that he forced her to help him, and she feared for her life. Would that be it?" She looked inquiringly at the magistrate.

He smiled and shook his head. "You have it precisely, my lady."

"That does somewhat limit our options," Will said. "I don't see how she can be charged with Frederick's murder. His words to your servants were not precisely a deathbed confession and could be dismissed as the ravings of a man out of his head with pain. And while I do not question the reconstruction of your gamekeeper, I doubt that his reading of marks in the dirt would convince a judge and jury."

"I fear you are correct. Unfortunately," Sir Thomas said, "under the law, I would not even feel entitled to send the case to the assizes."

"That leaves us with her part in the attempt on our lives," Will said.

"Really," Maria said, "you cannot possibly think there is any chance of persuading a jury to convict her."

Sir Thomas seemed startled by her vehemence. "The testimony of your husband would most assuredly carry weight with any jury in the land."

Lady Pellew looked at him sadly.

Maria raised her brows skeptically. "Tell me, does Lady Fanshaw agree?"

Will shook his head. "No. My wife is right. Oh, I know that in theory the testimony of a viscount would be almost automatically accepted. However, I am very much a newcomer to the district. Very few know me, and what others think they know may not be to my advantage."

"There is that," Sir Thomas acknowledged.

"In addition, such a trial would make us notorious. The scandal sheets would be full of it. We could never escape the obloquy."

"She will appear in court in her widow's weeds, looking frail and helpless, with tears trembling on her lashes," Lady Pellew said. "She is quite good at that. And no man on the jury will be able to think she could possibly have been prepared to shoot anyone."

"But she can't simply be allowed to get off scot-free!" Sir Thomas looked frustrated. "Would you allow her to return to living under your roof?"

"Absolutely not!" Maria burst out. "Are you mad? That . . . that *creature* attempted to murder my husband! He has shown her nothing but kindness, maintaining her and her shrew of a mother here in his home even when they did nothing but sneer and snipe at him. And when he was under no obligation to do anything for her."

Ah, she was in a fine fury, this wife of his. Will couldn't keep the smile from his face, but he did manage to say, "Well, she is my brother's widow."

"All the more reason for her to be grateful to you," Maria retorted.

Sir Thomas coughed apologetically. "Yes, I quite see your point, but the problem remains. What is to be done with her?"

Maria muttered something under her breath that sounded like "keelhauling."

"I think I have a solution." Will decided he actually felt like a viscount at present.

WILL ALLOWED ANOTHER DAY TO PASS before he went to see the women in the gatehouse. He had discussed his plans with Maria and her aunt. They had, grudgingly, agreed, though Maria would have preferred something with boiling oil. She declined to accompany him to his encounter with Isabella and her mother.

"I find I grow angrier and angrier the more I think about her actions," she said. "If I fly into a fury, they will think that all they have to do is wait until I have calmed down. If you explain to them, calmly and precisely, what their alternatives are, they will see that there is no chance of escape."

He strolled down to the gatehouse, walking stick in hand. It was not much more than half a mile. He was pleased to see that he and his leg had progressed enough that it was little more than a comfortable stroll for him.

Feeling reasonably confident, he knocked on the door. Lady Blackwell opened it and paused, startled.

"I had hoped it was one of the servants with some food for us," she snapped, stepping aside to let him in.

"I'm sure your bowl of gruel will arrive eventually," he said.

Isabella rose when he entered the room, obviously the main room of the cottage. Ignoring her, he selected a sturdy chair, turned it to face the women, and sat down.

"Please be seated," he said.

Every bit as offended as when she had opened the door, Lady Blackwell huffed her way to a seat. "I trust you have come to escort us back to our rooms."

He gave her a pitying shake of the head. "I'm sure you have heard by now that Frederick is dead."

Isabella sighed and touched a handkerchief to her eye. "Alas, poor man. He frightened me so, but I would not have wanted him to die a suicide, condemning his soul to eternal torment."

"I hardly think you need to worry about that. Just be grateful that he died before he could testify to your attempt to kill him. A rather successful attempt, as it turned out."

Lady Blackwell jumped up. "How dare you malign my daughter so! She has been much abused by your cousin. Only those consumed with jealousy like your ill-bred wife could possibly . . ."

"Madam!" Will thundered in the voice that had once made his orders heard even in the midst of cannon fire. "Sit down and hold your tongue. I know that your daughter was prepared to kill me, and I have no doubt that she succeeded in killing her partner in that endeavor."

Lady Blackwell sat.

Isabella raised her face and reached out a hand to him, her eyes limpid with tears. "I know it must look dreadful, but I swear I never meant you any harm."

Will shook his head. "You may stop the pretense, Isabella. I am not here to argue about your guilt. That is settled. I am here to offer you a choice about your future."

She straightened up and tilted her head to the side, studying him. "I am to have a future then?"

He studied her in return. It was amazing. She was still undoubtedly beautiful, but the young naïf had disappeared. The limpid gaze had been replaced by sharp calculation. Not at all a foolish child.

He was tempted to smile, but suspected that would be misinterpreted as weakness, so he spoke coldly. "Perhaps. In the interests of justice, you should be put on trial for attempted murder."

A glimmer of hope flickered in her eyes. "But that would certainly bring scandal down on you. Even more scandal were I to testify to what Frederick said about your parentage."

"What? That our fathers, his and mine, cuckolded each other? And your evidence for this would be that you heard him say it when he was, he thought, about to kill me? Because he cannot, now, corroborate your tale." Will shook his head in mock regret. "No. I doubt anyone would believe you."

She tightened her lips. "What, then?"

"You are right that I would prefer to avoid the scandal of a trial. I have no desire to feature in the scandal sheets." He shook his head when he saw her raise her head hopefully. "But no, I do not intend to simply let you return to Belford. It would be uncomfortable for my wife—and for me—to sit down to dinner every evening wondering if poison has been added to the soup."

Lady Blackwell looked outraged, but Isabella only offered a pitying smile as she shook her head.

Will continued. "Not only do I not want you in my house, I do not want you anywhere near me and my family."

"Family?" Isabella looked interested. "Is Maria expecting then?"

"That is not, and never will be, any of your concern." Frost dripped from his words. "No, I do not even want you in this country, in this kingdom. So, I offer you a choice. You and your mother may take ship and leave the country for any foreign port of your choosing. I will give you five hundred pounds to establish yourselves there."

"Mmm. Paris?" Isabella suggested.

Will shrugged. "If you wish, though I do not recommend it. This truce will not last much longer, and you may find yourself in the middle of a war."

"One could say the same of London."

"Do you fancy yourself as a reverse émigré?"

Lady Blackwell could restrain herself no longer. "How dare you, you *upstart*! You would exile us not just from our home but from our country as well?"

Exasperated, Will looked at her. "Madam, in no way could Belford Park ever be considered your home. You have been allowed to reside there, but that indulgence is quite finished."

Isabella ignored her mother. "You said you were offering a choice. What is the alternative to exile?"

"You may leave."

"And?"

He shrugged. "And anything you wish. My brother made no provision for you and neither did my father. I considered that shameful of them and was prepared to make you an allowance. However, you will understand that recent . . . developments have changed my mind. You may leave, but you can expect no assistance from me or from anyone in the neighborhood."

"You've told everyone, I suppose." A touch of bitterness had entered her voice.

"There was no need for me to say anything." He smiled. "The servants took care of that."

"Servants' gossip," Lady Blackwell sneered.

"But so often servants' gossip is the truth. And they relish it all the more when it concerns people who have not treated them well."

The lady turned to her daughter. "Aberdare will not listen to gossip. He is enamored of you and will gladly marry you."

Isabella smiled with surprisingly cynical wisdom. "No, Mama. If he were a duke or some other powerful nobleman, then he might scorn to listen to gossip. But wealthy as he may be, he is at heart still a shopkeeper, and gossip is precisely what he heeds."

She caught Will's quick, satiric smile. "How long do I have to decide?"

"Gibbs will be here in the morning. He will take you to a port where you will be able to find a ship going to your chosen destination. Or he will take you to the village inn. You will have to make your way from there."

She grimaced. "Very well. Let it be Paris."

"Are you sure? There is little doubt that war is coming, sooner rather than later. You might find the Americas safer."

She shook her head. "Safer, perhaps, but uncivilized. The French are reputed to be most chivalrous, and perhaps I may find more sympathy for a poor widow there than I do here."

He looked dubious, but then smiled cynically. "And war always creates a certain amount of confusion, does it not?"

She returned his smile but made no comment.

CHAPTER 36

Maria was appalled to hear that Isabella intended to go to Paris. "Is she mad? No one believes the truce will last much longer. She could find herself in the middle of a war. I am not vindictive enough to wish that on her."

Aunt Sophia was less surprised. "She probably considers Paris the most stylish place to go, now that they have stopped chopping off heads. So not entirely mad."

"Not mad," Will agreed with a half-smile. "I suspect she thinks that we may try to keep a watch on her. If she is in Paris and England is at war with France, that could be difficult."

Maria looked at him consideringly. "And would you keep a watch on her?"

"Oh yes, no doubt about it. I'd not trust her an inch."

That mistrust was shared by Gibbs, who was not delighted to be entrusted with the task of escorting the widow and her mother to Paris. "I'd as lief carry a trunk of vipers," were his precise words.

"And how do you suppose I should go about it," Gibbs asked in exasperation, "when the only bits of French I know are like to get me tossed out of any respectable place?"

Sinclair, who was equally suspicious of Isabella's motives, offered to accompany them. "My French will be a bit more useful than Gibbs' I imagine, and I wouldn't mind an excuse to visit Paris."

That, in turn, made Will suspicious, though he didn't offer any objections.

Two days later, when the party had all departed and he and Maria had the fireside to themselves, he turned to her with a crooked smile. "I suspect our Mr. Sinclair has his fingers in even more pies that I'd realized."

"I suspect you are right." She frowned at her needlework and put it down. "It is clear enough that he took the position as steward mainly to investigate the chicanery involved in wheat purchases, but that wouldn't send him to France. There's still more?"

"I'm sure there is. Lord Newbury is the sort of man who finds all kinds of information of interest. A bright young man like Sinclair, who keeps his eyes and ears open, can pick up a lot of information just sitting in a café. Especially if he can manage to hide how well he speaks French."

Maria was slightly shocked. Or rather, she was shocked. There was no *slightly* about it. "Do you mean to say that he is a *spy*?"

"Not precisely." Will shrugged. "But he seems to have something to do with St. Vincent and the admiralty, to say nothing of the ever-curious Lord Newbury. All of them would doubtless tell you it is best to know as much as possible about your enemies."

Maria opened her mouth. Realizing she had no idea what to say, she closed it again and returned to her needlework.

Everything seemed to settle down nicely. The household ran smoothly now that Lady Blackwell was no longer there to interfere. Even Hannah stopped sulking and made an effort to do her work with reasonable thoroughness.

Lady Fanshaw, Mrs. Maltby, Mrs. Upstone, and Mrs. Gilbert came to call and to get Maria's account of what had happened.

"It's not that we want to gossip," Mrs. Gilbert explained, blushing slightly, "but if we have the story from you, we can counter some of the more outlandish versions that are circulating."

"That's very true." Lady Fanshaw nodded approvingly at the vicar's wife, who continued to blush.

Maria smiled, suspecting that what Lady Fashaw approved of was a respectable excuse to ask for details, but she had no objection to recounting her adventure, especially since it enabled her to portray her husband in a heroic light.

Mr. Aberdare also came to call a number of times, and it soon became apparent that Lady Pelew was the object of his attentions. He invited her to dine, including Will and Maria in the invitation. Maria was amused to find herself chaperoning her aunt, but she was delighted to see her aunt blossoming under Mr. Aberdare's attentions.

Will and Maria, having come to see that they were indeed able to meet the demands of their new position, seemed to glow with happiness. They eventually acknowledged that part of that glow was due to the expected arrival of a child come autumn.

The ladies of the parish had suspected that long before it was announced.

AUTHOR'S NOTES

The Battle of Copenhagen

THE BATTLE OF COPENHAGEN, AT WHICH Will Dormer was injured, was a British victory. It was important in that it kept Denmark from allying with Napoleon. Today, however, it is best remembered for an anecdote about Admiral Horatio Nelson. At this battle, Nelson was second in command under Admiral Hyde Parker, a man best known for his caution. The delays in starting out for Denmark—Hyde Oarker was spending all his time ashore with his mistress—so infuriated the younger man that Nelson wrote letters to the Admiralty, and finally Lord St. Vincent, First Lord of the Admiralty, wrote a private letter telling Hyde Parker to get going.

When the battle was finally under weigh, two of the British ships were badly damaged. Hyde Parker could not see much of what was going on, but he saw their distress signals, and ordered a retreat. When told by his second in command about the signal to retreat, Nelson lifted his telescope to his blind eye and said, "I really do not see the signal." He charged ahead and the battle was won.

Mr. Potts' Leg

THE ARTIFICIAL LEG THAT WILL WEARS was invented in 1800 by a London carpenter, James Potts, who had lost his own leg and didn't want to have to rely on a peg leg and crutches for the rest of his life. He took out a patent for his device, but it didn't become famous until after the Battle of Waterloo. Henry Paget, Earl of Uxbridge and later Marquess of Anglesey, lost his leg in the battle, and was fitted for Potts' leg. The prosthetic device had a steel knee joint and an articulated foot with tendons made of cat gut. This made it possible for the foot to flex in accordance with the knee movement. In short, it enabled Will (and Anglesey) to walk with something approaching a natural gait.

Some improvements were made during the American Civil War, but this was essentially the prosthetic leg in use for a hundred years until World War I.

WHEN SHE RETIRED AFTER TOO MANY YEARS in journalism, Lillian Marek felt a longing for happy endings and stories where the good guys win and the bad guys get their just deserts. Having exhausted her library's supply of non-gory mystery stories, she started reading romance novels, especially historical romance. This was so much fun that she thought she'd like to try her hand at writing one. So she took her computer keyboard in hand, slipped back into the 19th century, and began.

She was was not mistaken—writing romance novels is as much fun as reading them. Especially when she can do it from the comforts of home, watching the ducks and swans on the pond and the deer and rabbits in the garden. If only they would stick to eating the weeds . . .

If she isn't working on a new book, she loves to read recipes (trying a new one every now and then) and to brag about her grandchildren.